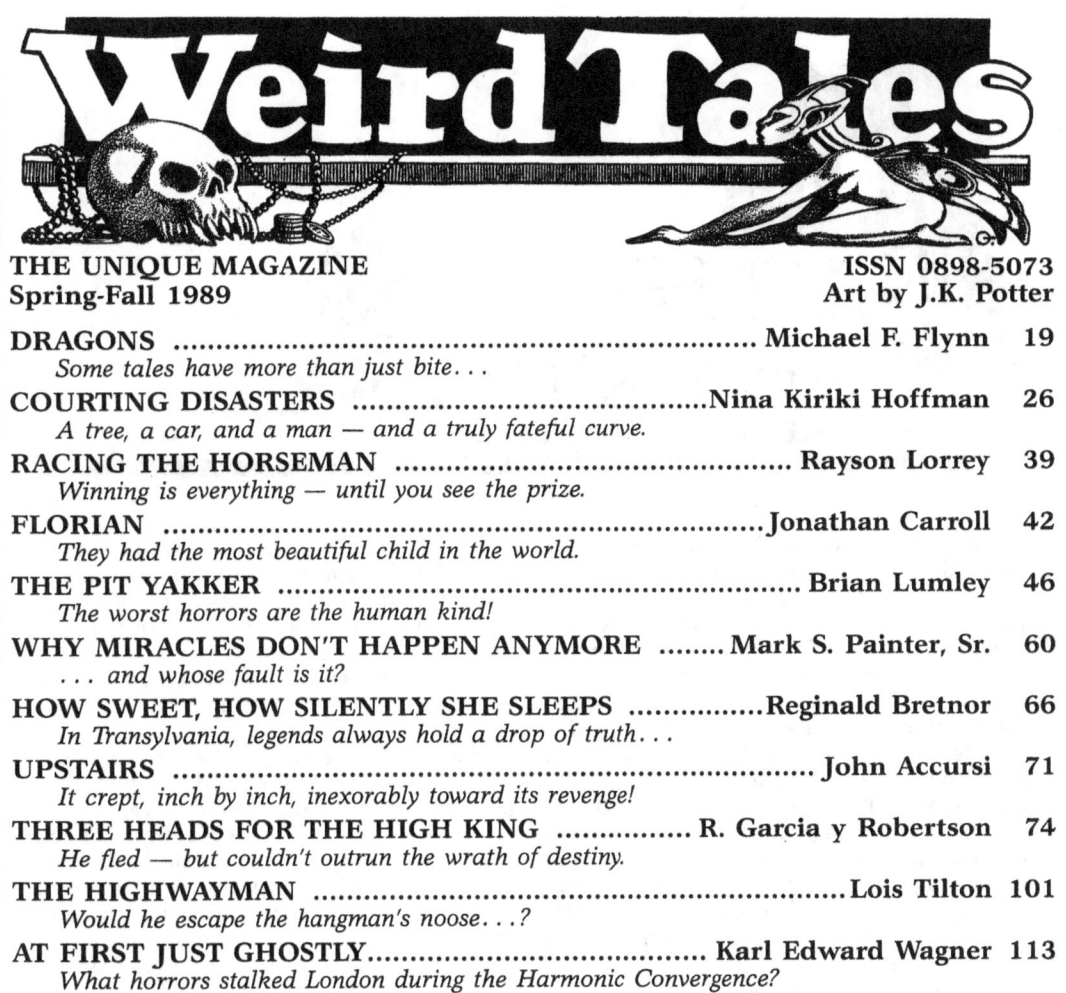

Weird Tales

THE UNIQUE MAGAZINE
Spring-Fall 1989

ISSN 0898-5073
Art by J.K. Potter

Published quarterly by the Terminus Publishing Company, Inc., P.O. Box 13418, Philadelphia PA 19101-3418. (4426 Larchwood Ave., Philadelphia PA 19104-3916.) Application to mail at second class postage rates pending at Philadelphia PA and additional mailing offices. Single copies, $4.00 (plus $1.00 postage if ordered by mail). Subscription rates: Eighteen months (six issues) for $18.00 in the United States and its posessions, for $24.00 in Canada, and for $27.00 elsewhere. The publishers are not responsible for the loss of manuscripts, although reasonable care will be taken of such material while in their possession. Copyright© 1989 by the Terminus Publishing Company, Inc.; all rights reserved; reproduction prohibited without prior permission. *Weird Tales*® is a registered trade mark owned by Weird Tales, Limited. Typeset, printed, and bound in the United States of America.

THE EYRIE

Welcome to the fifth issue of the revived (not exhumed!) *Weird Tales*®. Those doomsayers who were certain we would never get this far are invited . . . to renew their subscriptions. *Weird Tales*®, we are happy to say, seems to be sailing on an even keel now and the future looks quite bright. We are certain that our *Weird Tales*® will truly duplicate the experience that the original magazine gave its readers in the 1930s — that is, it will be a steady fixture, always there, year in and year out. In some of the previous incarnations, each new issue was something of a pleasant surprise. With ours, we hope that the mere existence of each number will be no more of a surprise than the changing of the seasons. (The *contents,* on the other hand, we hope will continue to surprise you. One of the great virtues of *Weird Tales*® of yore was that, for all it appeared month in and month out, its stories were never wholly predictable.)

On that note, we have some explaining to do . . .

But wait! **We haven't skipped any issues!** Various exigencies have played havoc with our schedule, we must admit, so you may have noticed that while the past issue was dated Winter, this one sports a much later seasonal label indeed.

Our Spring 1989 issue has gone the way of the December 1955 *Galaxy.* Collectors among you may have noticed that the run of H.L. Gold's celebrated science-fiction magazine follows an unbroken procession of months throughout the 1950s, save that there is no December 1955 issue.

Why? Because it happened that in the Fall of 1955 *Galaxy*'s distributor suddenly required that all magazines be dated one month further ahead of actual publication date. This is common in the magazine business. Remember that the date you see on the cover is the *off sale* date. Come June, the news agent or bookseller (theoretically) removes all June magazines from the shelf and sends them back unsold. A June issue published in mid-May would have, at best, two weeks on sale before it got shipped back.

Due to changing distribution patterns, *Galaxy* found it necessary to "skip" a month. Of course the January 1956 issue appeared thirty days after the November 1955 one, everybody's subscription was advanced one month, and the volume and whole-issue numbering remained undisturbed.

So it is with us. Our new distributor requires issues to be dated earlier. This is still issue number 294, appearing about three months after issue 293, for all it may be *dated* strangely. Remember that your subscription is keyed to a number of issues, not to seasons, so you haven't missed anything.

Robert Bloch reminds us of that we should say a word about the recent, sad death of the great **E. Hoffmann Price**:

. . . *surely one of* WT's *most cherished contributors, and deservedly so. In print as in person, he had unique qualities befitting to one who wrote for "The Unique Magazine."*

Indeed, E. Hoffmann Price was one of the great figures of the pulp era. He wrote, not

IO535886

THE EYRIE

merely for *Weird Tales®*, but for all the pulps from the 1920s on. He mentioned in one of his essays how, about 1940, he visited a newsstand and saw his name on the covers of fifteen different magazines. Price's first sale to *Weird Tales®* was "The Rajah's Gift," published in the January 1925 issue. He continued to write for the magazine off and on into the 1950s. His work was of high quality, and he showed a willingness to take risks, as when he took a dig at the Ku Klux Klan in the pages of *Weird Tales®* at the height of that organization's power, or when he brought Jesus Christ on stage (albeit invisible), chatting amiably with the Devil in "The Stranger from Kurdistan." He was a great traveler and raconteur, whose memoirs of the Pulp Era were always much prized by readers. He collaborated with the pulp giant Otis Adelbert Kline, and, perhaps more importantly, was the only professional writer to share a byline with H.P. Lovecraft — in "Through the Gates of the Silver Key" (here, July 1934). He was also the only member of the fantasy-writing fraternity ever to have met Robert E. Howard.

At the end of the Pulp Era, Price withdrew from writing for a time, then returned to science fiction and fantasy in the late 1970s with a series of paperback novels for Del Rey Books. He was a true storyteller to the end, and died at his computer, a writer at the age of ninety.

Two books of his pulp-era fiction (most of it from *Weird Tales®*) were published: *Strange Gateways* (Arkham House, 1964) and *Far Lands, Other Days* (Carcosa, 1975).

Brian Lumley writes:
292 came in and I'd like to comment. The issue had a few surprises, some good, some not so good. The artwork, I thought, wasn't up to scratch. Nothing much wrong with the cover, which contrasted well with the previous cover paintings and was undeniably "weird." But I thought the interiors were well below standard. The full-pager on p. 58 was good but it was the only one. The double-pager on pp. 116–117 said absolutely nothing and was a sheer waste!

Stories. There were two beauties here: "Emma's Daughter" — spoiled by a wholly contrived ending — a tear-jerker, alas, which could have been a real shocker. And "Little

Editors & Publishers:
John Betancourt
George H. Scithers
Darrell Schweitzer
Assistant Editors:
Leslie Smith
Dainis Bisenieks
Karl Würf
Vincent Evangelisti
Circulation Manager:
Richard Kabakjian
Computer Consultant:
David J. Williams III
Of Counsel:
Yale F. Edeiken
Photographer:
Advanced Litho, Inc.
Typesetters:
The Twin Company, Inc.
Campus Copy Center
Printer:
Malloy Lithographing, Inc.

SUBMISSIONS?

Like most editors, we get unsolicited manuscripts, *lots* of them. We survive, as do other editors, only by imposing Rules.

Yes, we read unsolicited manuscripts — *if* they are in proper manuscript format. Each must arrive with a self-addressed, stamped return envelope big enough to take that manuscript back to you, or with a stamped, addressed, business-letter-sized envelope *and* instructions to dispose of the manuscript if not bought. And no, we will not read manuscripts in unacceptable format.

This proper format is described in numerous reference works. One of them is *On Writing Science Fiction: The Editors Strike Back!*, by George H. Scithers, Darrell Schweitzer, and John M. Ford — which also goes into the whole art and practice of writing and selling fantastic literature. *On Writing* is available for $19.50, postpaid, from Owlswick Press, PO Box 8243, Philadelphia, PA 19101 (if you live in Pennsylvania, add $1.17 for sales tax).

Once," which gets my vote for the best (if shortest) story in the issue. *"Little Once"* is something you think about afterwards, and think about and . . . etc.! Congratulations to Nina Hoffman. Third place would go to Tad Williams's "Child of an Ancient City" for the high level of writing. And fourth spot gets taken by Quick's "Still the Same Old Story." Now, I know your issue was a Keith Taylor Special, but I just didn't find his stuff "weird" enough. Or perhaps, like Joe Christopher, I'm just a sucker for horror?

We suppose it's a natural consequence of The Unique Magazine's having something for everyone that we aren't going to please every reader with every story. In the old days, some readers just loved Edmond Hamilton's slam-bang space operas in the pages of *Weird Tales®*, while others hated them, and there was a decade-long debate over the scantily-clad ladies in Margaret Brundage's cover art.

Carl Lundgren's cover for issue 292 is certainly distinguished (not to mention much better executed than anything Brundage ever did!), and has already won several awards, such as (we paraphrase the ribbon) "Best of Show — Macabre" at the World Science Fiction Convention in New Orleans, shortly before the issue even appeared.

Bruce Moffitt of Box 350, Brookfield, MO, 64628 writes:

Weird Tales® was delivered by UPS yesterday, issues #291 and #292. I want to tell you how welcome they were: beautiful covers, quality paper, and as far as I've read in 291, excellent reading.

My tastes are Lovecraftian and I'm a low-budget book collector (or I was until 1982, when my collection was decimated by a fire which destroyed 85% of my moldering old Victorian house). I was able to salvage a few 1931 issues of Weird Tales® *but cannot afford to replace those I lost, or my huge collection of* Country Gentleman *magazines. Odd contrast, WT and CG, right? I still have* Weird Tales 50: A Tribute to Weird Tales *(1974), by Weinberg, a paperback that is undoubtedly out of print and scarce.*

If you'll search your files of ancient Weird Tales® *from 1941 or so, you'll find a fan letter from one Hugh Hefner of Chicago. Betcha never knew it! To this day, Christie Hefner prints decent fiction of the genre.*

I certainly wish you the best of success in perpetuating Weird Tales®.

I'd welcome correspondence from WT fans . . .

It just goes to show how far *Weird Tales®*'s influence has spread over the decades!

Connie Maria Plieger of Prince George, BC, Canada writes:

In the Fall issue (I haven't received the Winter yet) my favorite story was Tad Williams's "Child of an Ancient City." I much prefer this kind of eerie, atmospheric dark fantasy and horror, the kind that gives you chills and makes your hair stand on end, to the kind that tries primarily to dislodge your dinner. I realize this is just my taste, and overall feel you provide a good mix of subgenres. A poll of readers on this subject would be interesting, though. I also much liked Nina Kiriki Hoffman's "Little Once."

I'm looking forward with much anticipation (and trepidation!) to #293.

Many thanks for your kind words. Actually, we don't think we need a survey — *Weird Tales®* readers seem to be great correspondents, and keep writing to tell us what they like and don't like with the magazine. All comments, both positive and negative, are always welcome, and read by all three editors (and usually the rest of the staff).

Then again, there are letters which seem less than wholly constructive in their intent. **Bret Berman** of Monticello, NY writes:

Sorry, folks. I was reintroduced to your magazine with your Fall '88 issue and am sorely disenhearted. First — you perk me up with your schtick about trying to be non-derivative and fresh — then dollop out an issue of dated tripe, skillfully spun, perhaps, but nothing remotely modern.

With writers such as Rex (Slob) Miller about — how you can pay homage to a mediocretan like Keith Taylor is saddening.

Besides the W.T. Quick story, your Fall '88 issue was a batch of period pieces that belong in some "fantasy warrior homo-history" type magazine. Lovecraft is spinning in his grave!

Where is the ambiance of dread and mystery? Where is that inexplicable touch that rivets the reader's attention?

I think you should read more unsolicited

THE EYRIE

manuscripts regardless of the method of presentation. (Your hoity-toity attitude about "proper format" turns my stomach) (which is more than I can say about your choice of material).

In fact — I'd doubt if you even bothered reading this letter. (In today's society, one who doesn't type may as well be illiterate, eh?)

I hope you can bring Weird Tales® *back to life. I'll be watching.*

What can we say? Your letter couldn't help but leave us in a nasty mood, since it seems written with malice aforethought, and we were sorely tempted to print it for the sole purpose of putting you in the worst possible light. Instead, we decided that your very errors could be, in their own way, instructive to the rest of our readers.

You leave us several openings, coming off as decidedly retrogressive in your social attitudes ("homo-history," etc. etc.), which is a polite way of saying bigoted. And your sarcasm about proper manuscript format suggests that you are a determined amateur, the sort who won't do the right thing even when he's told.

Like it or not, there are standards in this industry. Perhaps *you* feel free to submit manuscripts handwritten in orange crayon on yellow, lined paper, rolled up and tied with a pretty pink bow, but don't think any editor is going to read them! Guidelines serve a distinct purpose in helping beginning or amateur writers move toward professional publication.

We also wonder if you're actually familiar with the old, traditional *Weird Tales*®, which did indeed publish a lot of sword and sorcery, historical adventure fantasy, and even lost-race stories. Keith Taylor would have been right at home there — but, as the success of his numerous paperback books shows, he is decidedly a modern, 1980s writer, not some sort of relic. Lovecraft might well have appreciated Keith's penchant for historical accuracy.

You mention Rex Miller as the sort of author you'd like to see in *Weird Tales*®. Miller is producing some of the most violent and distasteful horror fiction published nowadays — this opinion culled from reviewers we respect and our own attempts at reading his first novel, *Slob*. It seems to us that Miller's work merely means that the

horror field is in a period of degeneracy caused by splatter-movies and an increasing sensationalism in mass media everywhere. (In fact, this increasing sensationalism seems to be leading to the public becoming *desensitized* to violence and everything else repugnant. Therefore, the jaded thrill-seeker has to seek out greater and greater horrors. Isn't this the premise of Clive Barker's movie *Hellraiser*? We think Barker's warning is quite apt.)

We would not have rejected *Slob* for breaking our editorial taboos. We don't really have any for *Weird Tales*®. We would have rejected *Slob* because it violates — nay, *defies* — a principal rule of good writing: that the reader must feel sympathy for at least some of its characters. In *Slob* they are no more than so much lunch-meat to be sliced. The problem with the slash-and-vomit aesthetic is that once you have shown all, you have indeed *shown all*. There is nothing left to the imagination, or even to surprise the reader with later.

Charles Richard Laing of Newark, NJ is happier with us:
I would rate the stories in the very enjoyable Fall, 1988 issue in the following order:
1) "Child of an Ancient City"
2) "The Ordeal Stone"
3) "Men From the Plain of Lir"
4) "Emma's Daughter"
5) "The Haunting of Mara"
6) "Little Once"
7) "The Fool"
8) "Avatar"
9) "Still the Same Old Story"
I thought the Williams story was the finest you've published in your brief rebirth. (Yes, Virginia, there were vampires before Uncle Bela). It's good to see the traditional archetypes in unfamiliar settings.
Keith Taylor was a fine choice for Featured Author. In future issues I would like to see unjustly obscure writers such as Taylor featured, rather than the long-time marquee names such as Wolfe, Lee, or Davidson.

Kevin Filan of Montrose, PA writes:
Congratulations on the Fall '88 issue. While everything stood out as excellent, "Emma's Daughter," by Alan Rodgers, was more than excellent; it was incredible. I've rarely read anything so horrifying as that

7

story, or so well-written. I hope you have more from Rodgers in future episodes.

Alan Rodgers (former editor of *Night Cry* magazine) is a very slow and meticulous writer, but we keep encouraging him to send us more stories whenever we see him. We certainly expect — the muses willing — to someday have more. He keeps mentioning this novella about a Teddy Bear . . .

Dean Amantea of San Diego writes:
Weird Tales® *is incredible.*

I have a collection of science fiction magazines that covers one wall of my library (a collection which even includes some '30s vintage copies of your predecessor). But none of them come even close to the quality of your reincarnation of Weird Tales®. *I really just subscribed because it was there; but when I received your first issue I was delightfully shocked. From the simple physical quality of the paper and covers, through the excellent, imaginative prose, editing, and artwork, all tied together with headings and type face which so poignantly recall the Golden Era, the magazine almost sings. And not the least of the contributions to this imagery were Mr. Barr's excellent illustrations. (I'm older, but not old enough to remember many of the original pulp artists — but it seemed like Mr. Barr worked in various styles; also, perhaps, emulating the techniques of earlier artists? Some of his rendering reminded me of Virgil Finlay's work.)*

Your magazine is more than just a new version of the old Weird Tales®, *more than a paen to days gone by; it's a phoenix. Maybe you've started a whole new era: from pulps to digest to . . . quality?*

I hope so.

Gosh. [Blush.] Humility being the greatest of our many virtues, we are left speechless. Well, almost. Of course you're right that Barr was emulating various old-time grand masters. We counted pastiches of Bok, Finlay, Freas, and even Boris Dolgov.

Of interest to our more high-tech readers, John Betancourt runs a free computer bulletin board service (BBS) in Philadelphia. Telephone (modem only!) is (215) 889–0997, 1200 or 2400 baud. Please note: this is purely a discussion board, and we do not accept electronic submissions for *Weird Tales*®! You can, however, leave e-mail for the editors. Do mention *WT* when you sign up for access.

The Most Popular Story
Results are clearly in regarding the Fall 1988 issue. First place goes to Tad Williams for "Child of an Ancient City," followed closely by Alan Rodgers for "Emma's Daughter." Third place goes to Nina Kiriki Hoffman for "Little Once."

As we write this, subscription copies of the Winter '88–'89 issue have just been mailed, so we have yet to receive any votes on those stories. Next time.

Don't forget to write us! We really *do* read everything that comes in, and your opinions are valuable. Particularly welcome are suggestions for Featured Authors and Featured Artists, as we begin looking toward the eighth and ninth — and even farther future — issues of The Unique Magazine.

▲

MOVING?

Don't leave *Weird Tales*® behind! Send us your old address *(with ZIP code)* and your new address (also with Zip code). If you can give us all nine digits of your new Zip code, please do!

— Many thanks!!

THE DEN

by John Gregory Betancourt

The chairman of a large science-fiction convention recently invited a Big Name science-fiction writer to be Guest of Honor at his convention. When the SF writer accepted, local fans were delighted. However, when the chairman invited a Big Name horror writer to be a Special Guest at his convention too, trouble started.

Surprisingly, the trouble didn't come from either of the two writers (neither of whom is particularly temperamental). The trouble came from local fans. "There will be trouble," they predicted, "from horror fans who won't have anything to do at our convention." And — "This is a science-fiction convention, and horror fans and science-fiction fans don't mix." And — "I wouldn't go to a convention that had a horror guest."

The last statement is probably the most telling. For sheer xenophobia, for sheer insularity, for sheer ignorance, it's pretty well unmatched.

Don't fans realize that most writers work in more than one genre? That popular science-fiction writers like Fritz Leiber, David Drake, and George R.R. Martin write excellent horror and dark fantasy? That Stephen King has written everything from science fiction to horror to mainstream?

Clive Barker is best known for his *Books of Blood* — but *Weaveworld* is epic fantasy. Dean Koontz, F. Paul Wilson, Charles L. Grant, Thomas F. Monteleone, and S.P. Somtow all started as *science-fiction* writers before moving on to greater success in the horror field. And Koontz (in *Whispers*) and

King (in *The Tommyknockers*) continue to write science fiction.

Horror writers are often found at science-fiction conventions, enjoying the panels, the discussions, and the parties. (Perhaps fans whose reaction to horror writers is "Yuck!" don't read horror, and so don't recognize Wilson, Koontz, Monteleone, *et al.* as anything but old (and presumably retired) SF writers, and so they're "okay" to associate with.)

Citing a recent World Fantasy Convention as proof that you can't have both a Big Name science-fiction writer and a Big Name horror writer as guests at *any* science-fiction convention didn't particularly help. At that particular WFC, horror programming had predominated, and many people felt left out. But anyone who didn't dabble in horror felt left out that year. Bad programming is at fault: any well-thought-out convention would have strived for a balance between fantasy and horror.

If you went to a convention with Isaac Asimov (to pick a random Big Name SF writer) as Guest of Honor, and the only people who had a good time were Japanimation fans because the committee only programmed talks, panels, and videos/films on Japanese animation, would you say science-fiction writers are horrible and shouldn't be invited to *any* convention ever again? Would you threaten to boycott any convention which invited a science-fiction writer to be a guest? Of course not.

Ignorance and stupidity are everywhere.

But they're particularly loathsome in the field of the fantastic, where we're supposed to be above such things.

Brothers in Arms, by Lois McMaster Bujold
Baen Books, 338pp., $3.95 (pb)

Fantasist and science-fiction writer Lois McMaster Bujold is probably best known for her military SF novels about Miles Vorkosigan, the brilliant leader of the Dendarii Free Mercenaries. This book picks up a story about Miles begun in *Alien Stars*, Vol. III, edited by Elizabeth Mitchell — which is a problem because, unless you've read Bujold's novella in *Alien Stars*, you're going to have some trouble figuring out what's going on, and why.

The story, in brief: Miles returns to Earth to have his mercenary fleet repaired after a battle, but payments for his last job are mysteriously delayed. While he waits (and continues to wait), people begin trying to kill him. But which of his two identities are they after: Miles the Barrayaran, or Admiral Naismith, head of the Dendarii Free Mercenaries?

It's a good mid-series installment that could have been bettered by including the whole book. If you're already caught up in the series, you won't want to miss it; if you aren't, do yourself a favor and start with either *The Warrior's Apprentice* or *Shards of Honor*. Bujold is addictive enough that you'll eventually find your way to *Brothers in Arms*.

Madame Two Swords, by Tanith Lee
Donald M. Grant: Publisher, 128pp., $35.00 (hc)

Tanith Lee writes everything well, from science fiction to high fantasy to sword-&-sorcery, to horror. Her latest is a beautiful little book, published in a limited edition of 600 copies, all signed by Tanith Lee and artist Thomas Canty.

Like that of all of Tanith Lee's work, the style in *Madame Two Swords* is one of its most appealing facets: slowly, with attention to detail and characterization, Lee weaves the tale of a destitute young French woman obsessed with Lucien de Ceppays, a long-dead poet and instigating force in the French Revolution. Gradually, through happenstance and seeming coincidence, the protagonist is drawn to Madame Two Swords, an old fortune-teller who once ran a museum of the Revolution. Madame Two Swords is, like our heroine, obsessed with de Ceppays — to the point she cannot die because of her memories.

This story (which is actually very short because of each page's intricate border decorations) is, in this edition, more of a collector's item than anything else. For those who enjoy books with high production values, or die-hard Lee fans, this is the edition to get. For everyone else, just keep an eye out for "Madame Two Swords" — considering Lee's popularity, and the quality of the story, I would not be surprised to find it reprinted soon, either in one of the fantasy magazines or in a collection of Tanith Lee's work. Because of its limited edition status, expect this edition to sell out soon — if it hasn't already.

Up There and Other Strange Directions, by Donald A. Wollheim
The Nesfa Press, 148pp., $18.00? (hc)
Intuit, by Hal Clement
The Nesfa Press, 164pp., $18.00? (hc)

These two books are small, pocket-sized hardcovers published by fans from the Great Northeast (mostly Boston). NESFA seems to be the major small-press publisher for conventions these days. If only they'd bother to put prices on their dust jackets . . .

Up There was published for Nolacon II, where Donald A. Wollheim was Guest of Honor. It is a collection of his shorter work — mostly idea stories, well written and well presented, certainly interesting and well worth reading, if only because of Wollheim's importance to the science-fiction and fantasy fields.

NESFA published *Intuit* for Cactuscon, the North American Science Fiction Convention, which is the major U.S. science-fiction, fantasy, & horror convention when the Worldcon is held abroad. Hal Clement was an interesting (and very good!) choice for Cactuscon's Guest of Honor because he is too often overlooked. His hard-science SF books are few and far between, but almost all classics.

Intuit contains 4 stories: three reprints (one from *Astounding*, two from the *Stellar* anthology series), and one original to this volume. All share the same central character, Laird Cunningham, and deal with the problems he encounters and their *logical* solutions. It's a good collection, one which all of Clement's fans will enjoy.

The Last Deathship Off Antares, by William John Watkins
Questar Books, 204pp., $3.95 (pb)

I really wanted this book to be a new classic of SF in the Campbell school of problem-solving. But it isn't, despite a very promising premise: a group of human soldiers have been captured by aliens from Antares. They are being held in huge prisons — Deathships — where they are starved and forced to fight each other just to survive. Somehow, they must unite and defeat their captors.

The Last Deathship Off Antares isn't a novel; it's an outline for a novel. It's almost all synopsis, which automatically distances the characters: they aren't immediate enough to be involving, nor are they fleshed out enough to be real. All the elements of the story are here, from an archetypical blind genius, to a clever hero, to very alien aliens. I just wish Watkins had actually *written* the book!

The Blood Kiss, by Dennis Etchison
Scream/Press, 216pp., $22.50

Dennis Etchison is a deeply disturbing individual — which I mean as a sincere compliment. Of all the short stories and novels I've read, I can think of only one opening line that still leaps out and grabs me: "Today I put ground glass in my wife's eyes." For sheer horror, for sheer shock value, I've never met that line's equal. Of course, it's from an Etchison story that appeared in *Whispers* some years ago.

The Blood Kiss is Etchison's third collection, and includes stories from *The Magazine of Fantasy and Science Fiction*, *Whispers*, *Masques*, and other places, plus two originals: "Call 666" and "The Blood Kiss." I think I enjoyed "The Blood Kiss" most, with its dual action (part the script-outline for "Queen of the Zombies," part the story of a woman working on that script for a TV show). The claustrophobic stab-everyone-in-the-back feel is masterfully done.

You can order *The Blood Kiss* — and probably get a catalog of other Scream/Press titles, including two more Etchison collections — from: Scream/Press, PO Box 481146, Los Angeles, CA 90048.

Remembering Derleth: All About Augie
August Derleth Society, 112pp., $7.00 (oversized booklet)

Who was August Derleth?

That question would doubtless bring cries of shock from the August Derleth Society. But, slowly and surely, Derleth is sinking into obscurity. His mysteries, his regional mainstream, his horror, fantasy, and science-fiction collections and novels, his anthologies — they're not that easily found anymore.

Who was August Derleth? The August Derleth Society recently published a rather bizarre booklet, full of newspaper clippings, articles, photographs, playbills, remembrances, letters, biased appraisals of Derleth's fiction, and all manner of other ephemera about August Derleth. By the sheer volume of material, August Derleth must have been a famous person. And he must have been a truly great man, too, according to all the testimonials and obituaries.

Who was he, then? What was his importance to the fantasy field? The answers are buried in *Remembering Derleth*, and you have to dig for them. If you didn't already know Derleth wrote lots of fantasy and horror stories, founded Arkham House to keep Lovecraft's work in print, and kept a fairly well respected mainstream/regional fiction career going, then this certainly isn't the book for you. Somehow, it feels like something designed to preach to the converted. It even has recipes for Derleth's favorite foods!

I would be the first to admit a good book about Derleth is needed, and perhaps someone like Sam Moskowitz will write one. While there is a wealth of interesting material here, it's pretty well buried.

Those willing to dig for the interesting bits, or wanting to sample Derleth's favorite foods, can order from: Herb Attis, August Derleth Society Treasurer, 3333 Westview Lane, Madison, WI 53713.

The Once and Future Arthur, edited by Edmund R. Meškys
Niekas Publications, 72pp., $5.95
A Silverlock Companion, edited by Fred Lerner

WEIRD TALES

Niekas Publications, 52pp., $7.95

The ever-diligent people at Niekas Publications are doing a far better job at researching their favorite topics than is the August Derleth Society. The above two titles are examples of good fan scholarship.

The Once and Future Arthur, a special issue of the magazine *Niekas*, contains a few non-Arthurian columns that seem curiously out of place. The articles about King Arthur and the whole Arthurian mythos form the magazine's core, from such diverse talents as Diana L. Paxson (why is the Arthurian saga so powerful?), Marion Zimmer Bradley (did the Arthurian characters really exist?), Phyllis Ann Karr (was Merlin an instrument of Satan?), and others. I've been paging through it, reading bits and pieces, for the last month or so. Did you know, for example, that the British court in the 13th century had "round tables" where knights jousted, danced, and feasted in imitation of Arthur and his men? Did you know that Merlin's motive for spiriting Arthur away so shortly after his birth might have been to keep him unbaptized? Interesting thoughts, indeed!

A Silverlock Companion is a separate publication, not part of *Niekas*, and is intended to promote interest in the late John Myers Myers and his work. It contains an appreciation, interview, guide to source material for *Silverlock*, long bibliography, selection of Myers's verse, and more. If you are interested in John Myers Myers and his work, this is definitely a must-have volume. If you're not, try hunting down a copy of *Silverlock* and joining the rest of us.

Write to Niekas Publications, RFD 2 Box 63, Center Harbor, NH 03226–9729 for more information.

Those Who Hunt the Night, by Barbara Hambly
Del Rey Books, 296pp., $16.95 (hc)

There are books you simply cannot avoid. I had not read anything by Barbara Hambly before *Those Who Hunt the Night*, and I probably still wouldn't have, except for a local dentist named Henry Lazarus. (He's Philadelphia fandom's dentist-of-choice, and has worked on teeth belonging to such luminaries as George Scithers and Diane Duane. Can I have my five bucks now, Henry?)

Ahem. I digress.

Henry likes to come into the *Weird Tales*® office and talk about books, read the magazines, and generally gossip about the fantastic field. One day he insisted I absolutely *had* to read *Those Who Hunt the Night*. It was terrific, he insisted, and how soon did I want to borrow his copy?

With such a strong recommendation behind it, I decided to try the book. Word of mouth is often the best way to catch onto something good, after all, and it certainly sounded interesting.

And you know something? Henry was right. *Those Who Hunt the Night* is a first-class piece of fiction from start to end, with gripping action, characters you believe in and care about, and a completely convincing depiction of turn-of-the-century London — "the period of Sherlock Holmes" as the dust jacket calls it.

The story is straightforward enough. Ysidro, an ancient and powerful vampire, reveals himself to James Asher, Oxford professor and sometime player of the Great Game (he's a spy, in other words). It seems someone is systematically murdering the vampires in the city. Is it a human? Is it another vampire? Ysidro wants the answer before he becomes the next victim.

From there it becomes a sort of supernatural detective novel, with Asher and his wife forced to draw on their own vast skills and mental abilities to track down the murderer. Asher's training as a spy is what made him the obvious choice for the job — and, as a human, he can move both by night and by day.

Asher and his wife discover that vampires aren't just children's stories and that vampires are more dangerous than Ysidro has led them to believe.

Those Who Hunt the Night will be one of the best fantasy novels of the year. Don't miss it.

Blood Is Not Enough, edited by Ellen Datlow
Morrow, 319pp., $19.95 (hc)

If you haven't had enough vampires after *Those Who Hunt the Night*, this anthology is the obvious answer: 15 stories and 2 poems about vampires and vampirism, 8 of which are originals to this collection.

The line-up is good: Dan Simmons, Gahan

Wilson, Garry Kilworth, Harlan Ellison, Scott Baker, Leonid Andreyev, Harvey Jacobs, Sharon N. Farber, Edward Bryant, Fritz Leiber, Tanith Lee, Susan Casper, Steve Rasnic Tem (poem), Gardner Dozois, Jack Dann, Chet Williamson, Joe Haldeman (poem), and Pat Cadigan.

In some instances, the afterwords (written by the authors, concerning the incubation process of each story) are just as disturbing as the stories themselves. The collection provides a good overview of what contemporary writers think of the vampire myth, with a mix of classic stories by major author to serve (I would imagine) as a selling point to the general masses. The oldest story is from the early 1900s, by a Russian existentialist; the next oldest is Fritz Leiber's, from 1946.

It's not the definitive vampire anthology, but it's a start towards one.

DeadLines, by John Skipp & Craig Spector
Bantam Books, 309pp., $3.95 (pb)

Skipp & Spector are certainly at the forefront of dark fantasy's "splatterpunk" movement, which seems a shame considering *DeadLines*, their latest book. This time the violence seems less integral to the storyline, more tacked on as an afterthought, which (in my interpretation) means that they've become self-conscious about leading a "movement" and are now trying to write to their audience's expectations. Also, I found none of the characters particularly appealing — from the suiciding writer, to Colin the unfaithful lover, to Meryl the spoiled-bitch daughter. Katie, the woman whom Colin betrays, is the most appealing of the lot — but still a very flawed person, too credulous and yet too bland. And, the book's real-time action seems something of a framing device, with internal stories (presented as manuscripts which the characters read) doing much to break the pacing.

Dead Lines is simply self-indulgent. Which is too bad, because Skipp & Spector have a lot of talent, and don't need to write to anyone's expectations except their own.

The Null-A Worlds of A.E. van Vogt, by H.L. Drake
Chris Drumm, 30pp., $2.25 (booklet)

The latest in the Drumm Booklet series is very much a long interview with A.E. van Vogt (assembled from a series of interviews conducted between 1974 and 1985) concerning Dianetics and Korzybski's general semantics — both of which affected van Vogt's life and writing to a tremendous degree — as edited and clarified by H.L. Drake.

It's an interesting work, though I'm unsure how worthwhile it will be to future scholars. I would rather have had several complete interviews with van Vogt and been allowed to draw my own conclusions.

The publisher: Chris Drumm, PO Box 445, Polk City, IA 50226.

The Horror in the Museum, by H.P. Lovecraft
Arkham House, 450pp., $18.95

The dust jacket says it best: "Following S.T. Joshi's acclaimed three-volume critical edition of the Lovecraft fiction, this final supplementary collection includes all known revisions and collaborations undertaken by Lovecraft on behalf of his friends and clients. As with previous volumes in this series, the texts preserved herein scrupulously follow archival manuscripts, typescripts, or original publications, and constitute the definitive edition of these stories."

No horror library would be complete without Lovecraft, and no Lovecraft collection can be complete with anything *except* the definitive editions of The Master's work.

If you can't get them from your local bookseller, write to Arkham House for their catalog: Arkham House Publishers, Inc, Sauk City, WI 53583.

Swordsmen and Saurians, by Roy G. Krenkel
Eclipse Books, 152pp., $19.95 (trade pb); $45.00 (hc)

Roy G. Krenkel was one of the lesser-known but most talented of this century's fantasy and science-fiction artists — perhaps best remembered among comics fans for his work in the EC titles of the '50s and '60s. His influence can be seen in the work of such notables as Frank Frazetta and Al Williamson.

Swordsmen and Saurians is the second collection of his artwork in coffee-table book format, and presents — of course — many of his sketches of dinosaurs and fantasy swordsmen (from his illustrations of Edgar Rice Burroughs's books — the Barsoom titles especially), and others. He also drew nifty cities, otherworldly flora and fauna, and all manner of other things. Almost all are roughs, rather than finished drawings, which is just fine because what Krenkel left to the imagination is just as important as what he put into his pictures.

My only qualm is the cost: compared to the still in-print *Cities and Scenes of the Ancient World* [Owlswick Press, 1974, 82pp., $25.00 (hc)], this volume seems inaccessibly priced.

But — boy could Krenkel draw!

You can order from: Eclipse Comics, Forestville, CA 95436

The Dark Haired Girl, by Philip K. Dick Ziesing, 246pp., $19.95 (hc)

Yes, it's another posthumous PKD book — the supply still seems to be holding out, and I'm sure there are another dozen or so yet to come. (I'm waiting for some daring publisher to undertake putting Dick's mammoth *Exegesis* into hardcovers, and his complete correspondence in thirty volumes.)

This volume is the most interesting to me since Underwood/Miller assembled all of Dick's short fiction into a five-volume set. It's non-fiction, the core being "The Dark Haired Girl," an almost-narrative which Dick assembled from his letters in 1972. Also included are several essays, poems, and a minor short story which Paul Williams took from one of Dick's letters.

Philip K. Dick was a fascinating, complex man. Williams, in his introduction, says, "This is a tale told by an unreliable narrator, who recognizes his own unreliability and yet at the same time believes everything he says. If you in turn allow yourself to believe uncritically everything he says, you are a damn fool. Watch out. Especially if you think you are not a damn fool, watch out."

In his essay, "The Evolution of a Vital Love," Dick writes:

"Here is my first proposed extrapolation, then, of all this, into a science-fiction novel. The protagonist loses his happy but dull marriage, his middle-class little world, and plunges into the depths of violent excess: a subculture, covert and exciting and illegal. He has many lurid adventures but subtly descends until one day the vivid dream reveals a substratum of nightmare by insidious slow degrees leering through from within. That ugly underlying reality within this pleasure world seizes him remorselessly in the form of addiction to a specific drug he has been induced to take, possibly by a close ersatz-friend who is in reality a pusher . . .

"The true science-fiction element is the next step . . .

"In brief: the organization does not make you a captive by addicting you to the drug but by *saving* you from the drug." (pp. 180–1)

When I read Dick's non-fiction, a line from an old song runs through my head: *Paranoia runs deep.*

Mark Ziesing is to be commended for publishing this book. It's one that deserves to be read, and yet it's also one which I'm sure most publishers never would have dared to touch, because it's so *different* from everything else.

Ziesing's address is: P.O. Box 806, Willimantic, CT 06226.

Of Interest

For the beginning writer interested in the small press, I recommend *Scavenger's Newsletter*, a monthly update to the smaller markets in the fantastic field. A sample is $1.00 from: Janet Fox, 519 Ellinwood, Osage City, KS 66523–1329.

New things from those associated with *Weird Tales®: Another Round at the Spaceport Bar*, edited by George Scithers and Darrell Schweitzer, is now out from Avon Books. It's more fantastic stories with bar settings, a follow-up to last year's *Tales from the Spaceport Bar*.

And lastly, from Ace Books comes *The Dragons of Komako*, fourth in the Dr. Bones series (about a space-going archaeologist), by one John Gregory Betancourt.

▲

WEIRD TALES TALKS
WITH HARRY TURTLEDOVE

by Darrell Schweitzer

Weird Tales: You seem to have just come out of the blue with a story called "Death in Vesunna" in *Isaac Asimov's SF Magazine* some years ago. Was that the beginning of your career?

Turtledove: I had been *trying* to write since I was in high school. "Death in Vesunna" was the first thing that I sold. I sold it to the late, lamented *Cosmos.* I actually got paid for it, but the magazine died before the story ever showed up. By the time I got the rights to "Death in Vesunna" back and sold it again, it became my second story to appear in print. The first was a satire, an environmental impact story of Columbus's first voyage, which appeared in *Universe 10.*

WT: So, how long did it take you to break into print, from the start?

Turtledove: On and off, about thirteen years. This included about a five-year break while I was in graduate school doing a dissertation.

WT: Which leads us inevitably to the question of how one gets from Byzantine history to science fiction and fantasy.

Turtledove: It worked the other way around for me. I got to Byzantine history from science fiction. When I was in high school I read Sprague de Camp's *Lest Darkness Fall.* I got fascinated trying to find out what he was making up and what was real, because when I read it I knew nothing at all about this sort of thing. I was a red-hot science person. I knew nothing outside of U.S. history, that being what I was taught in public school, so the entire thing was a revelation to me. I went to Cal Tech, flunked out, and ended up at UCLA doing Byzantine history.

WT: You've written quite a lot about the Roman and Byzantine periods. What is the particular fascination with this? I know it is not unique to either of us. My own guess

is that we are fascinated by glitter, pomp, and spectacle, and the power of absolute monarchy as long as we don't have to live under it.

Turtledove: That's an excellent point. I would not want to live in the Byzantine Empire, for one thing, simply because I'm Jewish and would have a hard time automatically. But the amazing resilience of the people is what draws us to them, as well as their importance in transmitting to the West such things as defined Christian theology, which has played no small part in the world, though I don't share it; also the Roman law as codified under Justinian. Historically, Byzantium served as a bulwark against the Muslims for many hundreds of years; also most of what Western Europe knows of Greek literature and Greek philosophy comes from manuscripts preserved in Constantinople.

WT: Curiously, the West has only been interested in what Byzantium transmitted, not in what it created.

Turtledove: I think that's partly true because most of Byzantine literature, the high literature, was written and created for a court elite. When the elite broke down, first after the conquest of Constantinople in the Fourth Crusade and then especially as the Turks took more and more of the empire in the 14th and 15th centuries, no one cared about courtly tastes. Also, the Byzantines did not view themselves as improving on the ancients. They *modeled* themselves on the ancients. This is one of the differences between the West and the East. In the West the ancient models were so thoroughly lost that people were creating new things. In the East the shadow of the greatness of both the Roman Empire at its height, and also of classical Athens, was something that Byzantine authors were so conscious of that they felt that imitating these things rather than doing something different was the best way to go.

WT: This is probably part of the science-fictional fascination with Byzantium, which goes back to Asimov's psycho-history and all that. We have such a long view of the Roman state, from its birth to the death of its remotest descendants, that we can, in that context, imagine what it would feel like to have the weight of a thousand years of tradition on one's mind.

Turtledove: Yes. Byzantium was in a very interesting position, because it was the first non-Western society that was heavily affected by the expansion of Western Europe. Had the empire survived, Byzantium would have been in a better position to adapt itself. Byzantium understood what was happening. Toward the end of the empire, the Byzantines got very interested in the West. Cardinal Bessarion, who later converted to Catholicism and ended his life in Italy, urged the Byzantines to send some of their bright young men to the West to learn Western technical tricks. Possibly because they were closer to the West in origin, they were more willing to adapt than other civilizations which had longer to become set in their ways. But the Turkish conquest of course eliminated what might have been a very interesting change in Byzantium.

WT: A lot of people are writing fantasy about Byzantium of late. We feel sympathy for the Byzantines, for all we know that their government was in many ways harsh and the people were often intolerant.

Turtledove: I'm not so sure sympathy is the right word. Interest is. I think one of the reasons is simply that we have seen a great glut of Scandinavian fantasies, Greco-Roman fantasies, and Celtic fantasies, and people are looking for background which is relatively unexplored. This is one of the enjoyable things about having done the stuff professionally: because I've read some of the Byzantine texts in the original, I have access to material which is not translated into English. So when I write, it appears fresh and new, and yet it has the verisimilitude behind it because it is based on events that really happened.

WT: How did the Basil Argyros series start?

Turtledove: I had the idea in the back of my mind for a long time for an alternate universe in which Islam never happened and a Byzantine agent was going through the mountains in Spain, up toward the Franks who had discovered gunpowder. That was the first story that I wrote in the series. At the time, I thought it was a one-shot. Then I had another idea — what would happen if printing was discovered? — and after that, I started thinking about the man, Basil Argyros, about his life, until I had written a book-length series of stories which appeared in the "Asimov Presents" line as *Agent of Byzantium.*

WT: By an incredible coincidence — I'd guess you didn't see this — someone wrote in to *Worlds of If* sometime in the late '60s, suggesting that the magazine have a department in which readers offer their own ideas to any writers who cared to use them. This letter-writer suggested as his idea, to start things off, an alternate universe without Mohammed.

Turtledove: No, I never saw that. The phenomenal expansion of Islam is obviously one of the critical breaking-points in history. When you're looking to do an alternate history you try to find a point where, if things had happened differently, the world would start to look different fairly fast.

WT: It's not just a breaking-point, but yet another incredible coincidence. The whole expansion of Islam stems from a ruinous Byzantine-Persian war, which exhausted both empires beyond the point of being able to resist Islam. If Mohammed had come along ten years earlier or later, he wouldn't have gotten anywhere.

Turtledove: Possibly not ten years, but certainly fifty years either way, because the Byzantines and the Persians fought a series of wars from 572 to 592, and then again from 602 to 628. This last war almost resulted in the Persian capture of Constantinople and did result in the Byzantine sack of the Persian capital of Ctesiphon. It left both sides, especially the Persians, prostrate. They returned to the *status quo ante bellum,* but only because both were too exhausted to go on any more. It left them easy meat for the expansion of Islam. You're right. Islam could easily have remained a minor Arabian cult, had Mohammed come along at a different time.

WT: I can't help but wonder if various

other Arabian prophets did come along at different times.

Turtledove: There were others besides Mohammed. There was a man named Maslama, who came along, unfortunately for him, just *after* Mohammed and was suppressed by the rising Muslims.

WT: How would one take this awareness of the mechanism of history and project it into the future? Have you done much of that?

Turtledove: I've done a lot of it. It's a good question, and not an easy one to answer. You guess. Any alternate history is basically an informed guess. You try to do your best to figure out what would have happened and why. To use an example from another series I've done for *Analog* and *Asimov's* which was collected as *A Different Flesh*, I imagined a world where North and South America were settled, not by American Indians, but by *Homo erectus*. When the Europeans then discover America, what are the consequences? Well, the first *immediate* consequence is that Spain would probably not have become a great power in Europe, because Spanish power in the 16th and 17th centuries was based on the resources that they took from the Central and South American Indian civilizations. Those resources would not be collected by sub-human beings. Conversely, North America becomes easier to settle, because the sims, as I call the sub-humans, would offer much less resistance than the organized and more technologically sophisticated Indian tribes that the North American settlers had to push back. The next thing you have to ask yourself is, with North America easier to settle, what happens to England? With North America easier to settle, it would be easier to ship malcontents across the sea. I envisioned England becoming a divine-right monarchy on the order of Louis XIV's France, which in our history it narrowly missed doing.

WT: Finding *Homo erectus,* the Spaniards' ideas of what it means to be human would change enormously. Do sims have souls?

Turtledove: That's a question that I honestly don't have an answer to. But, yes, it would make us think of humanity in an entirely different way. In one of the stories I did, I envisioned — for one reason, because it was great fun to write — a pastiche of the diary of Samuel Pepys, and had him working out from the discovery of sims — and also from the discovery of chimpanzees, which occurred in Africa about the same time — the theory of evolution a couple of hundred years earlier than anyone really did. Another thing that discovering sub-human beings would do would be to make racial distinctions between various groups of *men* seem much less important: because compared to sub-humans, all people, no matter what color, are very much alike. I did a story about that too. It's called "Though the Heavens Fall."

WT: Wouldn't it also be possible for people to say that the despised group is "just like *them*"? I think that if twisted around, this perception could *strengthen* racism. We already have the old racist stereotype that black people resemble gorillas.

Turtledove: But when you compare blacks to sims, they are much more like other folk than like sims. Sims give *everyone* someone to look down on, black and white included. I think that the racism would be directed in their direction, rather than toward blacks.

WT: Most of your work seems to be alternate history rather than extrapolation from the real present. Why?

Turtledove: The majority of my work is alternate history. I've done some hard SF, mostly stories in *Analog*. I also have four volumes of a series called *The Videssos Cycle,* where I dropped three cohorts of Caesar's legionaries into a fantasy world modeled on 11th-century Byzantium. I have just finished for Del Rey a novel whose working title is *A World of Difference,* that is set in a universe identical to ours in every way, except that in this universe Mars, instead of being small, cold, dead, and bloody boring, is about twice the size that it is. The opening premise is that when Viking landed in 1976 on the world that I call Minerva — because it would appear bright and shiny from Earth instead of red — that the last picture Viking took was of a Minervan native getting ready to smash it to bits with a club. The book itself is set about fifteen years later, with U.S. and Soviet expeditions to Minerva to make contact with the natives.

The appeal of this sort of alternate history to me is that by operating in worlds different from ours, I can show ours and our beliefs and perspectives as if in a funhouse mirror. By looking how things might work if something had happened differently, you can get a better handle on the way things really have developed.

WT: What are the rules for writing alternate history? Obviously this must be done with some limits.

Turtledove: The rule that I use is to change one thing, make it a big change, and then try to follow as logically as possible the developments from that one single change.

WT: Would you ever contemplate doing a vast future history extrapolated from the real present?

Turtledove: No.

WT: Too difficult, or doesn't appeal?

Turtledove: Doesn't appeal. I find that, based on what I know, what I've studied, I tend to work better either in a past or an alternate present.

WT: What other writers have influenced you, other than, obviously, de Camp?

Turtledove: I'm not really coming out of a school of writers, but I seem to be doing some of the same things as Sprague de Camp and also Poul Anderson.

WT: What are you working on now and what's coming out in the immediate future?

Turtledove: I mentioned the book coming out from Del Rey with the alternate Mars. Right now I'm working on a novella in the parallel-novella series that Martin Greenberg is putting together, where classic novellas are published with sequels or prequels by younger writers. I'm doing a sequel to Sprague de Camp's "Wheels of If" called "The Pugnacious Peacemaker." After that, I have a contract with Del Rey for two more books in the Videssos universe.

WT: Thank you, Harry Turtledove. ▲

UNIVERSE

My face may be a Universe peopled by billions and billions
Of Lives which flame up and are extinguished while I draw a breath.
There may be continents and rivers,
Mountains and valleys.
I writhe the cosmic expanse of my lips
And earthquakes shake the nations and men die.
I clench my jaws and the muscles bulge —
Like Atlantis above the smooth oceans of my skin.

And while I clench my jaws
On the Atlantises of my jawbone muscles,
Generations thrive and live and die, all in a second.
I relax my jaws, my bulging muscles smooth out,
And continents have sunk into the depths
Bearing millions of screaming lives to oblivion.
I wonder if our universe is a man's face and if
Men, seeing afar the reflection of that face in some
Cosmic mirror, have dreamed of the face of God?

— **Robert E. Howard**

DRAGONS

by Michael F. Flynn

"Have you ever wondered where all the dragons have gone?"

Bennet Long asked me that one evening as we sat over brandy in my drawing room. Dinner had been filling but, for me, unsatisfying. I sat in my favourite overstuffed high-backed chair, savoring the liquor, and luxuriating in the warmth of the fire. I was enduring the long silence — enjoying it, even — although I knew it was but a prelude to some dreadful tale that Bennet had brought with him. I could see it in his face. Throughout the meal, as Bennet was eating his filet, I had had the impression, if I may be permitted the vulgarism, that something was also eating him.

I selected a cigar from the humidor on the table that sat between us. I offered him one, but he refused. I struck a wooden match with my right hand and paused while the chemicals burned out of the flame. "I should think," I answered him judiciously, "that the dragons haven't gone anywhere. That, since they have not been here at all, so to speak, it would be impossible for them to go somewhere else."

He nodded vigorously as if I had fulfilled his expectations. "Just so, Verril," he replied. "And most ecologists and biologists would agree with you. The dragons are gone, because they never existed in the first place. But!" He leaned forward in his chair and pointed a finger at me. "But, what if we were all wrong?"

I lit my cigar and sucked it into life. Bennet worried me. We had been colleagues at the University for many years. We had even published papers together. But Bennet was a changed man since his field trip into the Naga country some five years before. Something had happened to him there, something he never spoke of; yet, something that seemed to have changed his life. He abandoned his research, though it had been a very promising line of inquiry, boding well for our understanding of the eco-niches of tropical scavenger genera. And he began to delve into what I can most kindly characterize as "esoterica." Myths, legends, the magical bestiaries of forgotten savants. There was not a chimera fantasized by a medieval alchemist, nor a muckle brae' beastie imagined by some dull Scots peasant that did not excite his interest or engage his keen intellect. His obsession with cataloguing and arranging these creatures had possessed him to the point of destroying his marriage and most of his personal relationships. Out of respect for his brilliance I had made a determined effort to remain his friend. I am tolerant of most things, but Bennet's dragon monomania was becoming a bit of a nuisance.

"What about the second law of thermodynamics?" I told him with some aspersion. "You can't get around that, you know. There are no dragons, because a fellow named Maxwell said so." I smiled to myself at the witticism.

Bennet lapsed into sullen silence, so I pressed the point home. "Look here, Bennet. There is too much energy loss if you proceed too many steps up a food

19

chain. Plant life on the average manages to convert only 2% of the sun's energy into calories. Only 2%! All those sugar factories, covering virtually the entire earth, with their solar transducers straining to catch the sunlight — they are remarkably inefficient, as Transeau showed in his seminal study of Illinois maize. At best, and under ideal conditions, pampered by farmers with water and manure, they may manage 8% for a short while. And there they reach a limit set by the carbon dioxide content of our atmosphere. . . ."

"But, Verril . . ."

"Hear me out, Bennet. For your own sake." I took a sip of brandy and continued. "Now, of that minuscule 2% the herbivores harvest a mere 10%. The rest is lost. The plants use it themselves: for growth, maintenance, disease resistance, and the like. By diverting calories from these other functions into the edible parts of the plant, our genetic engineers can squeeze out a bit more nutrition. But — we must spend calories to do it! The farmer's own sweat is only one expenditure. So, there is an upper limit here, as well.

"The carnivores, in turn, harvest only 10% of the biomass of the herbivores, and *that* is the critical limit on your dragons. While herbivores may be large and numerous, big fierce animals must be rare. Because the carnivore must be big enough and agile enough to catch its prey. When Charles Elton made his classic observations of Arctic foxes on Spitzbergen, he found that predators typically outmass their prey by an order of magnitude. The foxes were many times larger than the sandpipers and buntings that they ate; and these, in turn, were many times larger than the worms and insects. Essentially, a kilo of prey must be hunted by 10 kilos of predator; and, since only a tenth of the prey's biomass is available, you must have 100 kilos of prey to support one kilo of predator." I smiled and made

20

a steeple of my fingers. "A Bengal tiger masses — oh, 200 kilos, I would imagine. So your dragons would mass up to 2000 kilos; and there could be only one of them for every hundred tigers." I spread my hands in appeal. "That is why the Top Predators are the lion, the tiger, the great white shark. Nothing larger and fiercer is thermodynamically possible. Don't you see? There simply aren't enough tigers — or lions — to support a self-sustaining breeding population of dragons. There is not enough profit to be had in the niche of tiger-hunting."

Long before I had finished I could see on Bennet's face that I had not convinced him. He was not listening, only waiting for me to finish.

"No, Verril, no. There are two things wrong with your argument. The first is that it is only true today. Humans have culled the great cats to the point that they can no longer sustain the dragons. That much is true. Where is the Lion of Nemea that Herakles hunted? The great cats pursued by the Babylonians and Mycenaeans? What of the European sabre-tooth? Gone even before the dawn of history. And the African lion and Indian and Siberian tigers are in decline, as well. But, Verril, *It wasn't always that way!*"

The way he said it made me shiver. I shifted in my seat and frowned at him. "What do you mean?"

"I mean that before primitive man came on the scene, the biomass of the great cats was sufficient to support a breeding population of dragons. I have identified four major species. There was the European Dragon, the traditional dragon of the fairy tales, that preyed on the now extinct European lion. Perseus was supposed to have saved Andromeda from one. Probably a dimly remembered legend of the prehistoric past. There was the closely-related African Dragon below the Sahara; the tiger-eating Asiatic dragon; and the

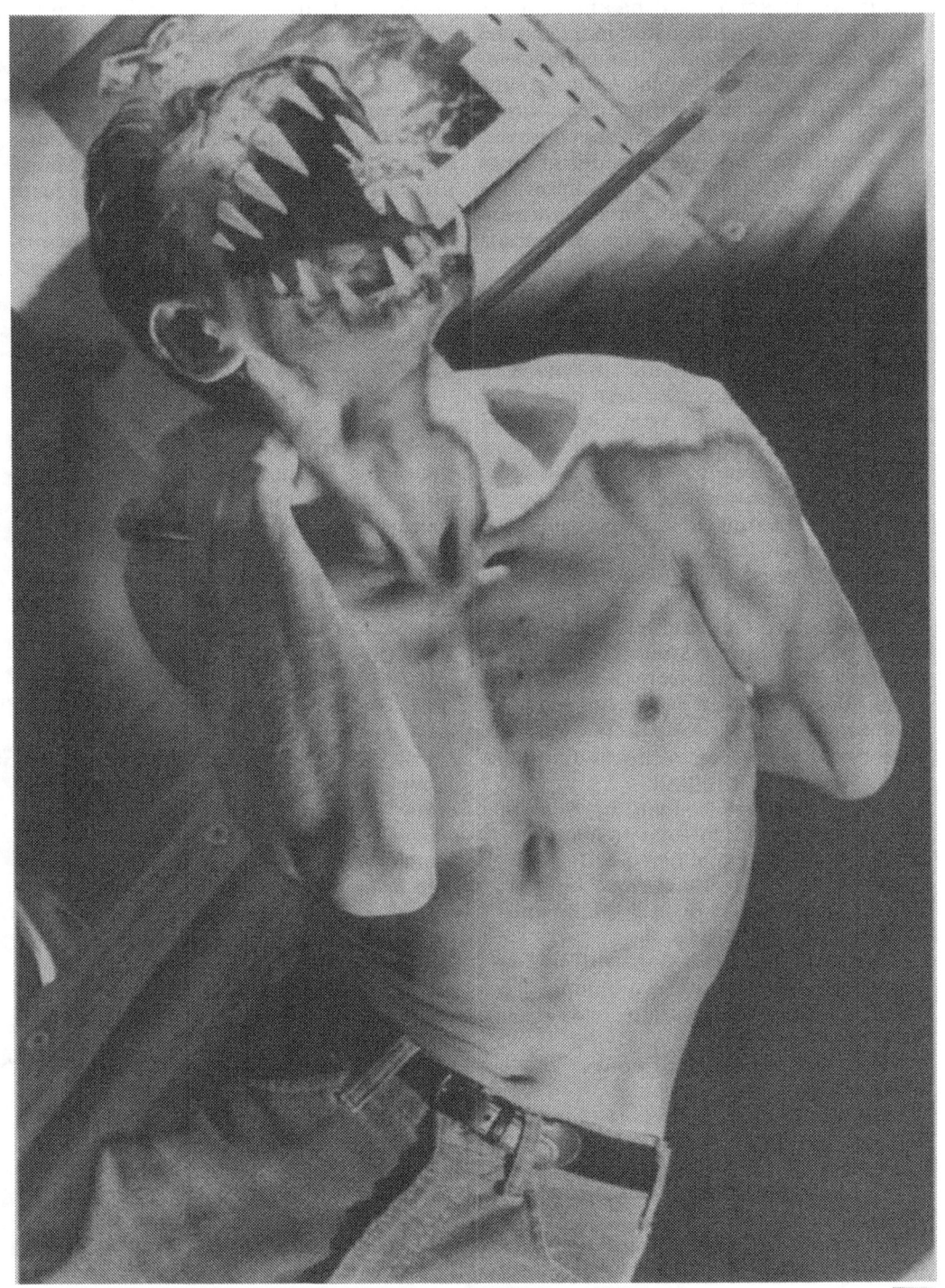

Mountain Dragon of China and Siberia that was long and thin and had a maned face and bulging eyes, like some creature out of Hell." He looked at me earnestly. "I have the figures, if you like."

I had no doubt that he had figures. How reliable they were would be anyone's guess. "Dash it all, Bennet," I scolded him. "You can't have giant reptiles chasing big mammals. Mammals are too fast, too agile. . . ."

"But dragons are also mammals! Oh, I know they are always pictured as scaly; but those are legends. Fantasy." He looked away from me, to the fire. "It has been a chore these past few years separating fact from fancy. Like fire-breathing. The European dragon was supposed to have breathed fire. Actually, it sprayed acid on its victims."

I sighed. "I suppose I cannot convince you otherwise."

"No. Because . . . because, I have seen . . ."

The door to the kitchen opened and Mrs. Robbins presented herself. She was a large woman from the West Indies. She normally wore the colorful blouses and turbans of the Islands, but just now she was clad in the mackintosh and galoshes of England.

"I have finished de cleaning of de dinner dishes, suh. If yo have no more need of me, I'll be going home befo' this storm breaks." As if to underscore her comments, a distant roll of thunder shivered the windowpanes.

"Yes, Mrs. Robbins, that will be fine. Have yourself a safe trip home. The meal, by the way, madam, was excellent, as always."

"Uh, yes," muttered Bennet. "It was quite good."

Mrs. Robbins thanked us and left. Bennet gathered himself together. "I suppose I should take my leave as well. This storm. I'm afraid I've made an awful pest of myself."

"Nonsense, Bennet. I won't hear of it. Mrs. Robbins lives nearby. Her son attends the University. Your digs are in Hampton, an altogether different trip. You'll stay. I insist."

I did insist. Bennet's theoretical ravings were one thing. Anyone could — and did — dismiss them. But he had intimated that he had seen something. I could not let him leave until he had told me about it. Whatever else he might have become, Bennet had always been a shrewd and careful observer. Perhaps, whatever it was, I could make him see it in a different light. I settled myself in my chair and listened to his story.

It was in the rhododendron forests of northern Burma [Bennet told me]. Five years ago. We had left Likhapani on the 15th of May and climbed the Patkai mountains from the Indian side. The trek was like a trek back into time. We left the teeming and well-ordered Bengali towns behind, with their market places and rice paddies, and passed through the villages of the Assamese tribesmen. The hill people, as you know, hate the Bengali townsmen and raid their settlements much as the Red Indians raided frontier towns in the American West — and for much the same reasons. The tribesmen watched us suspiciously as we passed and made occasional displays against us. The porters became nervous, but were more afraid of deserting and being caught alone than they were of staying with the group. Our guide, a small brown Hindu named Krishnamurthi, was equally contemptuous of both Bengali and Assamese.

When we left Assam and entered the Naga country I expected his contempt to increase. The Naga were still less civilized than the Assamese, not even possessing permanent villages. Oddly enough, it did not. Krish became strangely silent. He said only that the "children of the forest" remembered things that more civilized folk had for-

22

DRAGONS

gotten.

The Naga, of course, know nothing of India or Burma. When we crossed the Pangsan Pass and entered the Sangpang Bum we may have been the only humans for miles who knew that they had entered another country.

We were surrounded by an immense dark forest of maples and conifers, wildly festooned with magnolias and rhododendrons. Monkeys hung from the lower branches and scolded us as we passed. The smell of the flowers was sweet, almost cloying. It was as if we had entered another world.

We worked our way southwestward through the foothills, collecting samples as we went. Krishnamurthi never said what he thought of my careful collection and labelling of dung, or my classification of the parasites I found in my specimens. He had guided other scientific expeditions. The Bengalis and the two Assamese who had joined us surely thought I was crazy. Perhaps I was. It seems such a trivial pursuit in retrospect.

We made camp the fourth night near the headwaters of the Nampuk River. The Bengali porters had grown increasingly nervous and had shown a tendency to hang back during the day's hike. The two Assamese deserted us that night. When I asked Krish about it he shrugged and said, "Naga tales." He refused to elaborate, but I noticed a worried frown on his face. As a civilized man, he was trying to discount superstitions he had heard and was not being altogether successful.

It was in the early dawn, when the forest is lit in a strange unworldly light, that we were suddenly awakened by a hideous cry. We scrambled from our tents and stood looking about. It was a piteous cry: at once defiant and despairing. A snarl that was also a whimper. It went on and on and then rose into a screech and stopped in a bubbling gurgle. We stood there shaken. The jungle remained mute for long minutes afterward.

The cry, whatever it had been, was too close to our camp to be ignored. We steeled ourselves and went to investigate, clutching the rifles and handguns that we carried for self-protection. None of us wanted to venture out there. Not the Bengalis, not Krish, and least of all myself. But we were too frightened not to. The horrors of the imagination are worse than those that are real. The truth would calm our fears.

Or at least, so I believed at the time.

We probed our way cautiously through the undergrowth for fifteen minutes before we found it.

It was the corpse of a Bengal tiger. It lay on the jungle floor, twisted and broken, with its face twisted in a defiant snarl. Its hide was blackened in several places and reeked of sulfuric acid. Its throat had been ripped out and it was partially eaten.

We stared at that horrible sight for possibly a full minute. The realization came to all of us at the same time. I saw the others' eyes widen and Krishnamurthi's head come up and look around.

Something had hunted and killed a full-grown Bengal tiger. Something that spat acid and stood back and slashed its throat with a casual swipe.

And we had interrupted its feeding.

"Quickly," hissed Krishnamurthi. "Stop for nothing. Abandon everything. Meet at the ancient cairn where we made our first day's camp below the pass." He worked the action of his old Enfield rifle. I pulled my .45 from its scabbard. I carried it for snakes and pests. Its protection now seemed pitifully thin.

The next few days were a blur. At first we stayed together. We ran, night and day, never stopping to sleep. We only took wary pauses while some of us took turns resting fitfully. Then, off again up the trail toward the Pass.

It was after one such pause that

23

Krish counted heads and came up one short. One of the porters was missing. The man had been with us when we had stopped. Now he was gone. Something had reached quietly into our midst and snatched one of us away without alarming the others in the slightest.

It was pure panic after that. One man and I managed to stay together until we reached the cairn, but the rest scattered. From their viewpoint, I suppose we scattered. Once, during that ordeal, I thought I heard shots. Three of them, fired in measured succession, as from a bolt-action rifle. Twice I heard screams torn from the throats of living men.

My companion and I were the first to reach the cairn. The rest of the expedition dribbled in by ones and twos over the next few hours. All, save a few. Krish was not among them. I waited and I wanted to wait longer, but the other men insisted on leaving and threatened to leave without me. In the end, I gave in to their pleas. I knew I had seen the last of Krishnamurthi.

The fire crackled. The brandy sat untouched on the lamp table. I looked at Bennet over my fingertips.

"You did not actually *see* a dragon," I said.

He jerked his head around. The eyes were red and lined. He had relived the whole harrowing experience. "If I *had* laid eyes on one, I would not be here telling you of it. Krishnamurthi, I think, saw one."

I was disturbed. Bennet was a careful man. What he had seen might not mean what he thought it meant; but I could not doubt that he had seen it.

"Then, based on this one traumatic experience, you have developed an elaborate ecology of dragons."

"Yes," he responded eagerly, mistaking my tone for acceptance. "If we extrapolate from Top Predators, dragons must be very long-lived and must only

feed once a month. But as humans multiplied and spread, they undermined the dragon niche, hunting the lions and tigers themselves, until only a few pockets remained viable. Soon, the dragons turned on the humans as a new source of food and our legends were born. Who knows what a titanic struggle was fought in those long-forgotten days? We have only the memories of memories to guide us."

I saw an opening and I went for it. "But, then, if the dragons began to prey on humans, how could they have become endangered species, surviving in only a few remote areas? Four billion humans could support a population of, oh, forty million dragons. Today we may be able to defend ourselves against them. Humans are, after all, tenacious and fierce themselves. But in ancient Hellas or Babylon? No, your dragons died out too quickly."

I suddenly remembered my brandy. I picked it up and saw that the liquid was rippling. My hand was shaking. At some premonition of what Bennet had to say?

Bennet took his wallet and withdrew a folded newspaper clipping. He opened it up and handed it to me. It was from the *Times*. I glanced at the headline: **Tiger at Zoo Butchered. Satanic Cult Suspected.**

I laughed. "Come now, Bennet. Even you must admit that a two-thousand-pound dragon would be hard put remaining concealed in London Town!"

"Non-Eltonian hunters. The second flaw in your thermodynamic argument."

"Ah." I felt despair float through me. Bennet was all too convincing.

"Yes. Not all predators follow Elton's mass ratio. Take the great baleen whales. Compared to the krill they eat, they are absurdly large. But they hunt in non-Eltonian ways, lazily cruising the seas, straining the krill from the oceanic soup with their sieves of bone.

DRAGONS

And wolves. Normally, they take quail or rabbits like good Eltonians. But, on those rare occasions when they hunt the caribou, they hunt as a Pack."

"Then, you believe there are non-Eltonian hunters loose in London?" This was more upsetting than the dragons.

"Yes. The reason that dragons could not shift successfully from tiger-hunting to human-hunting was that *the human-hunting niche was already filled.* And now . . ." He indicated the newspaper clipping. ". . . the tiger-hunting niche is also open. After I read that story, I did some research. About great cats that die in zoos or simply disappear from game preserves. And people. Do you know how many people disappear every year? Mostly teenagers. Runaways, we say; but how many are ever found? And who notices if a few street people vanish? As is the case with any predator, our hunters prefer to take the young, the sick, and the weak. I have come to you for your advice."

"My advice."

"Yes. You are the foremost authority in England on animal mimicry."

The import of his words stunned me. I set my brandy carefully on the table. "You believe these, ah, hunters mimic the human form?"

"Of course. Could humans be hunted by monstrous *things* without some hint or rumor of it becoming common knowledge? No, there are only a few ways for mammals to make a living by predation: stalking, pack hunting, ambush, and so on. I believe that our hunters have done so with stealth, with mimicry, with — dare I say it? — *intelligence.*"

"And we never noticed?" I asked with some amusement.

"Would sheep notice fleecy white wolves? Wolves that baa'd like sheep? And yet, perhaps. There are other kinds of legends. Jack the Ripper. Werewolves. Vampires. Perhaps . . ."

I drummed my fingers on the table. "Have you told anyone of this?"

"No. Not yet. People would say I was crazy. But I have been collecting evidence. Yes. Evidence." He looked at me in appeal. "You believe me, don't you?"

This had gone too far. Lightning struck nearby and the lights went out for a brief moment. Bennet, distracted, looked at the lamp.

"Bennet?" I said.

"Yes?" He looked at me.

"I believe you." I smiled. And showed him my fangs.

▲

SIGHINGS

Such wonderful things
As ghosts,
And elves,
And witches,
Have passed, it seems,
To wiser realms.

And Arthur,
Deep in his hidden cave,
Has overslept.

— **Phil Emery**

25

COURTING DISASTERS

by Nina Kiriki Hoffman

Simon remembered the vision of the crash. He saw the windows shatter, the splash of glass, the crunching, inward impact. He was aware of the steering wheel smashing into his ribcage, the windshield battering his face, and the car's front end crushing his legs as the Ferrari and the redwood met, but he didn't feel the pain. There were certain sensations he allowed to travel from his body to his home, deep in his skull, but pain was not one of them. He had learned how to turn off the pain when he was eight.

But he didn't hear anything, either, and that disturbed him; he had never damped sound before. Hearing and sight were his favorite senses, vital to his job as well as to his off-hour pleasures. He recalled the mixture of desperation, abandon, and numbness he had felt; the pulse of the car around him, the cool night air blowing in the vents, the driving beat of rock music from the speakers behind him, the scent of wet and redwood as he mazed his way around the curves of the Avenue of the Giants.

When his control collapsed, when the road curved and his car did not, sound vanished. Instead, in the last moment before blackout, images battered his mind. He felt himself shaped and hammered in the heart of fire. He felt his feet had turned to hands with a million pale slim fingers, reaching downward into moist, fragrant earth.

In the blinking moment it took him to focus, Simon noted the colors around him: a muted sand-beige ceiling, warm gold curtains dangling from a host of bead-chains locked into a ceiling track that half-circled his bed on his left, light apricot walls to his right. According to the Lüscher color test, these colors should be relaxing yet slightly energizing, which seemed appropriate to the environment. He suspected this was a hospital, since the bed he lay in had rails.

He heard breathing: his own, and someone else's. The other person's breathing was slow, with long pauses between inhalation and exhalation.

Messages waited for him from outlying areas of his body, but he sensed the scream of pain in them and shunted them away. His glance fell on a tall machine beside the bed. It hummed and ticked very quietly. Red LED numbers flashed and changed on the face of a small blue box hanging midway down a chrome pipe. Drops travelled from a fat, clear hanging bottle down a plastic tube which vanished into the blue box, re-emerged from the bottom, and snaked under a bandage on his left forearm, which was taped to the bedrail.

Fueling up, he thought. Something about getting life-juice from a hose felt familiar to him. With his eyes shut he could imagine himself healthy, crouched upon asphalt, his rigid form encapsulating a power waiting to growl to life, a human heart locked inside him, the all-important spark that set everything in motion and brought him to waking life.

Simon lay and grinned beneath his bandages. His fantasies were usually

26

darker. He had never suspected his Ferrari loved him as much as he loved it. He lay imagining the warmth that entered the car when the human sat in its seat, turned the key, pressed pedals, shifted gears, and laid hands on the steering wheel. An almost unbearable thrill of anticipation simmered in him, like an unscratchable itch. The car did not care where it went. Movement excited it, the continual meeting and mating with the surface of the road.

Fueling up. The car understood.

When he woke the second time, there were flowers on the table by his bed. The flowers were color-coordinated with the walls: bronze chrysanthemums, sprays of pale everlasting, a sprinkling of strawflowers colored like the orange metal of cheap Far Eastern jewelry. The color reminded him of Rachel. She often wore large sun-colored pendants with snippets of metal dangling and jingling. He felt a momentary longing for her so intense it eclipsed everything else. Closing his eyes, he waited; eventually the desire eased its clutch. He opened his eyes again and looked at the flowers. The splayed, fingered chrysanthemum leaves were a green so dark it blotted light like black. The smell was strong, not flowery at all, but wet and aggressive and slightly swampy.

He began to remember what it was like to thrust upward among other trees, sun on his upper reaches, the light a liquor bringing life and wakefulness. His consciousness diffused between the green growing needles on the upside and the creeping roots beneath wet black soil on the down. Half of him strained toward the sun, the other half toward the center of the earth, with a tapestry of living tissue stretching along the length of the strong dead fibers of the trunk between. Information climbed slowly, riding chains of water during the day; he could think faster when the sun shone, yet moisture pleased him

too. Young fogs often gathered, thickening the air so one's messages could cross open space and reach others, instead of having to seep through soil, between root hairs.

Simon blinked. For a moment he frowned, wondering who this waking self was. He glanced at the IV again. Only a single root, he thought. Closing his eyes, he could almost track the spread of nutrients through his body. He had a growing awareness that lightning had struck him for the second time, cleaving and disrupting parts of his form. He rode his circulatory system, finding places where the gaps had been bridged, circumvented, or shut down. Processes of repair spun and crystallized, struggled, failed, restarted. Submerged in his systems, he explored, learned, lost himself.

The third time he woke, he smelled perfume. It was a delicate scent, like night-blooming jasmine at a distance. An image of the beach house he and Rachel had rented one weekend took on hue and texture behind his eyelids. He remembered waking in the morning to see her stand, a dark silhouette, against the window, with the glory of a morning sky and surf beyond her. Some strange mystery had opened in his mind then, a sense of forever, a feeling of peace and contentment.

One moment out of six months. Not enough.

A murmur of conversation came through the curtain to his left. "You're going to be *all right,* Chris. You are," said a woman in a tear-thickened voice.

"Don't lie to me, Mom." The boy's voice was very clear.

Simon looked at the ceiling. It was the color of ginger ale. He could faintly remember the explorations he, or someone, had made earlier. Without judging or evaluating, he had memorized himself, learned exactly which bones and organs were broken or damaged.

Today his detachment had lessened. He groaned.

"Simon?"

He turned his head. Rachel sat in a chair nearby, her dark hair raying out around her head, the freckles stark on her thin, pale face, her green eyes sunken. She wore a bronze-green Indian-print dress with dots of gold on it.

"Rae?" he said. He tried to reach for her, but his hand was taped to the railing. He wanted her. He remembered why he had run away from her. "What are you doing here?"

"Do you know where you are?"

"Obviously it's a hospital," he said, once again secure in the fortress of his skull, all input from below the neck reduced to proper second-class status. "No one has seen fit to inform me of its name or location. I never expected to see you again." His voice seemed raspy, and talking hurt.

She leaned forward and gave him a strained smile. "Same Simon," she said.

"No," he said, staring up at the ceiling. Stranger-thoughts had been passing through his brain. After two breaths, he looked at her.

She clasped the fingers of her left hand in her right.

"Then you know?"

He had never seen the skull so clearly beneath her skin before.

"Know? Oh, you mean the foot?" He heard his own detachment, then felt his stomach churn. He tasted bile, and felt a sinus ache around his eyes. The foot. One of his selves had recognized that his right foot was gone, but somehow it hadn't mattered to that self. Simon closed his eyes and tried to keep back tears. He had not cried since he was eight, the last time he had given his father any satisfaction during a whipping.

«It doesn't really hurt, having it replaced. First the jack, then a violation of the place under the hood where you hide the spare; but then you're back in

28

business.»

Simon smiled, heard a gasping laugh come from his throat.

"Simon?" Rachel reached for his free hand. "Are you all right? Can I get you anything?"

He swallowed, wadded up the pain and put it away. Years of practice made it easy. "Information. Where am I? How long since the accident? What are you doing here?"

"You're in a town called Hoodoo. You were in intensive care a week, then they moved you in here three days ago. They found my phone number in your stuff, Simon. They couldn't find any other addresses or phone numbers except the apartment you stayed in in Menlo Park. The landlady couldn't give them any information. They called me. I came up. Is there anybody you want me to call?"

"No," he said. "Nobody out there to wonder."

"Except me. How come you didn't say good-bye? The landlady didn't even know you were gone. Said you were paid through the end of the month. I called Express Communications and they said you had finished up and left. How could you?"

He looked at her, and knew the power he had tried to throw away was still with him. Leaving her seemed like the most beautiful thing he had ever done: he hadn't loved anybody so much since his mother died. Yet, intending to preserve her, he had hurt her, just like he had hurt the last two women he had gotten involved with.

She released his hand and rubbed her eyes, then gave him a trembling smile. "I'm sorry. You just woke up. I don't mean to accuse you of anything. I want to help. How can I help?"

He thought of the three white roses he had placed on his mother's coffin. Perfect and unstained. His wish for her heaven, a quiet place with no sign of the color red. Women should not suffer.

But his father was strong in him, pushing him against his will into relationships that led to suffering. "I wish you would go away," he said, and watched the tears spill down her cheeks.

Her chair was empty and the room was dark. He looked up toward the dim ceiling and listened to the boy breathe in the next bed. The nurse had shown him how to operate his bed; the controls lay under his hand. Earlier, he had elevated his knees. Now he wanted to lower them, but the bed made so much noise he was afraid it would wake the boy.

He considered pulling the needle from his arm. Not fast or drastic enough. He touched the bandages on his face, felt the ones encasing his chest. He thought about the space where a foot should be. Maybe his new appearance would not affect his job as an organizational behavior consultant that much. He could still walk into any office, — walk, or crutch, or wheel? Would they give him a prosthesis? — analyze the personal interactions, the colors, the atmosphere, the lighting, and figure out how to rechannel the energy into higher productivity. No bones pressing on his *brain*.

But his last assignment with Express Communications had convinced him that competence was no longer enough. Or maybe Rachel had. Both the job and the relationship had come too easily, followed too exactly in the footsteps of the ones before. Although Rachel had started out a little different. She had trusted him less — at first. He had hoped something outside of him would force change on him, since he had tried so often to change himself without success. Rachel's strength had given him hope. But hope was a poison in him that lifted him out of reality, making him vulnerable. He should have known better; he should have known he could trust himself to screw it up every time.

He began tugging at the adhesive on his face. He was just beginning to enjoy letting himself feel the little sharp pains as the bandages pulled at the scabs when his arm straightened, then dropped to his side. He could feel the texture of the sheets, but he could no longer move any of his muscles.

«This is what it's like when you turn off the ignition and take the key out. I put on the emergency brake. Leave the masking alone; we want the new paint job to work. Don't want to start with rust.»

His chest moved up and down of its own accord. His eyes blinked. His heart beat. He could feel the blood moving through him, but none of his muscles responded to him.

Body work.

"They said I could feed you," Rachel told him. She reached for the bed control and elevated his head and shoulders.

Simon licked his lips. The odd paralysis of the previous night had passed, leaving him afraid it would return. "I'm eating," he said, nodding toward his arm.

"Do you want to live, or not?" she asked. She stirred the bowl of chicken broth, looking down as floating bits of parsley swirled in the wake of her spoon.

"Not very much," he said, and felt the loss of control overtake him again. His mouth opened, but he had nothing to do with it.

She glanced up. "Make up your mind," she said. She fed him, and something in him ate. The next day, they took him off the IV.

Every morning a nursing technician came in at 7:30 to take his temperature and blood pressure. After one of her visits, the curtain to Simon's left twitched back, the beadchains rattling in their track above, and he found himself staring into the large gray eyes of a bald boy. Chris. Although he found himself participating in Chris's life vicariously, Simon had never been curious enough to pull the curtain aside. The child was wasting away, and he seemed more aware of it than his doctor or his mother.

"You're mean," Chris told him. "You're too mean to her. Don't you even care?"

"If you worked a little harder, you could convince her you're really going to die, and the relationship could move into a more comfortable stage for both of you," Simon said. He had read Kübler-Ross's work after his mother died, trying to label and reduce his feelings so they wouldn't overwhelm him. "You're already at acceptance, and she's still in denial. You going to let it go on until it's too late? She'll have to fight it all afterwards anyway."

"I know. There's time," said Chris. "I'll do it. So are you going to lighten up on your girlfriend?"

"I didn't ask her here."

"Aw, come on. You're giving life away with both hands. Why should you care who picks it up? When you were still asleep, she talked to me. She said some religions say suicides don't go to the next life, but get stuck in nightmares, hovering over this earth, never moving on. She believes that, you know. She's trying to pull you back from the edge. Maybe you don't care. Maybe you want to be on the edge. But you don't have to make it so hard on her."

"You're asking me to delude her? Take her back to stage one, while I'm at stage five?"

They stared at each other for a long moment.

"You're hurting her, and I don't like that," Chris said at last.

"The same to you," said Simon.

He fell asleep watching Chris stare at the ceiling.

In the dream, he glided down a road

as smooth and polished chrome. Night air cooled him, rushing along his lines, curling around and backwashing him. Ahead of him, up the hill, two arcs of paired red lights raced away, leaving traces of hot harsh breath, and the friction heat of tires on the road surface. Lines of paired white lights raced towards him on the left. Nothing else existed.

The road curved and he curved with it, delighting in the interplay of speed and grip and curve. Mined metal and mica had never dreamed of this as it lay under the earth, waiting only for water and rust and erosion. But since the furnace heat, the crafting and tempering and shaping, this was all his purpose. The world existed in only three dimensions — behind, ahead, and speed.

He raced on, meshing with traffic, riding for brief times in certain groupings, shifting and slowing or speeding to change patterns.

More curves.

And at last, a curve too tight. He went too fast and turned too slowly. He plunged off into the nothingness that was everything not The Road.

Ages earlier, a silence in the wood, broken only by the sound of dripping in the distance, and an occasional waterfall of birdcall. Salt mists rose, weaving through the trees. Seasons passed, some waterfat, some waterlean, each recording itself in the tree's trunk as it expanded outward, building and shedding bark as it grew, upper tips reaching ever towards the sun. A slow tangle of gossip came through the soil, ways to proof oneself against this moth or that moss, new mixtures of self to produce. The tree shed seed every season.

One storm season, lightning struck the tree, cleaving to the heart and leaving a burning in its wake that ate through many waterchains and foodchains, interrupting the pathways of life. An age the tree lingered between giving itself back to the soil and repairing itself, but the new green needles grew, roots spread beneath the soil, and life built new trails between.

Then the roads arrived, first logging roads, and small moving parts to a landscape that had never moved before, but the movers would not die no matter how much one poisoned the soil; then tar roads which fought back and carried more movers. This explosion of activity came late and happened quickly. The tree woke up more than it ever had before. Something about the noise, the enriched air the movers made, excited the tree. Trees farther back from the road did not understand. Questions took seasons to travel to the road, and answers seasons more to travel back. The tree observed, until at last a mover came and cracked it. Roots bereft of needles, needles bereft of roots, water-chains broken, no tissues still alive to carry the necessary information for healing.

«But now I am part of something that lives while it moves,» said the tree.

«But now I am part of something that lives while it is still,» said the car.

Simon sat up gasping out of the dream, and fell back, the full pain in his chest hammering at him before he shut off the message system.

«And we won't let you die,» they said. «This is too interesting.»

He lay and gasped.

"Are you all right? Should I call a nurse?" asked Rachel.

Simon trembled. He had bitten his cheek; the rusty taste of blood had a peculiar, violent vividness that both his ghosts savored. Blood thrummed in his head. "This building condemned," he said. "This building condemned."

"Are you delirious? Answer yes or no," said Rachel, touching his forehead with cool fingers.

"You smell like jasmine," he said.

"Simon?" The dent between her brows that appeared when she was worried looked much deeper than it used to. "Please. Are you okay?"

He drew in deep breaths, felt his heart calm inside him, no longer trying to knock its way free. "I'm all right."

She relaxed. He studied her, wondering what brought her up here after him, when he had come so close to beating her before he left. "Why did you come?" he asked at last.

"The doctor called me. She told me how badly hurt you were, and all alone. I thought — " She stared toward the door, beyond the open end of his curtain. "When you first asked me out, I thought, is this the one? You really noticed me. And you listened to me — such listening eyes. The men I've known before didn't listen like that. I think I got addicted to it."

"I can't give you that anymore."

"I know that," she said. She smiled. "I thought that if I helped you get well —"

"What? I'd be grateful, and marry you? That's not the way it works. I wanted to get away from you before you knew me any better, because — "

"That last date we had, you scared me," she said, and looked at the floor.

So she had sensed something.

"You started sounding like someone else. Another person's voice in your throat, Simon; another person's words in your mouth. Is that who you have nightmares about? That man, the mean one?"

"You don't understand. That's me, that's who I am underneath." The words were hard to say; once they came out, he shuddered, his secret fear at last given form. Sometimes when he turned around, he thought he threw his father's shadow. A man he had hated all his life, a man who taught him everything he knew about women, walked in his own shoes.

She touched his hand. "It doesn't

matter," she said, "because now you couldn't hurt me if you wanted to. First, you have to learn to walk, and I still know how to run."

"You didn't use to be a fast healer, did you?" she asked a few days later. "Remember that day you cut yourself shaving? I thought it was funny how upset you got, as if a little cut would ruin your whole appearance. You said it would take days to go away, too."

"The things I used to worry about." He could hear the laugh in his voice, and it troubled him. He was relaxing with her, and if he relaxed, his old habits would come back. Maybe she could escape physical harm, but he knew words could deal worse blows, and he hadn't been able to convince her to leave yet.

"Listen, they're going to take off the bandages today. The doctor can't believe how fast you're healing. I always thought attitude had a lot to do with it. You have one of the worst attitudes I've ever seen."

"But that's only a third of me. Two thirds of me want to get well and go mobile again."

"What?" She peered at the bandages on his head. "Maybe you *did* get a brain injury."

"Yes. I did." He leaned back and closed his eyes. This was the third day she had worn the red dress. He wanted to let go of everything going on, detach his mind, and analyze why she would wear something with a deep V neck and a high hemline to visit an incapacitated man in a hospital. She had never worn anything like that while he was seeing her in Menlo Park. Did she want to torment him or encourage him?

"Simon?"

One of the others opened his eyes and looked at her. Her face had started to flesh out a little. The shock had worn off and she was getting enough rest. "How can you leave school and spend

so much time up here?" he asked.

"I have my own set of priorities."

"You're getting something you need from this transaction?"

"If you start talking about system dynamics and quality circles and participatory management, I'm leaving." She stood up.

"Don't leave." He touched his throat. It was the first time one of the others had spoken aloud. He had wondered if they could talk. Most of their communication came in sensory images, though he suspected there was some translation mechanism, since neither of them had the same senses he had. "Why you wear that dress he wonders."

"What?"

Simon cleared his throat, trying to cough the other loose of it. "Chris? You awake?"

"Yes," said Chris from behind the curtain. He twitched the curtain open. "That was one of those *things*, wasn't it?"

"What things?" Rachel and Simon asked.

"Sometimes when you're asleep, you make these noises. They sound like other people trying to talk. They don't know how to do it, though. Are they in you when you're awake?"

"Yes," said Simon.

"The other two thirds of you?" Chris asked.

"Yes."

Rachel sat down again, hugging her purse. "Are you crazy?"

He took a deep breath. "I don't know." He made a fist.

"Is one of them the mean man?" she asked.

"No, oh no. This is something else. Something I don't want on my medical record." He frowned at Rachel.

"All right," she said. "I won't tell Dr. Kelsey if you don't want me to."

Simon gave Chris a long look. Chris nodded. Simon said, "I'm haunted. The car and the tree. They're both in my head." He knocked on his head. His breath came out in a restrained sob. "I've dreamed the accident from all three angles. When I wanted to pull out the IV or tear off the bandages, the car made me be still. When I wanted to die, the tree started healing me."

"Oh," said Rachel, her eyes wide. " 'Make up your mind.' "

"Yeah. Which one?"

"Well, that sounds pretty crazy to me," she said, "but I don't care. Maybe they'll talk to me, and say something besides telling me to leave." She leaned closer, her eyes bright. "Hey, one of you others, was he really wondering about this dress?"

"Yes," he said.

"Which one are you?"

"Still me," said Simon. "Why are you wearing a dress that's an open invitation when you know I'm practically tied to this bed?"

"Maybe I'm seeing someone else here; did you ever consider that?"

"Not yet." He began to weigh factors: time she had actually spent at his bedside while still wearing the dress versus time she had to spend sleeping, eating, traveling from the hotel and back; what he knew or suspected of her character and her actions . . .

Dr. Kelsey came in without knocking, pulled the curtain aside, set Simon's chart and a stainless steel tray on his bed table and rolled the table, with its pitcher of water, emesis bowl, deck of cards, cup, and a new purple flower in the jam jar away from the bed. She peered at him through thick-lensed glasses and took some tools out of the pocket of her white jacket, laying them on the tray. She was an enormous old woman with short red hair going white; Simon thought she must have studied medicine during the Depression. "Ready to have these off, son?" she asked, looming over him and tugging at the edges of the bandages on his face.

"If you say so." Simon had stared into his own eyes several times while shaving as much of his face as he could reach. He wondered what was left of what he used to consider an important asset. In odder moments he had wondered if half his face would be metal and the other half bark beneath the gauze.

"Would you rather the young lady left? You want Chris watching?"

"I don't care."

Dr. Kelsey looked at Rachel. "He's not going to be pretty yet."

"That's all right."

The doctor took a pair of long, slender, round-ended scissors from the tray. She began snipping the bandage along the curve of his cheek. The metal felt cold against his skin. He closed his eyes and waited.

She lifted an edge. "Wow," she said, as he felt clean air touch his cheeks and nose for the first time since he had awakened. "It comes away so clean. Usually there's some adherence. And these wounds look old."

He opened his eyes, reached his hand up to touch his face, but she caught his wrist. "Don't touch," she said. "Above all, don't scratch. There are still stitches in there. You can have little scars or great big ones; the choice is yours now."

"Can I see a mirror?"

She gave him a small round hospital-issue mirror and he stared at himself. Somehow, he had more trouble recognizing himself without the bandage than he had with it on. His eyes were harder to find amidst the maze of scabby scratches. "I look like a jigsaw puzzle," he said, and laughed for feeling like one too.

"You are a very odd boy," the doctor said, her eyes narrowing behind the large, thick lenses of her glasses. "If you're a puzzle, I put you back together, and I'm proud of my work. Provided you leave yourself alone, you should end up looking a lot like you used to."

"But how do I get rid of the extra

pieces?"

The doctor frowned at him, then retrieved his chart and made some notations on it. "If your ribs have healed as fast as the rest of you, it's time we started you on some physical therapy," she said. "You'll like that." She left.

"Do you really want to get rid of the extra pieces?" Rachel asked him when the door shut behind the doctor. "I want to talk to them."

"I don't know what I want." He felt himself at a balance point on a teeter-totter. He had a sudden image of Death at one end, his old life at the other. Whichever way the balance shifted, he would slide down towards an unbearable alternative. Silly. The tree, a red-brown girl, and the car, a midnight-blue boy, pulled him off the teeter-totter and led him away from the playground. "Silly," he said. "Where are we going?"

«There's road»
«There's sun»
«There's fuel»
«There's water»
«There's movement»
«There's interaction . . .»

"So what are you doing? You having a three-way conversation in your head?" Rachel asked. "No wonder you kept spacing out before."

"Do the creatures inside you say anything about being dead?" Chris asked. "Did it hurt?"

"It was a great shock," he heard himself say. "It was a great scream. It was just a translation . . . we are not dead yet." His voice independent of him was gaining intonation, Simon thought. His arm lifted; the fingers on the hand spread wide, then closed into a loose fist. "We could not do that before." One of them gave a delighted laugh. "Flexibility is very interesting."

"Quick, before he comes back, will you tell me why he crashed?" Rachel asked.

"The weight of history lay heavy on

him," said the tree in wondering tones. "He was searching for change." The tree knew things changed; the lightning had almost killed it, and afterwards it had a new shape; once there had been no road; then the road came, and later the road changed. But the tree had never imagined changing its own actions, because its actions were perfect.

Rachel sat back, hugging herself. "What history, Simon?" she said.

"Family history; the chain stretches from the past, through me; the strands shape me and lock me into a future —" He sucked in breath between his teeth. He opened his hand, looked at his palm, saw blood. "Flexibility is an illusion."

"No," said Rachel. "You always have a choice."

"That's what I tell all those executives, when I take them off on team-building weekends. Blow off the frustrations! Establish new lines of communication! Take another look at the overall picture and . . ." He sighed. He fingered his face, feeling the ridges of scab, the tiny prickly whiskers of the stitches. "I can't step back and see the overall picture when I'm in the picture myself. History takes over. Next time, I would have hit you. Then I would apologize and tell you not to trust me, but I would be very sincere, and you would trust me, and then I would hurt you worse."

"You must think I'm pretty dumb."

"I think you're locked into the history! You came here even after I scared you and left you without saying goodbye. Is that dumb? Or is it just what your mother would have done? Or what? I tried to choose away from my history, and you brought it back. It's inevitable."

"What! You're going to get better and follow me down the hospital halls and catch me and beat me? I don't think so. I think you've already chosen a new way out. These ghosts will stop you. How are your arms?"

Simon risked opening his mind to his body. His chest ached fiercely, his face prickled, and the end of his leg, where his foot no longer was, felt — strange. He could feel bandages against the skin of his calf, but there was no bottom to his leg, and yet there was. He frowned. As if he could feel the texture of the sheet, not very fine linen, against the sole of his non-existent foot.

He thought about his arms. He raised his hands and looked at them. The muscles in his shoulders pulled and hurt, but his arms responded. "My arms are fine," he said.

"All right." She rose and set her purse on the chair. She glanced at Chris, who lay and watched, his eyes very large in his thin face. "What's the sequence? I kiss you, and you hit me?"

Simon consulted his history. For a moment he could see it as clearly as if he were reading the instructions to a game. His father's patterns, repeated and locked into him. "No," he said. "I make impossible demands on you. You either refuse, or tell me the demands are impossible . . . then I go into a rage, tell you how worthless you are, and *then,* when I've convinced you you deserve it, I hit you. . . ."

She lowered the rail and sat beside him, staring at the wall above his head. "I remember," she said. "I remember that starting. I couldn't understand it. You seemed so sensitive when we first went out. Then, all of a sudden, you were asking me to give up a seminar I was really interested in and run away to the beach house for the weekend. 'If you really loved me . . .'" She looked at him. "And no other weekend would do. It had to happen *that* weekend. After I said no, you disappeared, and I thought, I can't let it end here. I didn't want to lose everything just because of a misunderstanding. I thought I could make you see my side, and everything

would get better."

He touched her hand, feeling its dry warmth. One of the others lifted her hand, bent the fingers, touched her nails, examined the articulation of her bones. He stayed behind his eyes and watched as the other explored, feeling the texture of her dress, her hair, her face.

She caught his hand and looked at him. "Are you trying to distract me?"

"Everything is new," said the car.

"You're one of the ghosts, huh? Stay there a moment." She let his hand go and scooted forward on the bed. She held herself away from him at first, touching only her lips to his, but he put his arms around her and hugged her to him before he remembered his ribs. He groaned and held her away again, more aware of himself than he had been since before the accident. So much of him hurt, and yet, pain was so connected to pleasure in his mind that he found himself aroused. Usually it was not his own pain that acted on him like this.

He stared into Rachel's face, excited with this new discovery, and thrilled to have her close enough to help him test it. He lifted his hands to grasp her shoulders. His arms froze, then dropped. His breathing slowed to normal. His eyes closed. The tree had decided it was time for another inventory, time to mend broken connections again.

The bed was flat when he opened his eyes. He wondered if Rachel had worked it, or a nurse. The light in his section of room was off, but a glow came through Chris's curtain, which was closed all the way again. "You have to accept it, Mom," said Chris. His voice, like the rest of him, had thinned. "Now, or later, but it would be easier if you could accept it now. Then we could talk about it. I don't want to leave you alone with this. You don't take care of yourself."

"You're getting better, Chrissie. Your

eyes are so bright, baby."

"I'm not getting better."

"Why you? Why my baby?" the woman asked, after a space of silence. She began to cry. "Such a good boy. Never harmed anyone. Why?"

"Why is no good now," he said. "This is happening. Mom . . . I love you. I love you. Don't hurt yourself about this. It's been worth it. Do you understand?"

"No," she said. Simon fell asleep to the sound of her quiet crying.

He had always found the Student Union Building cafeterias good hunting grounds. After all, that was where his father found his mother. . . . Father an army veteran, going to college after World War II on the G.I. bill. He had stayed in school only long enough to take Mother away from her library science courses before she got her degree. She used to talk about the moment when Father came to her table, stood above her and just looked at her. "He was so tall," she said. "Tall and quiet — I thought there must be some deep thinking going on in his head."

In the dream, Simon stood above Rachel, where she sat at the table in the cafeteria. Each time he started the cycle, he waited in the door of a cafeteria and let history fill him. Each time, he saw the right woman, went to her, stood and looked at her till his sense of himself as his father overcame him. The women never said anything when he sat down with them. They were always a little afraid — he never picked the really self-confident ones.

Rachel did not smile at him like the others. A glimmer of hope in that. He sat down and put his hands flat on the varnished pinewood table.

Between his hands, twigs began to sprout. Flat green needles grew from the tips of the branches. Some of the twigs grew right through his hands, rooting them to the table. The metal of the chair he sat on grew up and over

his legs, tendrils of it curling around him, as if the metal were vines.

Rachel gave him a slow, sweet smile. She rose, picked up her books, leaned forward to give him a lingering kiss, then walked away.

Helpless to follow, he watched her, wanting her, yet feeling relieved.

Then he felt release. He looked down at his hands. Twigs sprouted from their backs, but they were no longer pinned to the table. Metal banded his jeans, but no longer locked him to the chair. He stood up.

Rachel pushed open the glass door and walked out of the building, into a snow storm, or a light storm; each snowflake seemed like a light flake. He waited a moment for history to tell him what to do, but there were no precedents. He watched her walk off through falling light. After a moment, he followed her outside, but the light had become a blizzard, and he couldn't find her.

«Simon?»

"Chris?" Simon shook his head, trying to wake up. He elevated the bed head and grabbed his cup, swallowed a mouthful of water.

«Simon, I'm going now.»

He switched on his light and pulled back the curtain. Chris lay with his chin pointing at the ceiling. His mouth was slightly open, but his eyes were closed. He wasn't breathing.

"Chris? Chris!" Simon pressed the call button.

«Don't get so upset. I thought you, at least, would be ready for this.»

The tree began flooding his system with calmers. He lay back. "You're already gone?"

«Almost. I wanted to meet your ghosts. I really thought you made them up.»

"Did I?" Why hadn't that occurred to him? The most obvious explanation!

Chris laughed. «I'm glad you're going to get better. Will you please talk to my mother? If I had a will, I'd leave her to you.»

"Chris," he said. The nurse came in. She was frowning. Simon rubbed his eyes and pointed to Chris's bed.

There was a lot of activity in the room after that, behind the closed curtain. Simon lay in relative darkness and thought about roses. He thought about fishing with his father off the pier, using drop lines, tying hooks and lead sinkers onto rough green string, baiting the hooks with bacon. Fish scales stuck to his fingers; sometimes he found them on his clothes hours later.

Miniature golf and fractions. His father had been good at both. Miniature golf, fractions, and fishing were the only things his father ever taught him that he really liked. He had learned so many other things from his father.

When at last they took Chris's body away and shut off the lights, he thought about Chris. White roses, yellow roses, red roses, pink ones?

«How about a spray of pine needles?»

«You still here?»

«I'm going now. Tell her it didn't hurt. Tell her I love her. Tell her I was ready, and hanging on any longer would just be wasted time. Good-bye, Simon. I'm glad I knew you.»

«Good-bye.»

Chris's mother sat behind the curtain and cried. Rachel, in a dark blue dress, walked in, tossed her purse at the chair, then walked around the end of the curtain. She gasped. "Is he — is he — ?"

"He's gone," said Chris's mother.

Simon lay and tried to gather his strength. "Mrs. — Mrs. — ma'am?" he said. "Ma'am? He told me to tell you some things."

"What? They said he died in his sleep."

"He said he loves you, and that it didn't hurt. He said living any longer would be just wasting time. He asked me to talk to you."

She opened the curtain, and he saw her for the first time. She had Chris's gray eyes, but her hair was the same chestnut color his mother's had been. He felt the tangle of patterns trying to begin again, a murmur in his father's voice to leave her alone.

He held out his hand to her, and she took it.

"Are you going to let go of your ghosts now?" Rachel asked him later. His hand still tingled from the pressure of Chris's mother's clasp, and his mind was fuzzy from her stories about her child. She had stayed two hours, staring at nothing, and talking to him; Rachel wandered away early on, and only came back when Chris's mother left and the nurse brought in Simon's supper.

He flexed his fingers. "Do you want me to let go of them?"

She made a church of her hands, spread her thumbs as if they were doors, and wiggled the fingers inside. See all the people. "Do you need the ghosts anymore?"

"Yes." He touched his lips. "There's something I have to figure out. Something about pain." He felt the pain, letting it come through the barriers; the scabs on his face itched, but he didn't respond to them. His ribs ached, and he felt strange nerve firings from his legs. But he could also feel the satisfaction of movement, how each finger bent in answer to his thought, and his pleasure was amplified by the presence of the ghosts, who had never experienced anything like it. "Besides. Suppose I give up my ghosts, and you go away too. Then I'd be alone."

"And then what? Get better, get a job in some other city, pick up another student and start over again?"

He lay quietly and thought. Chris's mother had invited him to live in her house during his convalescence. She had a place on the beach, with trees all around. She would like to watch somebody get better, she said.

"I don't think I'm going to start over the same way," he said.

Rachel looked at her fingers for a long time. Then she looked up at him. "Simon, I'm going back to school."

"I thought you might."

"Is that in the program? Is that on the map of your past? Something you psyched out the way you psych out those businessmen?"

"No," he said. Tree felt calm, car felt calm, Simon felt calm. Something inside had shifted. He had lost all the old tactics, and hadn't had time to craft new ones.

Maybe when she walked off into the light blizzard he had known she would leave. Or maybe it was just the sense he had that she was attracted to danger; she would know he wasn't dangerous anymore, almost before he knew it himself. She was still trapped in her own history. She would have to look for someone else to replay it with.

She stood a moment beside his bed. "I miss you," she said.

"I'm still here."

"It doesn't feel the same," she said. She put her hand to her face, turned and left.

He touched his chest. Underneath the bandages, he knew there were bones of wood, bones of steel, and safe within, a human heart.

▲

RACING THE HORSEMAN

by Rayson Lorrey

Dexter ran on autopilot, his strides timed to the tempo of another runner two blocks ahead. The warm night air cycled smoothly in and out of his lungs, until the whine of tires on the pavement behind him interrupted his near trance.

Backlit by the approaching car's headlights, Dexter cast an elongated shadow, a caricature runner with flailing elbows and knees. The car kept to the middle of the street, granting him a generous leeway as it passed. Dexter would have smiled at the prominent tail fins on the old Cadillac convertible, except that he was already beaming because the Caddy's top was down and its seats were jampacked with coeds. A brunette in the back puckered her lips and gave him a wolf-whistle. The whistler's companions grabbed her and shouted, "Her name is Susan!"

Dexter committed Susan's face and her touch-me hair to memory. It would be great fun to meet her. They'd laugh over the wolf-whistle, and he'd ask her if it was his legs or his ass she had admired. The car sped away with the coeds laughing and blowing kisses. Women loved his body, and Dexter loved women — a gratifying arrangement. And since running was responsible for his well-muscled legs and the staying power the women so fancied, Dexter was diligent about his routine. He checked his watch. Its lighted face alternately displayed his pulse rate and the time. It was still early. He had run two miles to warm up, and he felt like doing another six or seven before cooling off.

Down the street, the headlights of the coeds' car spotlighted the back of the pacesetting runner. He wore gray shorts, gray Adidas, baggy socks, and a sweat shirt with a hood pulled up over his head. Sweat darkened the shirt over his backbone. The runner was tall and lean — no, more than lean; he was skeletal, anorexic. Dexter found it easy to imagine the anatomic details of the leg bones beneath the minimal layers of flesh and muscle. The guy would settle into a famine relief commercial without a ripple. Hell, he could be the very embodiment of Famine — the third of the Four Horsemen, minus his black mount. Dexter abruptly regretted skipping supper.

He closed some of the distance on the runner. A street light revealed liver spots and varicose veins on his legs. He had to be ancient. The runner's head swiveled around, pivoting like an owl's. *Limber old coot, aren't you?* Dexter thought, but he waved sociably, a gesture of runner-to-runner camaraderie.

The man's face remained expressionless, totally impassive, an emotional *tabula rasa*. Dexter dropped his hand. He'd seen plenty of similar faces at the nursing home. Doctor Barnard, the psychiatrist, would too often joke, "lack of affect," and describe a type of sociopath who was characteristically deadpan, regardless of his particular endeavor — be it eating a hamburger, strangling a cat, buying a magazine, or raping a schoolgirl. Then Barnard would giggle and stroll down the hall leaving Dexter

39

with the new patient. Dexter would push the man's wheelchair or help him with his walker or stay at his side as he shuffled down the wax-slippery hallway to physical therapy. Paralyzed facial muscles were usually a stroke victim's least worry.

The runner turned away and stepped up his pace, moving smartly from one yellow circle of street light to another. Dexter felt a tinge of envy; none of his patients had ever responded so well to therapy. Tooth-brushing was generally a major triumph. *Christ,* this guy didn't run like he had *ever* been stroked out. He covered ground with strength and authority, and if there was any readable sentiment in the sway of his back or in the set of his bony shoulders, it was disdain.

As the old man pulled away, Dexter felt a stirring that upset his rhythm; it was an urge to greater speed, a desire to sprint past the runner and to show him up. Only an undercurrent of shame held him back. He'd competed in high school and college, but not against gaffers. And now he ran for exercise; he didn't race. Still, some dormant competitive drive was waking, and Dexter wanted to test himself and push himself and *win.* He shrugged. Why not then?

His conscience answered faintly: Because he's just a senior citizen out for a jog, and maybe it's important to him to stay ahead of you. Maybe the running is all he has. Give him a break. You've outgrown one-upmanship games.

The old man glanced back — obviously checking on Dexter, almost daring him, and Dexter's conscience died in a surge of adrenalin. He lengthened and quickened his stride, his muscles responding eagerly. Thank you kindly, Horseman, for making up my mind.

The old man seemed to hear the charging footsteps behind him. He bore down, his tendons standing out like knife edges, and began to reclaim the distance Dexter had gained. Dexter

shook his head in awe. Hope I can do *half* that well when I'm your age. Then he laughed. But I'm not that age, yet. Not even close.

Dexter brought long-neglected nuances of good form into play. He held his head steady, evened his gait, and geared his breathing to his body's cadence. Soon he was flying, his feet brushing the pavement. He savored the sensation of acceleration and narrowed the gap on the Horseman with each stride.

The old man turned to look again. His eyes were vacant and cold. He had more speed in reserve, and he turned it on.

Dexter blinked, barely believing the geezer was holding him off. Okay, Horseman, you're some kind of triumph of geriatric medicine, but I'm comin' to get ya! No mercy. Dexter started to sprint.

So did the Horseman.

Dexter was still trailing as they entered the gentle curves of Poplar Street and zipped past small frame houses with yards that nurtured incongruous maple trees. The old man and Dexter flashed onto Sycamore's long straightaway side by side, their arms and legs pumping in unison — a pair of synchronic, manic metronomes. They raced neck and neck for five blocks with Dexter unable to seize an advantage. As they turned onto Elm, the old man retook the lead.

Dexter's lungs and the muscles of his legs and arms burned. He was pushing, maybe too hard, and he'd ache for it tomorrow. He shot a glance at his pulse meter and nearly stumbled. It read one-eighty, more than triple his resting rate. And despite everything, he was eating the old man's dust. To *Hell* with this, Dexter thought. When we turn the corner, you win, Horseman. I'll give it to you.

The corner was a hundred yards away. Dexter edged to the right to avoid a patch of gravel around a pothole, but the Horseman stayed on track. A flicker of hope made Dexter steel himself for one last push — just in case. The old man hit the gravel and faltered, missing a beat by losing and regaining his balance. It was opening enough. Dexter streaked by him and rounded the corner in the lead. Got him! I got him!

Dexter slowed to a walk, stopped, and bent over with his hands on his knees, trying to catch his breath. Behind him, he heard the old man approach. Dexter spoke between gulps of air, "Mister, you are some kind of runner. I'd like to shake your hand." He straightened up and turned, hand extended,

There was a skull inside the hood of the sweat shirt. The fleshless jaw worked, while a bystander in Dexter's head remarked that the bones should grate against each other. Nonetheless, only a tired voice emerged from the hood, "You weren't supposed to have caught me, young man . . . not yet." The Horseman shook his head. "Too bad. Too bad."

Dexter toppled to the pavement. One hand clawed at his chest where his heart jackhammered his ribs. The Horseman hobbled past him, still mumbling, "Too bad," like an apology.

Grit from the street coated Dexter's sweaty arms and churning legs. No breath would come to his straining lungs. The last thing he saw was his pulse meter flashing zero.

And his last thought was that he'd guessed wrong. It wasn't the third Horseman he had raced; it was the fourth, the rider of the pale horse. ▲

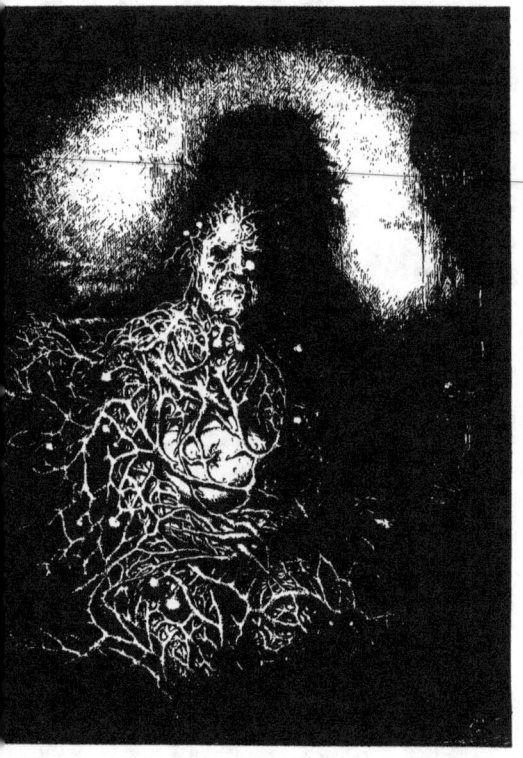

FLORIAN

by Jonathan Carroll

"They had the most beautiful child in the world. It was simply that. When still an infant in its baby carriage, people peeped in fondly and came away stunned. The parents grew permanently helpless expressions that silently told these passersby they couldn't understand it either: yes, the child was theirs, but its enormous ethereal beauty was as incomprehensible and impossible to them as it was to the awed observers. The Tibetans live with the Himalayas in their backyard, but they can take no credit — They're just lucky for the view.

"The father searched toy stores for things worthy of the child's attention: dolls that spoke four languages and answered difficult questions, balls that came when you called their name, crayons that lasted forty years. He bought it a cat named Fib that lied so well and entertainingly that none of them ever knew when it was telling the truth, but they didn't care.

"They lived in a small apartment by a railroad station in the country. Both parents worked at the station. The father sold magazines and cigarettes at the *Tabak,* the mother, in her waitress uniform, bustled from table to table serving railroad workers tureens of tea big and hot enough to steam open every envelope in the world. Harried travelers, not knowing how lucky they were to be there, asked her endless questions about the next train, how much coffee cost, who owned the child who, sometimes when bored, flew through the room in his bluebird-blue airplane.

"Locomotives taught it the secrets of iron and slowing gracefully. The child watched them with great care and came away filled with the capacity to pull a hundred and fifty cars, to lower crossing gates three miles away.

"In truth, there is no place on this earth for such a child. His name was Florian."

His wife came into the room and waited until he had stopped writing before she spoke.

"His temperature is the same."

The man looked at his own son's name — FLORIAN — typed on the paper in front of him. He closed his eyes and knew there was no hope. There was only small magic in the world. Never enough to go around, not nearly enough to write a dying child back to life.

Like the magical boy in the story, his own son had gone through early childhood untouched by the small pesky fingers of young diseases: mumps, measles, chickenpox. The parents considered this a small stroke of luck but nothing more. They assumed he would meet up with them sooner or later, and with little more than a face full of polkadot spots for a week, would glide on. He would grow up to ride a two-wheeler too recklessly and, falling, break an arm. A real hurt — a white cast or two to mark the passage from three wheels to two. Or climbing a tree, he'd slip and end up with a deep, small, lifelong scar on his chin, his perfect cheek.

But it was pneumonia. An autumn cough turned muddy and deep: fever hot enough to scare the fingertips. An oxygen tent — comical, monstrous cousin to the thing we store carrots in, in the refrigerator.

His favorite books lay unread in his lap. Happy stuffed animals alongside his hot unmoving hands inside the tent. Spots and drops of bright color inside the transparent, aseptic shell that would house him until he died.

The child looked at his parents with the pitying, ageless eyes of one who has seen the impossible and returned for a little while; war victims, hundred-year-old men, the dying. He never wanted anything — cool juice, a story read to him, his hand held. It made them frantic, it drove their uselessness home to them again and again and made them hate themselves, each other. It is easy to understand why.

"Write him a story. You're the famous writer. You could do that, couldn't you?" Her eyes accused him of everything and nothing. She was right, however. He could write his son a story.

They lived far out in the Austrian countryside near a railroad station where two tiny trains a day stopped for a few minutes on their funny crawl to and from Vienna. He had always wanted to live near a train station. With the success of his book, he suddenly had the means to buy a Hansel and Gretel house, complete with solid, rustic furniture, low ceilings with bare beams, 1849 chiseled over the front door. And best of all, a clear view of the train station across a field of fledgling pine trees. It pleased him to know that some day his son would have the choice of cutting down the trees for the view, or else keeping them and having his own small forest.

But the child died before the man's story was finished. The fingers never moved, the breath just decided one day to stop rather than fight its way to the boy's hot, tired skin.

"When Florian was five, his father took him to Vienna one Sunday to visit the Prater. The boy wanted to climb the cables of the *Riesenrad* and look out over the city he would someday possess. But his father said no. Instead, they paid their fares and rode the ferris wheel the proper way. The boy was bored. When his father turned to admire the wonders of the Wienerwald, Florian pushed open a window and slid out into clear space, lined only by the pigeon-gray spars and steel cables that held the gigantic wheel together. When the father turned back, he was not at all surprised to see the boy was gone. There was no way to hold lightning in a fist or on a leash."

He read that section to his wife and then put it down to sip his tea. Her hair was the color of tea — old tea now that the boy was gone, brown more than the warm, autumnal red it had been when the child was alive.

"Why do you make me listen? Don't you know how much it hurts? It was his story. He's dead now! Why don't you stop and write something else, for God's sake? He doesn't need stories any more. Every time you even say 'Florian' it cuts right into my heart."

"But it *is* Florian, don't you see? Since I started it when he was alive, if I continue to write, he still lives on, in a way."

"Oh really? Where?" The words were a vicious froth on her lips. "I don't hear him, do you? His toys aren't all over the floor. They're in that *box* in the cellar. His clothes are *always* so *clean* now!" She got up and fled the room, the pain of loss making her wish she were dead, he were dead, everything dead.

The man put on his coat and walked out into the early spring night. The weather had been beautiful for three days; a rare warmth at that time of year when, usually, it was much grayer and colder.

The sweep of stars across the country night made him feel empty and lost. The only thing he felt like writing was a story for his dead son.

He walked towards the trees; dark, short shadows against the moon-blue earth. A lone dog barked in the village, a car drove away into the night.

The night so full of secret gifts for him; the smell of dew-covered pine, shooting stars, animal sounds . . . But he stood there too alone and afraid to accept them. He was too young and successful to think about his own death, but the balance had tipped and he had no desire to support the weight that had been cast upon him. His son was dead, his wife walled off in impenetrable guilt.

The door opened and his son came in, dressed for bed.

"Pa-pa, I bring you present."

He put the pen down and looked at the smaller version of the child he had been writing about in the story.

"Mama says you working but I bring you present."

The boy, his hair recently cut in a summer-y monk's bowl, handed the man a cockeyed construction of blue Tinkertoys.

"A plane, Papa. I show you." He put it on his father's desk and pushed it back and forth, making a three-year-old's version of airplane sounds. He ran it up and over the pages the man had already written, across the empty ashtray and red unopened package of cigarettes.

His wife called from the other room, warning the child Papa was working and he'd better come out of that room right now — Or Else!

The little boy looked naughtily at his father and ran out of the room, victorious.

The television was on in the other room. He heard its murmur of German voices, his son's bangings, then his wife's footsteps much heavier and slower now that she was nearing the end of her pregnancy.

As always, he had read her the story as it developed. She made good and helpful suggestions, but he wondered how she really felt about it. How could she stand to hear of even the fictional death of their beloved son, of the bitterness and approaching madness he'd assigned her in this strange and, ultimately, unnecessary story?

He had taken the boy to the park to play in the sandbox several days before. It was just after dinner and no other children were around. The boy, agile and fearless, jumped up on the monkeybars and crawled around and over the red iron maze. A line came to the man as he watched his son play. "They had the most beautiful child in the world." It came out of nowhere but he liked it and rolled it around like a single marble in his hand. ▲

BACK ISSUES STILL AVAILABLE

#290 (Spring, 1988) — our special 65th Anniversary Issue, with Gene Wolfe as Featured Author and George Barr as Featured Artist. Plus F. Paul Wilson, Ramsey Cambell, T.E.D. Klein, and Tanith Lee, $3.50 + $1.00p&h. (Trade hardcover: $20.00; signed, limited edition hardcover is *sold out!*)

#291 (Summer, 1988) — Stephen Fabian as Featured Artist, Plus Brian Lumley, Morgan Llywelyn, Harry Turtledove, Nancy Springer, $3.50 + $1.00p&h. (Trade hardcover: $20.00, Signed/limited hardcover: $50.00.)

#292 (Fall 1988) — Keith Taylor as Featured Author and Carl Lundgren as Featured Artist. New Stories by Alan Rodgers, W.T. Quick, Tad Williams, $4.00 + $1.00p&h. (Trade hardcover: $20.00; Signed/limited hardcover: $50.00.)

#292 (Winter 198/89) — Avram Davidson as Featured Author and Hank Jankus as Featured Artist. Plus Robert Sheckley, Keith Roberts, Carl Jacobi, Ian Watson, $4.00 + $1.00p&h. (Trade hardcover: $20.00; Signed/limited Hardcover: $50.00.)

Order from: *Weird Tales®*, PO Box 13418, Philadelphia, PA 19101-3418.

THE PIT-YAKKER

by Brian Lumley

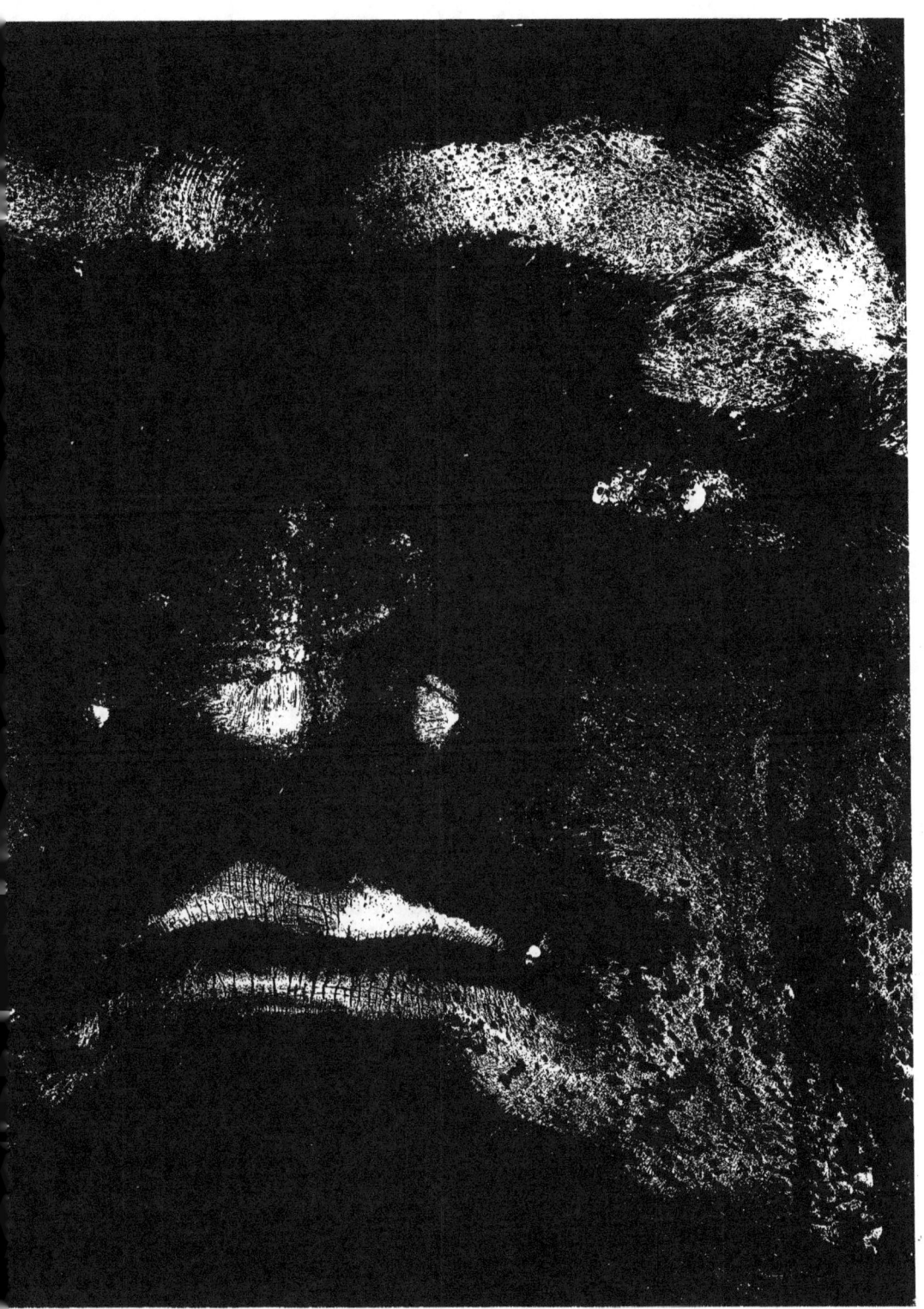

When I was sixteen, my father used to say to me: "Watch what you're doing with the girls; you're an idiot to smoke, for it's expensive and unhealthy; stay away from Raymond Maddison!" My mother had died two years earlier, so he'd taken over her share of the nagging, too.

The girls? Watch what I was doing? At sixteen I barely *knew* what I was doing! I knew what I wanted to do, but the how of it was a different matter entirely. Cigarettes? I enjoyed them; at the five-a-day stage, they still gave me that occasionally sweet taste and made my head spin. Raymond Maddison? I had gone to school with him, and because he lived so close to us we'd used to walk home together. But his mother was a little weak-minded, his older brother had been put away for molesting or something, and Raymond himself was thick as two short planks, hulking and unlovely, and a very shadowy character in general. Or at least he gave that impression.

Girls didn't like him: he smelled of bread and dripping and didn't clean his teeth too well, and for two years now he'd been wearing the same jacket and trousers, which had grown pretty tight on him. His short hair and little piggy eyes made him look bristly, and there was that looseness about his lips which you find in certain idiots. If you were told that ladies' underwear was disappearing from washing-lines, you'd perhaps think of Raymond. If someone was jumping out on small girls at dusk and shouting *boo!*, he was the one who'd spring to mind. If the little-boy-up-the-road's kitten got strangled . . .

Not that that sort of thing happened a lot in Harden, for it didn't. Up there on the north-east coast in those days, the Bobbies on the beat were still Bobbies, unhampered by modern "ethics" and other humane restrictions. Catch a kid drawing red, hairy, diamond-shaped designs on the school wall, and

wallop!, he'd get a clout round the earhole, dragged off home to his parents, and doubtless another wallop. Also, in the schools, the cane was still in force. Young people were still being "brought up," were made or at least encouraged to grow up straight and strong, and not allowed to bolt and run wild. Most of them, anyway. But it wasn't easy, not in that environment.

Harden lay well outside the fringes of "Geordie-land" — Newcastle and environs — but real outsiders termed us all Geordies anyway. It was the way we spoke; our near-Geordie accents leaped between soft and harsh as readily as the Welsh tongue soars up and down the scales; a dialect which at once identified us as "pit-yakkers," grimy-black shambling colliers, coal-miners. The fact that my father was a Harden greengrocer made no difference: I came from the colliery and so was a pit-yakker. I was an apprentice wood-cutting machinist in Hartlepool? — so what? My collar was grimy, wasn't it? With coal dust? And no matter how much I tried to disguise it I had that accent, didn't I? Pit-yakker!

But at sixteen I *was* escaping from the image. One must, or sex remains forever a mystery. The girls — the better girls, anyway — in the big towns, even in Harden, Easingham, Blackhill and the other colliery villages, weren't much impressed by or interested in pit-yakkers. Which must have left Raymond Maddison in an entirely hopeless position. Everything about him literally shrieked of his origin, made worse by the fact that his father, a miner, was already grooming Raymond for the mine, too. You think I have a down on them, the colliers? No, for they were the salt of the earth. They still are. I merely give you the background.

As for my own opinion of Raymond: I thought I knew him and didn't for a moment consider him a bad sort. He loved John Wayne like I did, and liked to think of himself as a tough egg, as I did. But nature and the world in general hadn't been so kind to him, and being a bit of a dunce didn't help much either. He was like a big scruffy dog who sits at the corner of the street grinning at everyone going by and wagging his tail, whom nobody ever pats for fear of fleas or mange or whatever, and who you're sure pees on the front wheel of your car everytime you park it there. He probably doesn't, but somebody has to take the blame. That was how I saw Raymond.

So I was sixteen and some months, and Raymond Maddison about the same, and it was a Saturday in July. Normally when we met we'd pass the time of day. Just a few words: what was on at the cinema (in Harden there were two of them, the Ritz and the Empress — for this was before Bingo closed most of them down), when was the next dance at the Old Victoria Hall, how many pints we'd downed last Friday at the British Legion. Dancing, drinking, smoking, girls: it was a time of experimentation. Life had many flavours other than those that wafted out from the pit and the coke-ovens. On this Saturday, however, he was the last person I wanted to see, and the very last I wanted to be seen with.

I was waiting for Moira, sitting on the recreation ground wall where the stumps of the old iron railings showed through, which they'd taken away thirteen years earlier for the war effort and never replaced. I had been a baby then but it was one of the memories I had: of the men in the helmets with the glass faceplates cutting down all the iron things to melt for the war. It had left only the low wall, which was ideal to sit on. In the summer the flat-capped miners would sit there to watch the kids flying kites in the recreation ground or playing on the swings, or just to sit and talk. There was a group of old-timers there that Saturday, too, all looking out across the dark, fuming colliery toward the sea; so when I saw Raymond hunching my way with his hands in his pockets, I turned and looked in the same direction, hoping he wouldn't notice me. But he already had.

"Hi, Joshua!" he said in his mumbling fashion, touching my arm. I don't know why I was christened Joshua: I wasn't Jewish or a Catholic or anything. I *do* know why; my father told me *his* father had been called Joshua, so that was it. Usually they called me Josh, which I liked because it sounded like a wild-western name. I could imaging John Wayne being called Josh. But Raymond occasionally forgot and called me Joshua.

"Hello, Ray*mond!*" I said. I usually called him Ray, but if he noticed the difference he didn't say anything.

"Game of snooker?" It was an invitation.

"No," I shook my head. "I'm, er, waiting for someone."

"Who?"

"Mind your own business."

"Girl?" he said. "Moira? Saw you with her at the Ritz. Back row."

"Look, Ray, I —"

"It's OK," he said, sitting down beside me on the wall. We're jus' talking. I can go any time."

I groaned inside. He was bound to follow us. He did stupid things like that. I decided to make the best of it, glanced at him. "So, what are you doing? Have you found a job yet?"

He pulled a face. "Naw."

"Are you going to?"

"Pit. Next spring. My dad says."

"Uh-huh," I nodded. "Plenty of work there." I looked along the wall past the ground-keeper's house. That's the way Moira would come.

"Hey, look!" said Raymond. He took out a brand new Swiss Army penknife and handed it over for my inspection. As my eyes widened he beamed. "Beauty, eh?"

And it was. "Where'd you get it?" I asked him, opening it up. It was fitted with every sort of blade and attachment you could imagine. Three or four years earlier I would have loved a knife like that. But right now I couldn't see why I'd need it. OK for wood-carving or the Boy Scouts, or even the Boys' Brigade, but I'd left all that stuff behind. And anyway, the machines I was learning to use in my trade paled this thing to insignificance and made it look like a very primitive toy. Like a rasp beside a circular saw. I couldn't see why Raymond would want it either.

"Saved up for it," he said. "See, a saw. Two saws! One for metal, one for wood. Knives — *careful!* — sharp. Gouge —"

"That's an auger," I said, "not a gouge. But . . . this one's a gouge, right enough. Look," and I eased the tool from its housing to show him.

"Corkscrew," he went on. "Scissors, file, hook . . ."

"Hook?"

"For hooking things. Magnetic. You can pick up screws."

"It's a good knife," I told him, giving it back. "How do you use it?"

"I haven't," he said, "— yet."

I was getting desperate. "Ray, do me a favour. Look, I have to stay here and wait for her. And I'm short of cigs." I forked out a florin. "Bring me a packet, will you? Twenty? And I'll give you a few."

He took the coin. "You'll be here?"

I nodded, lying without saying anything. I had an unopened packet of twenty in my pocket. He said no more but loped off across the road, disappearing into one of the back streets leading to Harden's main road and shopping area. I let him get out of sight, then set off briskly past the groundkeeper's house, heading north.

Now, I know I've stated that in my opinion he was OK; but even so, still I knew he wasn't to be trusted. He just

might follow us, if he could — out of curiosity, perversity, don't ask me. You just couldn't be sure what he was thinking, that's all. And I didn't want him peeping on us.

It dawns on me now that in his "innocence" Raymond was anything but innocent. There are two sides to each of us, and in someone like him, a little lacking in basic understanding . . . well, who is to say that the dark side shouldn't on occasion be just a shade darker? For illustration, there'd been that time when we were, oh, nine or ten years old? I had two white mice who lived in their box in the garden shed. They had their own swimming pool, too, made out of an old baking tray just two and a half inches deep. I'd trained them to swim to a floating tin lid for bits of bacon rind.

One day, playing with Raymond and the mice in the garden, I'd been called indoors about something or other. I was only inside a moment or two, but when I came back out he'd gone. Looking over the garden wall and down the street, I'd seen him *tip-toeing* off into the distance! A great hulk like him, slinking off like a cartoon cat!

Then I'd shrugged and returned to my game — and just in time. The tin lid raft was upside-down, with Peter and Pan trapped underneath, paddling for all they were worth to keep their snouts up in the air trapped under there with them. It was only a small thing, I suppose, but it had given me bad dreams for a long time. So . . . instead of the hard nut I considered myself, maybe I was just a big softy after all. In some things.

But . . . did Raymond do it deliberately or was it an accident? And if the latter, then why was he slinking off like that? If he had tried to drown them, why? Jealousy? Something I had which he didn't have? Or sheer, downright nastiness? When I'd later tackled him about it, he'd just said: "Eh? Eh?" and looked dumb. That's the way it was with him. I could never figure out what went on in there.

Moira lived down by the high colliery wall, beyond which stood vast cones of coal, piled there, waiting to fuel the coke ovens. And as a backdrop to these black foothills, the wheelhouse towers rising like sooty sentinels, coming into view as I hurried through the grimy sunlit streets; a colliery in the summer seems strangely opposed to itself. In one of the towers a massive spoked wheel was spinning even now, raising or lowering a cage in its claustrophobic shaft. Miners, some still in their "pit black," even wearing their helmets and lamps, drew deep on cigarettes as they came away from the place. My father would have said: "As if their lungs aren't suffering enough already!"

I knew the exact route Moira would take from her gritty colliery street house to the recreation ground, but at each junction in its turn I scanned the streets this way and that, making sure I didn't miss her. By now Raymond would have bought the cigarettes and be on his way back to the wall.

"Hello, Josh!" she said, breathlessly surprised — almost as if she hadn't expected to see me today — appearing like a ray of extra bright sunlight from behind the freshly creosoted fencing of garden allotments. She stood back and looked me up and down. "So, you're all impatient to see me, eh? Or . . . maybe I was late?" She looked at me anxiously.

I had been hurrying and so was breathing heavily. I smiled, wiped my forehead, said: "It's . . . just that there was someone I knew back there, at the recreation ground, and —"

"— You didn't want to be seen with me?" She frowned. She was mocking me, but I didn't know it.

"No, not that," I hurriedly denied it, "but —"

And then she laughed and I knew she'd been teasing. "It's all right, Josh," she said. "I understand." She linked my arm. "Where are we going?"

"Walking," I said, turning her into the maze of allotments, trying to control my breathing, my heartbeat.

"I know *that!*" she said. "But where?"

"Down to the beach, and up again in Blackhill?"

"The beach is very dirty. Not very kind to good clothes." She was wearing a short blue skirt, white blouse, a smart white jacket across her arm.

"The beach banks, then," I gulped. "And along the cliff paths to Easingham."

"You only want to get me where it's lonely," she said, but with a smile. "All right, then." And a moment later, "May I have a cigarette?"

I brought out my fresh pack and started to open it, but looking nervously around she said: "Not just yet. When we're farther into the allotments." She was six months my junior and lived close by; if someone saw her smoking it was likely to be reported to her father. But a few minutes later we shared a cigarette and she kissed me, blowing smoke into my mouth. I wondered where she'd learned to do that. Also, it took me by surprise — the kiss, I mean. She was impulsive like that.

In retrospect, I suppose Moira was my first love. And they say you never forget the first one. Well, they mean you never forget the first *time* — but I think your first love is the same, even if there's nothing physical. But she was the first one who'd kept me awake at night thinking of her, the first one who made me ache.

She was maybe five feet six or seven, had a heart-shaped face, huge dark come-to-bed eyes which I suspected and hoped hadn't yet kept their promise, a mouth maybe a fraction too wide, so that her face seemed to break open when she laughed, and hair that bounced on her shoulders entirely of its own accord. They didn't have stuff to make it

51

bounce in those days.

Her figure was fully formed and she looked wonderful in a bathing costume, and her legs were long and tapering. Also, I had a thing about teeth, and Moira's were perfect and very, very white. Since meeting her the first time I'd scrubbed the inside of my mouth and my gums raw trying to match the whiteness of her teeth.

Since meeting her . . .

That had been, oh, maybe three months ago. I mean, I'd always known her, or known of her. You can't live all your life in a small colliery village and not know everyone, at least by sight. But when she'd left school and got her first job at a salon in Hartlepool, and we'd started catching the same bus in the morning, that had opened it up for us.

After that there'd been a lot of talk, then the cinema, eventually the beach at Seaton which the debris from the pits hadn't ruined yet, and now we were "going together." It hadn't meant much to me before, that phrase, "going together," but now I understood it. We went places together, and we went well together. I thought so, anyway.

The garden allotments started properly at the end of the colliery wall and sprawled over many acres along the coast road on the northern extreme of the village. The access paths which divided them were dusty, mazy, meandering. But behind the fences people were at work, and they came to and fro along the paths, so that it wasn't really private there. I had returned Moira's kiss, and in several quieter places had tried to draw her closer once or twice.

Invariably she held me at arm's length, saying: "Not here!" And her nervousness made me nervous, too, so that I'd look here and there all about, to make sure we were unobserved. And it was at such a time, glancing back the way we'd come, that I thought I saw a face hastily snatched back around the

52

corner of a fence. The thought didn't occur to me that it might be Raymond. By now I'd quite forgotten about him.

Where the allotments ended the open fields began, gradually declining to a dene and a stream that ran down to the sea. A second cigarette had been smoked down to its tip and discarded by the time we crossed the fields along a hedgerow, and we'd fallen silent where we strolled through the long summer grass. But I was aware of my arm, linked with hers, hugged close against her right breast. And that was a thought which made me dizzy, for through a heady half-hour I had actually held that breast in my hand, had known how warm it was, with its little hard tip that felt rough against the parent softness.

Oh, the back row love-seats in the local cinema were worthy of an award; whoever designed them deserves an accolade from all the world's lovers. Two people on a single, softly upholstered seat, thigh to thigh and hip to hip, with no ghastly armrest divider, no obstruction to the slow, breathless, tender and timid first invasion.

In the dark with only the cinema's wall behind us, and the smoky beam from the projector turning all else to pitch, I was *sure* she wasn't aware of my progress with the top button of her blouse, and I considered myself incredibly fortunate to be able to disguise my fumblings with the second of those small obstacles. But after a while, when for all my efforts it appeared I'd get no further and my frustration was mounting as the tingling seconds ticked by, then she'd gently taken my hand away and effortlessly completed the job for me. She *had* known — which, while it took something of the edge off my triumph, nevertheless increased the *frisson* to new and previously unexplored heights.

Was I innocent? I don't know. Others, younger by a year, had said they knew everything there was to know. Every-

THE PIT-YAKKER

thing! That was a thought.

But in opening that button and making way for my hand, Moira had invited me in, as it were; cuddled up together there in the back row, my hand had moulded itself to the shape of her breast and learned every contour better than any actor ever memorized his lines. Even now, a week later, I could form my hand into a cup and feel her flesh filling it again. And *desired* to feel her filling it again.

Where the hedgerow met a fence at right-angles, we crossed a stile; I was across first and helped Moira down. While I held one hand to steady her, she hitched her short skirt a little to step down from the stile's high platform. It was funny, but I found Moira's legs more fascinating in that skirt than in her bathing costume. And I'd started to notice the heat of my ears — that they were hot quite apart from the heat of the sun, with a sort of internal burning — as we more nearly approached our destination. My destination, anyway, where if her feelings matched mine she'd succumb a little more to my seductions.

As we left the stile to take the path down into the dene and toward the sea cliffs, I glanced back the way we'd come. I don't know why. It was just that I had a feeling. And back there, across the fields, but hurrying, I thought . . . a figure. Raymond? If it was, and if he were to bother us today of all days . . . I promised myself he'd pay for it with a bloody nose. But on the other hand it could be anybody. Saying nothing of it to Moira, I hurried her through the dene. Cool under the trees, where the sunlight dappled the rough cobbled path, she said:

"What on earth's the hurry, Josh? Are you *that* eager?"

The way I took her up in my arms and kissed her till I reeled must have answered her question for me; but there were voices here and there along the

path, and the place echoed like a tunnel. No, I knew where I wanted to take her.

Toward the bottom of the dene, where it narrowed to a bottleneck of woods and water scooped through the beach banks and funnelled toward the sea, we turned north across an old wooden bridge over the scummy stream and began climbing toward the cliff paths, open fields, and sand holes that lay between us and Easingham Colliery. Up there, in the long grasses of those summer fields, we could be quite alone and Moira would let me make love to her, I hoped. She'd hinted as much, anyway, the last time I walked her home.

Toiling steeply up an earth track, where white sand spilled down from sand holes up ahead, we looked down on the beach — or what had been a beach before the pit-yakkers came — and remembered a time when it was almost completely white from the banks and cliffs to the sea. On a palmy summer day like this the sea should be blue, but it was grey. Its waves broke in a grey froth of scum on a black shore that looked ravaged by cancer — the cancer of the pits.

The landscape down there could be that of an alien planet: the black beach scarred by streamlets of dully glinting slurry gurgling seaward; concentric tidemarks of congealed froth, with the sick, wallowing sea seeming eager to escape from its own vomit; a dozen seacoal lorries scattered here and there like ticks on a carcass, their crews shovelling pebble-sized nuggets of the wet, filthy black gold in through open tailgates, while other vehicles trundled like lice over the rotting black corpse of a moonscape. Sucked up by the sun, grey mists wreathed the whole scene.

"It's worse than I remembered it," I said. "And you were right: we couldn't have walked down there, not even along the foot of the banks. It's just too filthy! And to think: all of that was pure

53

white sand just, oh —"

"— Ten years ago?" she said. "Well, maybe not *pure* white, but it was still a nice beach then, anyway. Yes, I remember. I've seen that beach full of people, the sea bobbing with their heads. My father used to swim there, with me on his chest! I remember it. I can remember things from all the way back to when I was a baby. It's a shame they've done this to it."

"It's actually unsafe," I told her. "There are places they've flagged, where they've put up warning notices. Quicksands of slag and slop and slurry — gritty black sludge from the pits. And just look at that skyline!"

South lay the colliery at Harden, the perimeter of its works coming close to the banks where they rolled down to the sea, with half-a-dozen of its black spider legs straddling out farther yet. These were the aerial trip-dumpers: conveyor-belts or ski-lifts of slag, endlessly swaying to the rim and tripped there, to tip the refuse of the coke-ovens down onto the smoking wasteland of foreshore; and these were, directly, the culprits of all this desolation. Twenty-four hours a day for fifty years they'd crawled on their high cables, between their spindly towers, great buckets of muck depositing the pus of the earth to corrode a coast. And behind this lower intestine of the works lay the greater pulsating mass of the spider itself: the pit, with its wheel-towers and soaring black chimneys, its mastaba cooling towers and mausoleum coke-ovens. Yellow smoke, grey and black smoke, belching continuously into the blue sky — or into a sky which looked blue but was in fact polluted, as any rainy day would testify, when white washing on garden lines would turn a streaky grey with the first patter of raindrops.

On the southern horizon, Blackhill was a spiky smudge under a grey haze; north, but closer, Easingham was the same. Viewed from this same position

at night, the glow of the coke-ovens, the flare-up and gouting orange steam when white hot coke was hosed down, would turn the entire region into a scene straight from Hell! Satanic mills? They have nothing on a nest of well-established coal mines by the sea. . . .

We reached the top of the banks and passed warning notices telling how from here on they rolled down to sheer cliffs. When I'd been a child, miners used to clamber down the banks to the cliff-edge, hammer stakes into the earth and lower themselves on ropes with baskets to collect gull eggs. Inland, however, the land was flat, where deep grass pasture roved wild all the way from here to the coast road. There were a few farms, but that was all.

We walked half a mile along the cliff path until the fields began to be fenced; where the first true field was split by a hedgerow inside the fence, there I paused and turned to Moira. We hadn't seen anyone, hadn't spoken for some time but I suppose her heart, like mine, had been speeding up a little. Not from our efforts, for walking here was easy.

"We can climb the fence, cut along the hedgerow," I suggested, a little breathlessly.

"Why?" Her eyes were wide, naïve and yet questioning.

I shrugged. "A . . . shortcut to the main road?" But I'd made it a question, and I knew I shouldn't leave the initiative to her. Gathering my courage, I added: "Also, we'll —"

"— Find a bit of privacy?" Her face was flushed.

I climbed the rough three-bar fence; she followed my example and I helped her down, and knew she'd seen where I could hardly help looking. But she didn't seem to mind. We stayed close to the hedgerow, which was punctuated every twenty-five paces or so with great oaks, and struck inland. It was only when we were away from the fence that I remembered, just before jumping down, that I'd paused a second to scan the land about — and how for a moment I thought I'd seen someone back along the path. Raymond, I wondered? But in any case, he should lose our trail now.

After some two hundred yards there was a lone elder tree growing in the field a little way apart from the hedge, its branches shading the lush grass underneath. I led Moira away from the hedge and into the shade of the elder, and she came unresisting. And there I spread my jacket for her to sit on, and for a minute or two we just sprawled. The grass hid us almost completely in our first private place. Seated, we could just see the topmost twigs of the hedgerow, and of course the bole and spreading canopy of the nearest oak.

Now, I don't intend to go into details. Anyone who was ever young, alone with his girl, will know the details anyway. Let it suffice to say that there were things I wanted, some of which she was willing to give. And some she wasn't. "No," she said. And more positively: *"No!"* when I persisted. But she panted and moaned a little all the same, and her voice was almost desperate, suggesting: "But I can do it for you this way, if you like." Ah, but her hands set me on fire! I burned for her, and she felt the strength of the flame rising in me. "Josh, *no!*" she said again. "What if . . . if . . ."

She looked away from me, froze for a moment — and her mouth fell open. She drew air hissingly and expelled it in a gasp. *"Josh!"* And without pause she was doing up buttons, scrambling to her feet, brushing away wisps of grass from her skirt and blouse.

"Eh?" I said, astonished. "What is it?"

"He saw us!" she gasped. "He saw you — me — like that!" Her voice shook with a mixture of outrage and fear.

"Who?" I said, mouth dry, looking this was and that and seeing no one. "Where?"

"By the oak tree," she said. "Half-way up it. A face, peering out from behind. Someone was watching us."

Someone? Only one someone it could possibly be! But be sure that when I was done with him he'd never peep on anyone again! Flushed and furious I sprinted through the grass for the oak tree. The hedge hid a rotting fence; I went over, through it, came to a panting halt in fragments of brown, broken timber. No sign of anyone. You could hide an army in that long grass. But the fence where it was nailed to the oak bore the scuff marks of booted feet, and the tree's bark was freshly bruised some six feet up the bole.

"You . . . *dog!*" I growled to myself. "God, but I'll *get* you, Raymond Maddison!"

"Josh!" I heard Moira on the other side of the hedge. "Josh, I'm so — ashamed!"

"What?" I called out. "Of what? He won't dare say anything — whoever he is. There are laws against —"

But she was no longer there. Forcing myself through soft wooden jaws and freeing myself from the tangle of the hedge, I saw her hurrying back the way we'd come. "Moira!" I called, but she was already half-way to the three-bar fence. "Moira!" I called again, and then ran after her. By the time I reached the fence she'd climbed it and was starting back along the path.

I finally caught up with her, took her arm. "Moira, we can find some other place. I mean, just because —"

She shook me off, turned on me. "Is that all you want, Josh Peters?" Her face was angry now, eyes flashing. "Well if it is, there are plenty of other girls in Harden who'll be more than happy to . . . to . . ."

"Moira, I —" I shook my head. It wasn't like that. We were going together.

"I thought you liked *me!*" she snapped. "The real me!"

My jaw fell open. Why was she talking to me like this? She knew I liked — more than liked — the real Moira. She *was* the real Moira! It was a tiff, brought on by excitement, fear, frustration; we'd never before had to deal with anything like this, and we didn't know how. My emotions were heightened by hers, and now my pride took over. I thrust my jaw out, turned on my heel and strode rapidly away from her.

"If that's what you think of me," I called back, "— if that's as *much* as you think of me — then maybe this is for the best . . ."

"Josh?" I heard her small voice behind me. But I didn't answer, didn't look back.

Furious, I hurried, almost trotted back the way we'd come: along the cliff path, scrambling steeply down through the grass-rimmed, crumbling sand pits to the dene. But at the bottom I deliberately turned left and headed for the beach. Dirty? Oh, the beach would be dirty — sufficiently dirty so that she surely wouldn't follow me. I didn't want her to. I wanted nothing of her. *Oh, I did, I did!* — but I wouldn't admit it, not even to myself, not then. But if she did try to follow me, it would mean . . . it would mean . . .

Moira, Moira! Did I love her? Possibly, but I couldn't handle the emotion. So many emotions; and inside I was still on fire from what had nearly been, still aching from the retention of fluids my young body had so desired to be rid of. Raymond? Raymond Maddison? By *God*, but I'd bloody *him*! I'd let some of *his* damned fluids out!

"Josh!" I seemed to hear Moira's voice from a long way back, but I could have been mistaken. In any case it didn't slow me down. Time and space flashed by in a blur; I was down onto the beach; I walked south under the cliffs on sand that was still sand, however blackened; I trekked grimy sand dunes up and down, kicking at withered tufts of crabgrass which reminded me of the

grey and yellow hairs sprouting from the blemishes of old men. Until finally I had burned something of the anger and frustration out of myself.

Then I turned toward the sea, cut a path between the sickly dunes down to the no-man's land of black slag and stinking slurry, and found a place to sit on a rock etched by chemical reaction into an anomalous hump. It was one of a line of rocks I remembered from my childhood, reaching out half a mile to the sea, from which the men had crabbed and cast their lines. But none of that now. Beyond where I sat, only the tips of the lifeless, once limpet- and mussel-festooned rocks stuck up above the slurry; a leaning, blackened signpost warned:

DANGER! QUICKSAND!
Do Not Proceed
Beyond This Point.

Quicksand? Quag, certainly, but not sand . . .

I don't know how long I sat there. The sea was advancing and grey gulls wheeled on high, crying on a rising breeze that blew their plaintive voices inland. Scummy waves broke in feathers of grey froth less than one hundred yards down the beach. Down what had been a beach before the invasion of the pit-yakkers. It was summer but down here there were no seasons. Steam curled up from the slag and misted a pitted, alien landscape.

I became lulled by the sound of the birds, the hissing throb of foamy waters, and, strangely, from some little distance away, the periodic clatter of an aerial dumper tilting its buckets and hurling more mineral debris down from on high, creating a mound which the advancing ocean would spread out in a new layer to coat and further contaminate the beach.

I sat there glumly, with my chin like lead in my hands and all of these sounds dull on the periphery of my consciousness, and thought nothing in particular and certainly nothing of any importance. From time to time a gull's cry would sound like Moira's voice, but too shrill, high, frightened, or desperate. She wasn't coming, wouldn't come, and I had lost her. We had lost each other.

I became aware of time trickling by, but again I state: I don't know how long I sat there. An hour? Maybe.

Then something broke through to me. Something other than the voices of the gulls, the waves, the near-distant rain of stony rubble. A new sound? A presence? I looked up, turned my head to scan north along the dead and rotting beach. And I saw him — though as yet he had not seen me.

My eyes narrowed and I felt my brows come together in a frown. Raymond Maddison. The pit-yakker himself. And this probably as good a place as any, maybe better than most, to teach him a well-deserved lesson. I stood up, and keeping as low a profile as possible made my way round the back of the tarry dunes to where he was standing. In less than two minutes I was there, behind him, creeping up on him where he stood wind-blown and almost forlorn-seeming, staring out to sea. And there I paused.

It seemed his large, rounded shoulders were heaving. Was he crying? Catching his breath? Gulping at the warm, reeking air? Had he been running? Searching for me? Following me as earlier he'd followed us? My feelings hardened against him. It was because he wasn't entirely all there that people tolerated him. But I more than suspected he *was* all there. Not really a dummy, more a scummy.

And I had him trapped. In front of him the rocks receding into pits of black filth, where a second warning notice leaned like a scarecrow on a battlefield, and behind him . . . only myself behind him. Me and my tightly clenched fists.

Then, as I watched, he took something out of his pocket. His new knife, as I saw now. He stared down at it for a moment, then drew back his arm as if to hurl it away from him, out into the black wilderness of quag. But he froze like that, with the knife still in his hand, and I saw that his shoulders had stopped shuddering. He became alert; I guessed that he'd sensed I was there, watching him.

He turned his head and saw me, and his eyes opened wide in a pale, slack face. I'd never seen him so pale. Then he fell to one knee, dipped his knife into the slurry at his feet, commenced wiping at it with a rag of a handkerchief. Caught unawares he was childlike, tending to do meaningless things.

"Raymond," I said, my voice grimmer than I'd intended. "Raymond, I want a word with you!" And he looked for somewhere to run as I advanced on him. But there was nowhere.

"I didn't —" he suddenly blurted. "I didn't —"

"But you did!" I was only a few paces away.

"I . . . I . . . "

"You followed us, peeped on us, messed it all up."

And again he seemed to freeze, while his brain turned over what I'd said to him. Lines creased his brow, vanishing as quickly as they'd come. "What?"

"What?!" I shouted, stepping closer still. "You bloody well *know* what! Now Moira and me, we're finished. And it's your fault."

He backed off into the black mire, which at once covered his boots and the cuffs of his too-short trousers. And there he stood, lifting and lowering his feet, which went **glop, glop** with each up and down movement. He reminded me of nothing so much as a fly caught on the sticky paper they used at that time. And his mouth kept opening and closing, stupidly, because he had nothing to say and nowhere to run, and he knew I was angry.

Finally he said: "I didn't mean to . . . follow you. But I —" And he reached into a pocket and brought out a packet of cigarettes. "Your cigarettes."

I had known that would be his excuse. "Throw them to me, Ray," I said. For I wasn't about to go stepping in there after him. He tossed me the packet but stayed right where he was, "You may as well come on out," I told him, lighting up, "for you know I'm going to settle with you."

"Josh," he said, still mouthing like a fish. "Josh. . . ."

"Yes, Josh, Josh," I told him, nodding. "But you've really done it this time, and we have to have it out."

He still had his knife. He showed it to me, opened the main blade. He took a pace forward out of the slurry and I took a pace back. There was a sick grin on his face. Except . . . he wasn't threatening me. "For you," he said, snapping the blade shut. "I don't . . . don't want it no more." He stepped from the quag onto a flat rock and stood there facing me, not quite within arm's reach. He tossed the knife and I automatically caught it. It weighed heavy in my hand where I clenched my knuckles round it.

"A bribe?" I said. "So that I won't tell what you did? How many friends do you have, Ray? And how many left if I tell what a dirty, sneaky, spying —"

But he was still grinning his sick, nervous grin. "You won't tell," he shook his head. "Not what I seen."

I made a lunging grab for him and the grin slipped from his face. He hopped to a second rock farther out in the liquid slag, teetered there for a moment before finding his balance. And he looked anxiously all about for more stepping-stones, in case I should follow. There were two or three more rocks, all of them deeper into the coal-dust quicksand, but beyond them only a bubbly, oozy black surface streaked

58

with oil and yellow mineral swirls.

Raymond's predicament was a bad one. Not because of me. I would only hit him. Once or twice, depending how long it took to bloody him. But this stuff would murder him. If he fell in. And the black slime was dripping from the bottoms of his trousers, making the surface of his rock slippery. Raymond's balance wasn't much, neither mentally nor physically. He began to slither this way and that, windmilled his arms in an effort to stay put.

"Ray!" I was alarmed. "Come out of there!"

He leaped, desperately, tried to find purchase on the next rock, slipped! His feet shot up in the air and he came down on his back in the quag. The stuff quivered like thick black porridge and put out slow-motion ripples. He flailed his arms, yelping like a dog, as the lower part of his body started to sink. His trousers ballooned with the air in them, but the stuff's suck was strong. Raymond was going down.

Before I could even start to think straight he was in chest deep, the filth inching higher every second. But he'd stopped yelping and had started thinking. Thinking desperate thoughts. "Josh . . . Josh!" he gasped.

I stepped forward ankle-deep, got up onto the first rock. I made to jump to the second rock but he stopped me. "No, Josh," he whispered. "Or we'll both go."

"You're sinking," I said, for once as stupid as him.

"Listen," he answered with a gasp. "Up between the dunes, some cable, half-buried. I saw it on my way down here. Tough, 'lectric wire, in the muck. You can pull me out with that."

I remembered. I had seen it, too. Several lengths of discarded cable, buried in the scummy dunes. All my limbs were trembling as I got back to solid ground, setting out up the beach between the dunes. "Josh!" his voice reached out harshly after me. *"Hurry!"*

And a moment later: "The first bit of wire you see, that'll do it. . . . "

I hurried, ran, raced. But my heart was pounding, the air rasping like sandpaper in my lungs. Fear. But . . . I couldn't find the cable. Then —

There was a tall dune, a great heap of black-streaked, slag-crusted sand. A lookout place! I went up it, my feet breaking through the crust, letting rivulets of sand cascade, thrusting myself to the top. Now I could get directions, scan the area all about. Over there, between low humps of diseased sand, I could see what might be a cable: a thin, frozen black snake of the stuff.

But beyond the cable I could see something else: colours, anomalous, strewn in a clump of dead crabgrass.

I tumbled down the side of the great dune, ran for the cable, tore a length free of the sand and muck. I had maybe fifteen, twenty feet of the stuff. Coiling it, I looked back. Raymond was there in the quag, going down black and sticky. But in the other direction — just over there, no more than a dozen loping paces away, hidden in the crabgrass and low humps of sand — something blue and white and . . . and red.

Something about it made my skin prickle. Quickly, I went to see. And I saw . . .

After a while I heard Raymond's voice over the crying of the gulls. "Josh! *Josh!*"

I walked back, the cable looped in my lifeless hands, made my way to where he hung crucified in the quag; his arms formed the cross, palms pressing down on the belching surface, his head thrown back and the slop ringing his throat. And I stood looking at him. He saw me, saw the cable in my limp hands, looked into my eyes. And he knew. He knew I wasn't going to let him have the cable.

Instead I gave him back his terrible knife with all its terrible attachments — which he'd been waiting to use, and which I'd seen no use for — tossing it so that it landed in front of him and splashed a blob of slime into his right eye.

He pleaded with me for a little while then, but there was no excuse. I sat and smoked, without even remembering lighting my fresh cigarette, until he began to gurgle. The black filth flooded his mouth, nostrils, the circles of his eyes. He went down, his sputtering mouth forming a ring in the muck which slowly filled in when he was gone. Big shiny bubbles came bursting to the surface. . . .

When my cigarette went out I began to cry, and crying staggered back up the beach between the dunes. To Moira.

Moira. Something I'd had — almost — which he didn't have. Which he could never have, except like this. Jealousy, or just sheer evil? And was I any better than him, now? I didn't know then, and I don't know to this day. He was just a pit-yakker, born for the pit. Him and me both, I suppose, but I had been lucky enough to escape it.

And he hadn't. . . . ▲

WHY MIRACLES DON'T HAPPEN ANYMORE

by Mark S. Painter, Sr.

The Reverend Billy-Joe Murphy — pastor of Maranatha Independent Baptist Church of Buena Vista, Virginia, host of two of the most watched religious-TV programs in America, *The Gospels Revealed* and *The Word at Work,* public figure, political activist, and spiritual father to millions — was in a quandary. The board of directors of Full-Time Gospel Ministry had voted to upgrade the transmitter of Billy-Joe's TV station, WBVV in Buena Vista, but he could not decide from which manufacturer to buy the new equipment. The Westinghouse model had twice the wattage, meaning, according to the arcane formulas employed by broadcast engineers, it would reach nearly 100,000 more heathens than the GE transmitter, but GE offered their equipment for less than half the price. The board had already examined the competing proposals, but ultimately voted not to make a recommendation, which left Billy-Joe to ponder the difficult question of whether the additional souls were worth the additional cost.

So Billy-Joe did what he always did when he felt crushed beneath the responsibilities of his ministry: he retired to his private retreat in the mountains of West Virginia. There, isolated except for the long rows of carefully tended oak and maple saplings on the estate — his many detractors thought it hypocritical that Billy-Joe, who regularly predicted the imminent end of the world, had

landscaped his retreat with trees that would not grow to their full effect for thirty years, which just went to show how little his detractors understood of the subtleties of theology — he prayed, waiting for a sign from the Lord.

On the desktop before him, he spread the Westinghouse and GE sales brochures, then clasped his hands and prayed fervently. "O, mighty Lord," said Billy-Joe, "give me Your sign, that I might know which transmitter to buy for the TV station, that I may be seen and heard by as many people as possible, in Your Name. Amen."

Then he picked up a pencil and, closing his eyes, waved it randomly over his desk. Just as he was about to bring the point down, a still, small voice said, "Billy-Joe."

Startled, Billy-Joe jumped to his feet, scattering the sales brochures. "Who is that?" he demanded.

"It is I," the voice replied. "The Lord your God. Creator and Sovereign of the Universe. The world is tired, Billy-Joe. People have lost faith. You will work miracles in My Name, and give them hope."

Billy-Joe was understandably suspicious. His gardener had an odd sense of humor and was not above the occasional practical joke. "I've spoken with You many times before, O Lord," said Billy-Joe doubtfully, "but You have always spoken in great booming words that I feared would shake this mighty house to its foundations. So why are

You whispering this time?"

"That was not My voice," God replied, "for I have never directly spoken to you before. Rather, it was your own voice, which, in your vanity, you took for Mine. Imagining that you were following My commands, you were, in fact, merely surrendering to the whims of your own pride."

"There's no need to get so personal," Billy-Joe objected.

"That's what Ezekiel used to say," warned the Lord, "and I told him he'd just have to get used to it. So will you, if you want to be My prophet. It goes with the job."

But Billy-Joe hadn't heard anything the small voice said after 'prophet.' "So," he breathed, eyes glazing, "I am to be Your prophet."

"Yes," said God. "You have to warn the people that they have gone far astray. You will speak for me, Billy-Joe. Tell them I hold each of them personally responsible for the mess the world is in. I am tired of their endless campaigns, movements, and crusades, which are largely devices for shifting the blame. You must tell them that there is no purifying the world until they first purge the evil that dwells in their own hearts, and that is a lifetime task."

"It'll never sell," said Billy-Joe. "It's a downer."

"It's *supposed* to be," God said. "My patience is wearing thin. If I take My vengeance, no one will escape."

"But I can't get on TV and say something like that," Billy-Joe objected. "They'll change the channel on me. They want to know what Christianity can do for them, like get them a better job, or help them get along with their wives, or just to feel good about themselves. They don't want to hear about tribulation; they want to know how to *escape* tribulation."

"Christianity does none of those things," said God. "It was never intended to."

"On the other hand, if I'm going to be Your prophet, that means I should go with the more powerful transmitter, I suppose." Billy-Joe picked the Westinghouse brochure off the floor. "It'll cost more, but I'm sure You can help me out there."

"I'm not interested in television," said God. "You can't work miracles on television. For all your television broadcasts, you've saved but a paltry handful of souls. As I said to Ezekiel, the people cannot follow your example unless you set one. I want you to go out among the people, like the prophets of old, traveling from town to town, subsisting on locusts and honey, one step ahead of the mobs who would stone you —"

"Locusts?" Billy-Joe's voice trembled. *"Stone* me?"

"You said yourself that the message would be unpopular. Forget money. From now on, you have no need of money. You will work miracles in My name: healing the sick, calling down fire from the heavens. Your world hungers for miracles, Billy-Joe. Together, we will provide them."

Billy Joe fingered the pages of the Westinghouse brochure, smiling beatifically. "The Westinghouse transmitter," he said. "Definitely. I will tell them that it is Your Will, O Lord."

"And, by the way, Billy-Joe, tell them I said you're overdue for a cost-of-living increase in your salary," a voice told him. But it was the loud voice that came from within. Of the still, small voice he heard no more, then, or ever.

Hojjatoleslam Hashemi Farajzadeh, an Iranian mullah, looked with satisfaction at the bomb parts spread on the table before him. In the next two weeks, a dozen Iranians would enter Morocco, each carrying one of these pieces. In Rabat, they would be assembled, and detonated on a busy street at rush hour. If Allah was with them, many would be slain. Thus warned, the Moroccans would surely rise up against the infidel King Hassan, who was but a puppet of the hated French, who were pawns of the despised Americans, who served the cause of the loathsome Zionists and the despicable Saudis.

Jews, Americans, French, Arabs. Islam faced so many enemies. Praise Allah for men — well, boys, to be precise — like Muhammad. Hojjatoleslam Farajzadeh offered a prayer that Muhammad would be accepted into Paradise for his service.

"Hashemi," said a still, small voice.

Hojjatoleslam Farajzadeh seized his blessed M-16 rifle, a piece of military booty left over from the time of the accursed shah, spun around, and fired five rounds into the doorway behind him.

"Don't sneak up on me like that," he said, after the bullets finished ricocheting. "It makes me nervous."

That there was no living person in the doorway did not surprise him. But neither was there a dead one, which was distinctly strange.

"Hashemi," the voice repeated.

The failure of the voice to be silenced by gunfire worried Hojjatoleslam Farajzadeh, but he was determined not to let it show. "Who dares call me by my first name? I am 'Hojjatoleslam Farajzadeh' to you, whoever you are."

"I am Allah," replied the voice.

Angered by the blasphemy, Hojjatoleslam Farajzadeh fired another burst from his rifle.

"I want you to work miracles in My name, Hashemi," continued the voice, unfazed. "The world is weary, and needs something to believe in. Together —"

"The world already has something to believe in," Hojjatoleslam Farajzadeh replied. "The glorious Islamic Republic."

"— for I want you to be my next Imam," the voice concluded.

"Well, why didn't You say so in the first place?" Hojjatoleslam Farajzadeh flung the rifle into the far corner of his study. "So I am to be the next ruler of Iran? How marvelous! When do I start?"

"The Imam is not the ruler of Iran," said the voice. "Rather, he rules the community of Islam in My name. Since the vast majority of Muslims are not Persian, you must first discard all loyalties to your native country. You cannot serve both Iran and Me."

This blasphemous suggestion made Hojjatoleslam Farajzadeh wish he had not cast away his weapon so hastily. But, as Hojjatoleslam Farajzadeh often said, where firepower is unavailable, one must make do with words. "What's the point in being Imam," he asked, "if not to purge the Faith?"

"I created Islam — the word means 'submission to Allah,' which you sometimes seem to forget — to show people how they might perfect their own souls. Now I find too often that it is misused as a tool to persecute both unbelievers and fellow Muslims. As my new Imam, you will tell them that Islam is the path to self-perfection, and not to the forcible perfection of people whom you happen not to like."

Hojjatoleslam Farajzadeh tried to imagine himself saying such a thing on the streets of Mecca — or in Teheran, for that matter. "They'll kill me!" he objected.

"Of course," the voice replied blandly. "Your predecessors, Ali, Hasan, and Husein, the first three Imams, all died violent deaths at the hands of My enemies. Why should you be any different?"

"But — but —" sputtered Hojjatoleslam Farajzadeh.

"In the city of Rabat at this very moment," continued the voice implacably, "waits a seventeen-year old Lebanese boy, Muhammad Jadhi. When that

63

bomb on the table behind you is assembled, he intends to detonate it by hand, killing himself as well as the passersby on the street. You told him to do so. You told him I would open the gates of Paradise to him if he martyred himself in My name. Should I expect anything less of my Imam?"

"Don't be ridiculous!" Hojjatoleslam Farajzadeh shouted. "Muhammad's just a kid, and dumb as a Turk, to boot. But I'm a Hojjatoleslam! How do you suppose the Ayatollah Khomeini managed to hang on for eighty-seven years? By blowing himself up every chance he got?"

"Islam needs a miracle, Hashemi," the voice insisted. "The re-emergence of the hidden Imam, to show My believers the way from internecine strife and bickering toward enlightenment and self-perfection."

"This must be a hallucination," Hojjatoleslam Farajzadeh told himself. "No doubt the CIA has been spiking my coffee again." He stuck his head out the door. "Saleh!" he called. "The bomb's ready."

Professor Rachel Garvey, lecturer in women's religion at Union Theological Seminary, came across a burning bush during her lunchtime stroll through Central Park.

"Rachel," said a still, small voice.

Rachel jumped, briefly considering the possibility that the bush and the voice were a ruse employed by a particularly crafty mugger or sex pervert. "Who's that?" she demanded.

"It is I," the voice said. "The Lord your God. The world is troubled, Rachel. I want you to be My prophet. Through you, I will work miracles: healing the sick, feeding the hungry, restoring sight to the blind. Together, we will give the people back their hope."

64

"Fat chance," Rachel sneered. "Not in *Your* Name. You're hopelessly sexist. You never picked anyone but men to be Your prophets in times past. Beg and plead all You want; it won't do You any good. Today's women will never forgive You for the persecution You brought upon our foremothers."

The flames crackled huffily. "I hadn't intended to beg or plead."

"You even have a man's voice," Rachel continued angrily. "You are symbolic of everything that's wrong with contemporary society: dominant, aggressive, militarist, technocratic, and life-hating. What the world needs is a new goddess, whose gospel has meaning in a revolutionary context. Women theologians are crafting a new, female deity — one that is worthy of modern females. You are obsolete, You . . . You . . ." Rachel groped for a suitable expletive. "You *man!*"

"I am neither male nor female," the voice said. "If you choose to place femininity on an altar and worship it, you worship not Me, but a false idol of your own invention. Equally wrong are those who worship masculinity, insisting that only a man can represent Me. I created humanity male and female, as I am. My image is too awesome to be reflected in any one person. Combine all the five billion men and women alive today, and you still have only a tiny fragment of what I am — for the whole would encompass not only the billions alive today, but the billions who have already lived and the billions yet to come. Eliminate any individual and the image is incomplete, because every member of your species is an indispensable part of it."

Rachel cocked her head in thought. "It sounds very much like an article I read in *Christian Century* a few years back. 'Re-Interpreting the Image of God in a Contemporary Context,' by Walter Jason, who used to teach at Drew. It was all the rage for a while, back in the days of first-generation feminism, but no one does that kind of theology today. Where would you publish it?"

"I don't become obsolete," said the voice. "I am eternal."

"Nope. The post-Christian church demands a goddess. Have you read *GynEcology: The Meta-Ethics of Radical Feminism,* by Mary Daley?"

The burning bush grew redder, sullen. "No."

"That's pretty much where we're at today on the gender thing. Wait a minute! Suppose there are *two* gods, one male and one female. The female one makes trees and oceans and stars, while the male one makes nuclear wastes. . . ." Lost in her own thoughts, she wandered down the path.

Behind her, the bush burned unnoticed.

Al Kurtz flopped into his overstuffed easy chair and pushed a button on his remote control. The TV set came to life. It was 9:30 and his two boys, Alfie and Mike, were finally in bed. His wife was over at the church, so he finally had the TV all to himself.

A cop drama squealed its tires at him. Al didn't like cop dramas, and that was all there seemed to be on TV these days. With the push of a button, he switched to a sitcom in which two cute kids said funny things. That was a little better. He watched for a while, wondering why his own boys never said anything clever, instead of just whining at him all the time.

He watched the sitcom until the next commercial, then was bored again. It was tough, now that the football season was over. Al didn't know much about the prime-time schedule; TV shows seemed to come and go so fast these days. Alfie and Mike had all the TV schedules memorized, but they were asleep, and good riddance to them.

God, he thought, *why can't there be something better than this on TV?*

As if in answer, the sound cut off, and the screen abruptly filled with bright, swirling colors.

"Al," said a still, small voice. "I want you to become My prophet. The world is tired, and hungers for something to believe in. You will work miracles in My Name, and give them hope."

Al stabbed at the remote control, and the TV set died. "Television's getting dumber all the time," he muttered.

Thank God there were only a few more weeks until the baseball season started.

The rains began to fall. ▲

HOW SWEET,
HOW SILENTLY SHE SLEEPS

by Reginald Bretnor

Listen! This is what befell Vlad Hra-zovar, Voivode of the Eastern Mountains, Lord of the dread Fortress Drakul, here in this castle when it was not quite as crumbling as it is today. Our kings had become dissolute and weak, so that the voivodes were a law unto themselves, and Radu, Vlad's grandfather, was the worst of all. He possessed the rich foothills with their forests, their vineyards, but it was not enough, for he had been infected by the cruel rapacity of the nomads against whom it was his duty to defend us, here in these once-verdant valleys. His was a rule of terror—none of those he ruled ever could forget his dungeons with their instruments of torture, his wild rages, his dark suspicions, his joy in others' agonies. None were exempt—nor man nor woman, nor child nor beast.

It was not enough. In the seventh year of his reign, he stormed down into these valleys, looting, burning, raping, slaying. Vlad, as a boy, often thrilled to his boasting of how he had ridden in triumph through the open gates of our Count's city, now dead and decaying at this castle's feet. In the outskirts, he had seen a peasant's infant crawling among a stable's horse-turds. He had speared it, and he had ridden in waving it, still alive, like a bloody pennant. And when he told of it, his harsh laughter had always rasped against the stone walls of the great hall, and he had slammed his drinking horn against the oaken table-top. "Then," he would shout, "then they knew what I had come for, their gold and their women and their pretty boys! Men are not ruled by mercy, Vlad—no, nor women neither! *Especially* women—" Here his laughter would burst out again, for all knew his women were nothing more than breeding animals.

He ruled by brute strength, and guile, and savagery, and Vlad admired him, far more than he admired his own father, Laza, who resembled Radu only

as a shadow. He grew up patterning himself after the old man, cherishing his tales of blood and rapine and triumphant terror. There was one tale especially, about the too-gentle Count who had ruled the valleys from this city, and his wife the Lady Naliyana, whose beauty was famous the length and breadth of all the land. Radu stormed this castle and took it easily, for none had expected one charged with their protection to turn on them. At her lord's behest, then, the Lady barricaded herself into her tower with her handmaidens, and all Radu's demands, all his false entreaties, were met with silence. So he impaled her husband on the battlements in her full view, promising him an easy death if she would unbar the door. But even that promise, she knew, was false.

Finally, after the Count had breathed his last, Radu burst into the tower by main force—and found her there, beautiful on her bier; and each of her maidens died loyal to her, telling how she had taken poison. There is no need to mention how they died. But the mere telling always threw Radu into such a terrible rage that he would break the back of a dog or two or, more often, hurry to his dungeons to refresh himself.

Often, Vlad would tell the old man that he too, when he was grown, would descend on those rich valleys, and reap as fine a harvest; and Radu, winking at him slyly, always cautioned him to patience. "We must give the dumb brutes time to get fat again, to forget a little, to let down their guard. Ten years is not enough. No, it will take twenty to make it worth our while."

When Vlad was thirteen, when only eleven years had passed, Radu Hrazovar was murdered in his sleep by Laza, his son and heir, and his right-hand man with him. It was cleverly done, but Vlad did not admire his father for it. He said nothing, biding his time.

HOW SWEET, HOW SILENTLY SHE SLEEPS

Prematurely, then, Laza moved against the valleys and the city, and the harvest he reaped was by no means as rich as Radu's. Enraged, he spent a fortnight there, destroying blindly, before he rode back again.

Vlad grew up the very image of his grandsire: a forehead like a tub, lowering brows, small, deep-set unclear eyes, a jaw like a rock, and the strength of four ordinary men. When he was eighteen, he in turn slew his father and was admired for it, and became Voivode. His pleasure was in combat, and in drinking, and in the bed of every woman—and indeed every likely lad —his eyes happened on. Yes, and in the dungeons and the amusements they afforded him.

Not until his twenty-eighth year did he in turn mount his raid against the people of the valleys.

He rode forth with a great force of men, advancing directly on the city, and they found—nothing. Every field was fallow. Not a beast cropped the neglected pastures. Every hut and cottage, even the houses of petty noblemen, lay deserted, stripped of everything worth taking. And the city itself was as silent and as utterly abandoned. Someone, perhaps the good Count's heir, had persuaded all the people to flee to the King's more immediate domain, for whatever protection he and his barons might afford them.

Vlad Hrazovar's soldiery began to grumble, and only their fear of him prevented them from abandoning the expedition. They were forced to content themselves with the petty pickings of the greater houses, with stray barnyard creatures, broken pieces of cutlery or jewelry, overlooked casks of sour wine.

Vlad, grim-faced, turned the haunted city over to them, forbidding them to follow him, and rode his horse to the high hill on which this castle stands. Who knows what he thought he'd find?

He rode across the drawbridge, its floor riven, its chains hanging lax. Leaving his mount in the forecourt, he strode into the empty, echoing great hall. It was not then as cobwebbed, as damp and mouldering, as it is today, but abandonment already had begun to take its toll. Owls flew out, hooting, at his footfall. In disgust, he saw that nothing of value had been left, not so much as a pewter flagon, so—thinking that possibly at least some precious sacred vessels might have been left behind—he stamped through the flagstoned halls and found the chapel.

He entered. He halted, frowning. In the center, before the high altar, stood a granite tomb, a tomb with great brazen doors. There was no dust here, no spider-webs, no bats clinging to the dark beams overhead.

He loosened his long sword in its great jeweled scabbard. Slowly he approached.

Over the tomb's door, in bronze, he read the words:

How Sweet, How Silently She Sleeps

And instinctively he knew who was buried there.

Then he heard a voice, cracked and aged, almost at his elbow. He whirled, sword flying free.

The crone who stood there was bent and withered, old almost beyond belief, her gray hairs sparse and straggling.

"Yes, Lord," she said, "it is the Lady Naliyana who lies there."

He seized her with one huge hand, sword's edge at her throat. "Do you lie to me, hag?" he growled, touched momentarily by apprehension. "Lie to me and I'll have your head."

"I would not lie to you, Lord. See—it is I who care for her resting place, as I have for uncounted years. But she is not dead, Lord." She cackled strangely, and Vlad Hrazovar caught the sound of her senility.

"Not dead? Damn you, she was well dead before old Radu ever left this place, and well for her she was!"

Again she cackled. "No, no! It was through witchcraft that she escaped him. She had women in her service who knew all such things, who prepared the potion. He-he-he! And wasn't he angry though? Shall I tell you what he did, Lord?"

"You have lied to me!"

"Lord, I have not lied. Look, here is the key." From somewhere in her ragged robe, she pulled a vast bronze key. "She simply sleeps, still locked in her enchantment. Here, take this. Open those doors if you do not believe me. Read what it says over them. Lord, it is true."

Vlad stared at her with unclear eyes. There was an age-old silence all through the chapel, a waiting silence; and suddenly, remembering how his grandfather had described the Lady Naliyana, he seized the key, thrust it into the right hand door, turned it savagely. He thought, *Perhaps I should kill this creature first?* But the doors were opening.

He gasped, forgetting the old woman —for the doors had not opened on a constricted sepulchre. A soft, golden light poured through them, and it came from a chamber far larger than that tomb could hold, a chamber hung with tapestries of gold and pale blue and silver. No bier stood there. In the chamber's center was a bridal bed, and on it, clad only in a thin silken gown, her feet bare, her golden hair streaming over the richness of her pillows, the Lady Naliyana lay.

The last of Vlad's apprehensions vanished. He was conscious only of her beauty, of her flooding perfume, of the raw juices of his manhood, his grandfather's manhood, burning in his loins.

"Waken her, Lord!" whispered the old woman.

He took one step forward.

The Lady Naliyana stirred.

Instantly he forgot all caution. He ripped his swordbelt off, tossed it aside, sword and all. As her eyes opened, he advanced, stripping off his jerkin, tearing at his breeks.

"Now," he shouted, *"I shall finish what my grandsire began!"*

Instantly he was upon her, forcing her back against the bed. He knew she had recognized Radu's face in his. She made no sound, but she fought him, fought him ferociously. She bit his hand, his cheek, deeply, drawing blood. He forced her legs apart, forced his way into her against her desperate muscles.

Triumph surged through him as he felt the first onset of his terrible climax. He never reached it. Nor did he see the exultant smile with which she looked at the swiftly closing granite walls. His destroying hands closed on her throat —and suddenly there was no throat there. She was no longer under him. Abruptly he understood that his hands were crushing only dry bones and shreds of hair, and long-rotted cloth, that there was no longer perfume in the air, but the smell of grave-dust.

The last sound that he heard was the key turning in the lock of the brazen door.

How do I know these things? There are some things only old women know. And yes, you are right. Now that *she* is gone, the words over these doors are changed. Now they simply say, *Who knows? Perhaps he sleeps.*

Stranger, are you curious? Would you like to know?

Here is the key.

▲

UPSTAIRS

by John Accursi

The hand is the sickly white of old chalk, still wrapped in bloody, dragging bandages, and it is making its way through the house with horrifying quickness.

It is too light to make a sound as it creeps across the cold wooden floor, and not one of the family even stirs in their beds as the twitching thing passes by each of their open doors, fingers trembling in anticipation and urgency. In the darkness it finds its way through the family room, and its long, cracked nails make a rustling sound as they drag over the thick carpet. In their guilty, nervous sleep, the family does not hear it.

It crosses over and out of the cool, white-tiled kitchen, into another hallway, toward another door.

The door to its father's room.

Father seems to be sleeping peacefully enough, tired after a hard day's work.

Yes, the axe was very heavy for your tired, old arms, wasn't it, Father?

THANKSGIVING DAY. I CAN HEAR THEM DOWN THERE, ALL OF THEM, THEY'RE SITTING AT THE IMMENSE OAK DINING TABLE THAT STANDS IN THE LIVING ROOM AND IS NEVER USED, EXCEPT ON THIS DAY. I HEAR LAUGHTER. FULL, RICH, DEEP VOICES. I WANT TO BE WITH THEM SO VERY BADLY. EVEN IF IT IS FOR ONLY A MOMENT.

MY HAND REACHES THROUGH THE DARKNESS, SEARCHING FOR MY DOOR. THERE IS NO KNOB FOR ME TO TURN, NO WAY FOR ME TO LEAVE. THE WOOD IS VERY HEAVY, MAYBE MADE OUT OF THE SAME WOOD AS THE DINING TABLE. IF I TRY TO SHOUT FATHER WILL COME FOR ME, SO I AM SILENT. I HAVE NOT TRIED TO KNOCK THE DOOR AWAY FOR MANY MONTHS, BECAUSE FATHER HAS TOLD ME WHAT WILL HAPPEN IF I TRY THAT AGAIN. IT DOES NO GOOD ANYWAY, THE DOOR IS TOO STRONG, STRONGER THAN ME.

BUT I WANT TO BE DOWNSTAIRS. I TRY TO PUSH THE DOOR AWAY, ANYWAY. WORRY ABOUT FATHER LATER.

IT IS A MIRACLE. THE DOOR DOESN'T FALL AWAY, BUT IT IS OPEN PLENTY FOR ME TO SQUEEZE OUT AND ONTO THE STAIRS. TO SEE THANKSGIVING.

The hand catches moonlight as it crosses the den towards the front door, and it is like a great, robed spider hunting in the darkness for prey.

Finally it reaches the front door, and to the right of it, the stairs.

The stairs.

You tried, but you couldn't kill me, Father. You couldn't. Too much fear.

I COME THROUGH THE DOOR INTO THE DINING ROOM. THE TABLE IS EVEN MORE BEAUTIFUL THAN IN MY DREAMS. THERE IS MORE FOOD ON THAT TABLE THAN

I HAVE EATEN IN MY LIFE. I TAKE ALL THIS IN AT ONCE, FOR I ONLY HAVE AN INSTANT BEFORE FATHER HAS LEAPED OUT OF HIS CHAIR AND RUN TO HIS ROOM. MOTHER IS CRYING. THE OTHERS ARE JUST SCREAMING. I WISH I HADN'T COME DOWNSTAIRS THEN. LOOK WHAT I'VE DONE.

I RUN OUT OF THE DINING ROOM. NOW I'M SCREAMING EVEN LOUDER THAN THE OTHERS. I CAN STILL HEAR MOM CRYING AND SAYING NO NO NO NO. I'M ON MY WAY BACK TO MY ROOM WHEN I SEE FATHER WAITING BY THE FOOT OF THE STAIRS. HE'S HOLDING AN AXE.

The hand rests a long time at the foot of the stairs, momentarily unsure why it is there. But as the steady, impatient chatter bellows out from somewhere at the top of the stairs, it begins its ascent with an almost frantic urgency.

Climbing upward, toward the sound at the top of those stairs. The quiet, whimpering sound that seems so familiar. The sound of hatred.

You tried, Father, but I'm not dead. Hate is so much stronger than fear. Not dead.

THE AXE COMES DOWN. IT COMES DOWN. IT COMES DOWN. ALL I CAN SEE IS REDNESS. REDNESS ON THE CEILING. REDNESS ON THE FLOOR. ON EVERY INCH OF EVERY WALL. THERE IS NO PAIN, ONLY ICY COLD DIZZINESS. THEN FATHER SCREAMS AND BLACKNESS FINDS ME AS THE AXE ENTERS MY BRAIN.

FATHER PICKS ME UP AND BRINGS ME BACK TO MY DARK ROOM. HE DOES NOT SEE THE HAND THAT HAS ROLLED INTO THE SHADOWS UNDER THE OLD COUCH. LUCKY FOR ME.

The hand takes the steps one at a time, step after painfully slow step. It is just over halfway up when it stops, its muscles burning and beginning to lose control. Then something in the room upstairs kicks a door angrily, and the hand begins to climb once again.

Near dawn, it reaches the upstairs landing, and makes its way to the battered door of the single room of the forgotten upper floor. The door is cracked and uneven, leaning within the frame, after endless nights of beatings and hammerings from within.

My room. Yes, my room.

The hand climbs the door. Up the splinters, hanging onto the grooves, somehow. It climbs the door. And when it is high enough, it grasps the tarnished brass doorknob that Father has left on the outside. And turns it. Slowly. Quietly.

Pleasant dreams, Father. I'm coming. Coming.

And the door swings open, the door to the *mad* room, the bloody room. The room where there had never been a beam of light, a breath of air, or a single, gentle breeze that hadn't carried the strong stench of madness.

From the darkness, there comes a small sound: the voice of something that had once been a little boy, a long, forgotten time ago. It repeats a few words over and over, as though they had been burned into its mad little mind, sending all else into an obscure abyss.

Look what you've done to me, Father. Look what you've done to me.

And then the little boy comes out, a piece at a time, and begins to climb down the stairs to his father.

A handless arm is the first to emerge from the blackness of the room, but the stump of a leg follows much more quickly, travelling in an awkward hopping motion. Other, smaller pieces also follow, but it isn't until they have all reached the foot of the stairs that the greatest horror emerges.

At first it is nothing more than a partially obscured image — two spider-belly orbs of black glass hovering there, watching. Then shape becomes evident, and the monster's face totters at the top of the steps, choosing its treacherous path down. It will be long.

Getting down the hallway to Father will be easy, though. Even with the axe still in its head. ▲

IMPROBABLE BESTIARY: THE NIGHTMARE

When I am alone, then the Nightmare comes,
Introducing itself with a grin.
It bestraddles my head, and persistently drums
On my skull, while it shrieks: *"Let me in!"*
It unfastens the latch on the doors of my mind —
It steps over the threshold, its glee unconfined —
And it drags several sinister satchels behind
As it props up its feet on my brain.
Then I ask why it sits, tucked away in my wits,
And the Nightmare replies: *"You're insane."*

When I am in crowds, then the Nightmare broods,
And it whispers dark thoughts in my ear.
And no person who looks at me ever concludes
I am other than as I appear.
But the Nightmare has secretly taken control
Of my voice and my body, my thoughts and my soul;
It unbuckles my flesh, and it swallows me whole,
Then it tries on my body for size.
And the man people see, whom they fancy is me,
Is the Nightmare in human disguise.

When I am asleep, then the Nightmare rides
Through a dark and foreboding terrain.
And the alien shores of the land it explores
Are the valleys and shoals of my brain.
And the Nightmare wears faces I don't want to see;
It pursues me eternally, howling with glee,
And it traps me in places where I cannot flee
From the Nightmare within, which inhabits my skin.
And before I can ask
Why its face is concealed
By a hideous mask,
All at once it's revealed:
And the form of the Nightmare has steadily grown
To resemble myself . . . *and its face is my own.*

— F. Gwynplaine MacIntyre

73

THREE HEADS FOR THE HIGH KING

by R. Garcia y Robertson

One night at winter's end I dreamed I saw dawn through a window. My mother's sod house had no windows, just a smokehole in the roof and a leather door that faced the sea and sunset. The house was windowless because it was dug into the head of a deep valley. Tall cliffs enclosed the valley, guarding us from the black winds howling off the Frozen Sea. Our barn was a natural cave that vanished into these cliffs; I never knew how far until I found a fear worse than darkness.

I asked Mother what the dream meant. I was youngest daughter and slept far from the door. How could I see dawn from our big bed, when we had no windows and the door faced the sunset? Taking all questions seriously, Mother put on her night-blue cloak with the moons and stars, her black lambskin hood, and her hairy calf-skin boots with the long laces. She wound a snakeskin belt around her waist, then slipped on the white catskin gloves with the hair turned inside. Holding her Blackstaff, she sat on a three-legged stool and went into a trance. When she returned from the trance Mother said that I must meet the first ship that sailed into the fjord from out of the sunrise. There would be a man aboard who would help me know my dream. If he was not on the first ship, I should not despair, but should try the next instead.

What was the use of ritual, I asked her? I meant to meet the ships anyway, since how else would we women find men? She set down the Blackstaff and stripped off her catskin gloves, saying,

"Caer, even on the simplest questions I listen first for the Goddess, or else what is the use of being a Priestess?"

You may call me Caer. I was born on Ultima Thule, an island that sits on the sunset edge of the world and is still emerging from Ocean. At fifteen winters I had already seen Mother Earth give birth: heaving her thighs, throwing molten stone from her mountain flanks, and gnashing her rocky teeth. Much of Thule is half-formed, a lifeless welter filled with the raw elements of creation: sharp peaks and lava flows, snow fields, drift sands and cinder deserts. There are even newer islands just off shore, still warm from the fires that formed them. Fulmars and black-backed gulls bring seeds in their feathers, and tufts of lyme grass slowly turn the dark lava sands into dunes. Life springs from life.

Each year more snow comes down from the Frozen Sea, smelling of salt and mist. In places it never melts, piling season upon season into great snowfields. Even where deep fires warm the gray ground snow clings in white patches throughout spring and into summer. Thule's seaward edges have been worn into soil by winter frost, spring shoots, and falling water, but most of this green shore is utterly empty; with no fences, no farmsteads, just hills pressed down by the weight of many winters. Our homes, hidden in bays and inlets, offer the only warm landfall.

My dream stayed with me while the moon waxed and waned. Then one afternoon three men came walking up

74

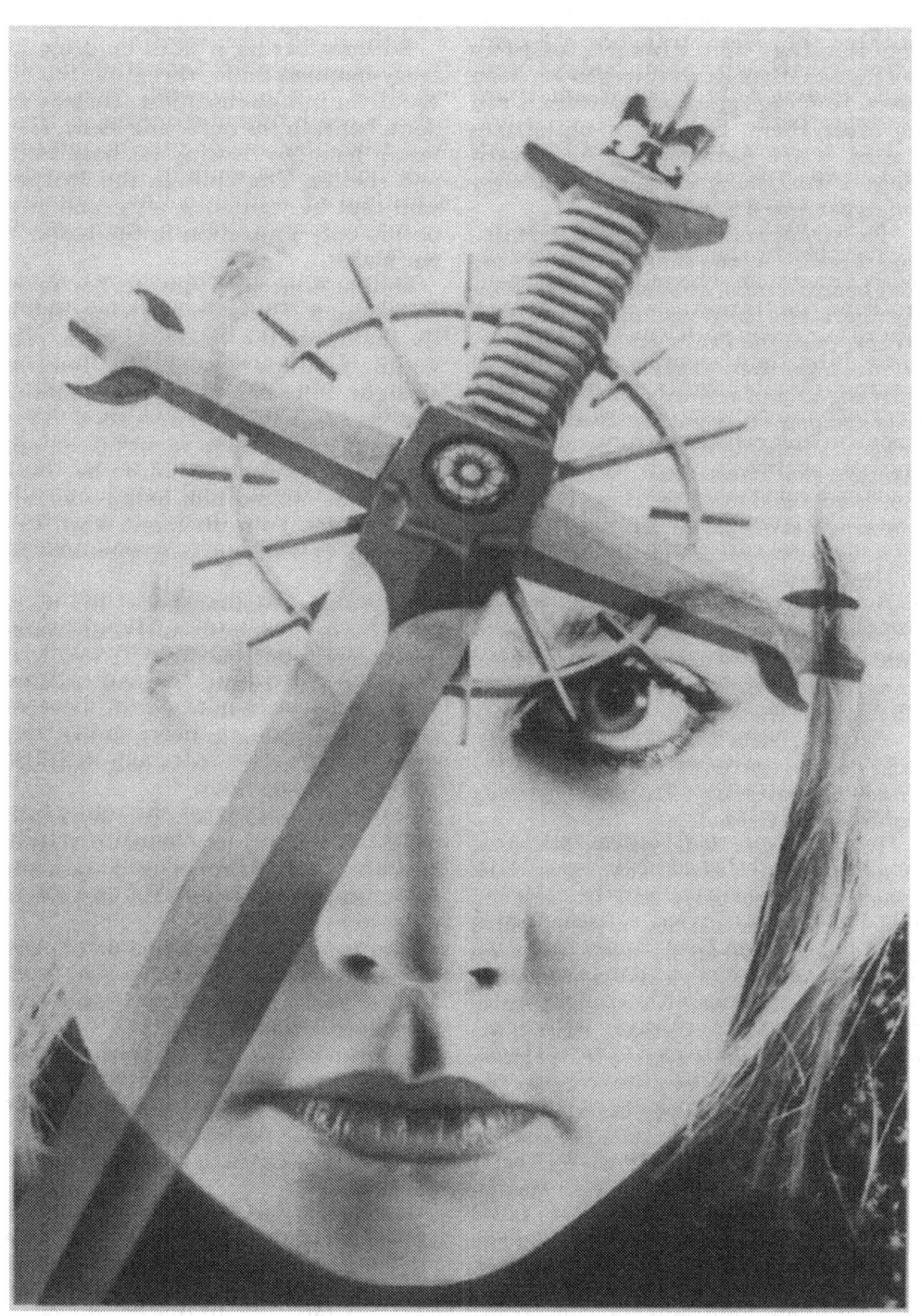

from our fjord. You could see by their gait that they were strangers tossed up by the sea, though no ship had yet been seen. Holding tight to my dream, I ran to greet them. Several of my sisters called, "Caer, come back," but I played deaf. I was youngest daughter, everyone's pet and free to roam.

The strangers stopped and stood talking together by the shore. Two were big red-bearded men who might have been brothers, the third was slim and blond. Where our green valley meets the gray-white hills they separated, the blond turning inland towards our farmstead. His companions went westward where other settlements were strung out along Thule's southwest coast, warm amber beads on a cold stone necklace. I watched the single stranger climb past the sheep pens and tiny cornfields that fell down to the water. Spring had turned the hills on either hand into half-greened bronze, tarnished almost black in places and golden brown in others. Behind him the restless sea rolled and beat at the foot of the valley. Half my family — women, sons and fathers, children and dogs — gathered on the slope behind me watching him make his way up from the fields.

This stranger was young, tall as a king's son, with broad shoulders, dark eyes, and thick curly hair the color of pale honey. He carried a pack and a staff, but no weapons aside from an ivory-handled knife tucked in his leather belt. He greeted me with a quick smile and a few words in a heavy British accent from somewhere east of Eire. I took his hand, leading him gravely to the threshold where I presented him to Mother. She had taken time to change and was wearing her great full skirt trimmed with glass beads, her wooden arm rings, and her leather boots laced high up her calf. From the waist up she wore only an ivory necklace, a crown of spring flowers, and red ocher on her nipples. She held her beaten iron **76**

Blackstaff lightly in one gloved hand.

Without saying a word he drew his ivory-handled knife, thrusting the silver sliver into our doorpost. Then he sat down beneath the quivering blade. Here was a bold boy, asking for hospitality and shelter. The knife in the doorpost said that he wanted to stay, and gave up his only protection to the power of our house.

Mother welcomed him to her farmstead and to Thule, in her name and in the name of the Sacred Queen. The young stranger stood up, looking straight into her eyes and thanking her, just as though he were used to ceremony. Parting a sea of curious daughters and sons she led him to her table where she offered him bread and salt. He accepted both, then sat down to a full meal of fish, onions, greens, and oat cakes.

As he ate, Mother asked his name and where he was from. He answered her second question first. "I was born and bred in Britain. You can call me Hands, because hands are all I have to offer. I am hoping to find a family that needs a pair of hands to help with the lambing and the wool."

Mother leaned across the table, taking his wrists, turning them up to study his palms. "Fair-Hands would be a better name, these palms have never done farm work."

The young man laughed at his new name, saying it was a lucky one in his Mother's family; and as for farm work, he was willing to learn.

Mother reached up, slipping slender white fingers under his collar, pulling forth a white-gold chain with a silver cross hanging from it. Then she said a few words in Latin, a language I never mastered.

Hands replied in his thick British accent that he was indeed a Christian.

"Then swear by your cross that you mean no harm to my people and that in this valley you will live by its laws."

He took the cross between his palms and swore, "By this cross, by Jesus who died on it, and by the Holy Mother who bore him; I mean no harm to this valley and will live by its laws while I am here. I have committed no crimes out of the ordinary. I have forced no women, and killed no men except in battle."

Mother said he was welcome to work for food, shelter, and a share in the shearing, but that for the rest of the day and evening he was our guest. His chores would began in the morning. At dinner he talked freely of his travels in Eire and his arrival in Thule, but refused to give any hint of his name and family. My sisters and I served him, heaping his platter though he looked askance at our meat.

Hands asked, "This is certainly not beef; is it mutton?"

Boann, my eldest sister, assured him that it was not mutton either.

"Then perhaps it is pork," said Hands.

Except aboard visiting ships, I had never so much as seen a pig. Brigit, the second oldest, tartly told him that his own Scriptures proscribed pig-meat. Though we were heathens, we did not mean to insult a guest.

Hands grew worried, "I have heard that some heathens eat human flesh, which is also not advised in Scripture."

Brigit became very prim. "The meat is fresh, do we look like we are in mourning? Even if we had just lost a loved one, we would never serve a family member to a stranger. We eat our dead only during the hardest of winters, when the Sacred Queen has sprinkled salt on our tongues and the Goddess has given us leave. Have you never eaten seal before?"

Hands forced on a smile, but went at his meat with more enthusiasm.

Night settled, and we sisters waited to see if this strange boy would become our father. Mother had nine children, three sons and six daughters. Aside from the twins, Maeve and Macha, no two could boast the same father. Instead we looked back on a long succession of fathers: fisher fathers, hunter fathers, stranger fathers. When Hands arrived we even had a pair of fathers living with us. The custom on Thule was to call any man who had copulated with your Mother your father. That this boy was half her age hardly mattered. She was then nine and thirty, a lucky age and hardly old. Her body was white as ivory, carved in full flowing curves and worn smooth as an ancient Goddess image handed down through a thousand generations. She was more beautiful even than the Sacred Queen, and good at getting on with strangers.

Nothing happened that night, and Hands went off to sleep in the barn. While Mother smothered the seal-oil lamps we all gathered around to see what she thought. The red embers in the firepit turned her skin pale rose. "He is noble," she said, "that is for sure."

"I could see that in his eyes," said Brigit, who fancied she could look straight into men's souls.

"He spoke Latin like a noble, and is too pretty to be a priest," sad Boann. As eldest daughter Boann was training to be a priestess and already familiar with sacred tongues.

"And he is a Christian," said Etar, "all the best people in Britain are Christians." Sailing to Eire had made Etar an authority on the wider world.

"His nobility was in his hands," Mother replied. "They had only one callus, and that one never came from oar or plow. It is a little ridge on his sword hand, right where a hilt rubs on the knuckle."

Despite his doubtful background Hands emerged at dawn, as willing to work as if he were born to do it. Mother set him to repairing winter damage to the windbreaks that bordered the oat fields. The work stretched out and the day heated up. Soon his shirt came off, and between my own chores I would watch his hard young muscles ripple in the ripening sun. His body was strong but his skin looked smooth, almost feminine, and very appealing; I thought that men's skin was rougher than need be and wanted a lover with a gentle hand, his skin like eiderdown. Etar swore that the children of British princely houses bathed in milk.

After waiting a full quartermoon Brigit broached the subject of fatherhood with Mother, asking how she fancied the boy. Mother's reply sounded soft, a mild breeze blowing off drift ice. "Fair-Hands is handsome enough, but I now have nine children and it would be less than lucky to break that holy number with a Christian. This winter I had two husbands hanging about, and I am approaching the age where it is easier to handle two husbands than three."

Brigit said she was happy to hear that answer, for she herself was still at the age when two men were better than one, and three even better than two. Boann and Etaine said they felt the same.

We were used to having men descend on us in the spring. Hunters came seeking seal and sea-ivory, fishermen came seeking land food and dry beds. Behind them came the sea-brigands, hunters and fishers of other men. All who would keep the peace were welcome. Many of these men landed with an eye for women, being bored by whatever it is men do when they are alone together. The handsome ones all had wives in Eire or Brittany, and thought they were getting the better of both them and us. Etar had returned from Eire with similar stories about Irish girls. Men who failed to become our fathers were suitable as husbands or lovers.

My greatest hardship in growing up was having five older sisters, each determined to have as many lovers and husbands as she could manage. This hungry brood left not even scraps be-

78

hind. Every handsome lad within walking distance and every man who wandered by was instantly taken, or tested and found wanting. All his virtues and faults lay exposed like a scapegoat gutted and examined for omens. So I was fifteen and still a virgin. That spring I would have settled for even a hand-me-down, if only I could have discovered his faults for myself.

My condition was not surprising considering the advantages my sisters had. Boann and Brigit were broad-breasted and wide-hipped, with dark hair and full lips; each had proven her womanhood by bearing children. Next was Etaine, nineteen and without child, but having a great riot of red hair and a saucy smile inherited from an Irish father. If men wanted younger women they needed look no farther than Maeve and Macha, slim blonde twins as fair and wild as spring dandelions. Any man who could resist them separately had to face the formidable inducement that the twins, two halves to a single soul, did everything together. None of my sisters was much more attractive than me, but the accumulation of advantages was crushing.

I had been born and raised in a single-room sod house, seeing two brothers, along with several nieces and nephews, made and born after me. By now I knew all that went between women and men, or fancied that I did. There had been a few drunken offers, and a couple of angry ones from fellows spurned by my sisters. None of these attracted me, and playing naked in the brush with my younger brothers was becoming demeaning. That winter I had decided to dedicate my maidenhead to Diana, the virgin huntress.

Hands drove Diana and younger brothers from my mind. His body had a special sort of beauty, supple as a woman's and strong as steel. I cried as Boann and Brigit crowded around him. Being the eldest they expected us to

THREE HEADS FOR THE HIGH KING

give them room to work. They took him in hand, showing him every household task from weeding the garden to gathering wild honey, making it plain the whole time that they would be pleased to teach him other things as well. Nothing came of all this instruction. One night when Hands was sleeping alone in the barn, Brigit announced that though he had a strong young body Hands was obviously the type who favored boys. "There is nothing to be done about it," she said. "It is something you are born with, like a tongue for singing or one foot shorter than the other."

I knew better than to correct Brigit, but I had watched Hands's eyes. He was friendly enough with the boys, but we were the ones his looks lingered on. Hands hid it well, though I had seen him studying Etaine and even the twins, then crossing himself afterwards.

Etaine was both excited and daunted by Boann and Brigit's failure. She put on her best dress of soft leather, tanned white with the hair off and slit up the sides. On her head she wore the tooth-and-bone headdress that she had inherited from our Grandmother. The effect was startling. Her scarlet hair seemed even wilder, like the mane of some young beast of prey.

It was a holy day, one moon before Beltaine. No one was working and Hands had gone hiking in the hills. Etaine took me along for support, and I put to use all the skills I had practiced as a virgin huntress. Like two lithe foxes we stalked him far up the slope of an old volcano. From the flanks of the cinder cone our sod house became a little mound grazed by tiny sheep. The valley seemed empty in the clear morning light, and I could make out only the few lines of stone that marked our fences. Beyond the fields, our fjord slithered toward the sea, a deep-blue snake penned by the stone cliffs. At its mouth, serpent-tooth islands rose our

of the world-circling Ocean.

When we found him Hands was down on one knee, picking through the litter beneath the trees. Etaine ordered me to wait behind a screen of white birch, saying I should not breathe until she was done, though I was welcome to watch and learn. Then she strolled out, with hands clasped behind her and breasts thrust forward, asking how he was wasting his free time.

I knelt among the birch leaves smelling acid bark mixed with dank soil and salt sea wind. Each time I dared to peek around the rough trunk nothing special seemed to be passing between them. The sun climbed and my stomach turned hungry. Still nothing. After an endless space Etaine returned.

"What happened?" I asked.

"Nothing happened, he is looking for rocks."

"What sort of rocks?"

Etaine described a certain crystal, then swore me to secrecy. No one must know that he had passed her up for some pebbles.

I was too excited to betray Etaine. Sex I knew only in the abstract, but in my short life I had turned over millions of stones. Thule was alive with rocks; new ones were being made all the time. Volcanoes spewed forth every sort of stone from tiny cinders to great boulders and long beds of ropy lava. Running home, I shook my rock collection out of its leather sack. I had stone shells and fish bones taken from ancient seashores high in the hills. I had stone wood and leaf prints pressed flat by the ages. I had rocks that floated in water and rocks that shone in the sun. From among my crystals I selected just the stone Hands was searching for. Here was an advantage not even the twins could compete with.

I was wise enough to pick a small broken crystal, not the best of its kind. I wanted to whet Hands's appetite, so he would follow me into the hills for

79

more. On seeing the stone, Hands wanted to know at once where the crystal had come from. When I showed him the spot his caution fell away, "This is half the reason I came to Thule, to collect stones such as these."

"Whatever for?" I wanted to know.

We sat back against a boulder that had been tossed playfully onto the hillside by a forgotten eruption. "These are sunstones," Hands said, "by looking through them a pilot can find the sun through overcast and fog. I need them to find my way to Avallon. The River in the Sea runs between here and Avallon, bringing mists and fog down from the Frozen Sea."

Few people sailed as far as Avallon, and fewer still came back. I was sickened to discover that all my ingenuity was only helping Hands sail away. "Why do you want to go there? Avallon lies beyond the Land of the Ogres, over the sunset sea. It is in the direction of death." Sunset is the gateway to the Shadow Lands, just as sunrise is the direction of rebirth. Our ancestors came out of the sunrise and someday we shall all go into the sunset, but Hands was rushing his end.

"I am searching for a woman." His gaze was fixed on the westward rim of Ocean.

That made me feel even worse. "Your lover?"

"No," Hands smiled and shook his head. "I am searching for my Mother, who is a witch of Avallon. Surely a heathen girl like you can respect that."

I said I could, and asked who his Mother was. "Perhaps my Mother has heard of her and can help you avoid the journey."

He shook his head again. "Then you would know who I was, and that would not be safe for you nor me."

I moved closer and plucked at his leggings. "You owe me something for finding the sunstones."

He said he did, and offered to tell me a story about Britain instead. That was not the reward I would have named, but I was too shy to say so. Instead I sat beside him, feeling miserable, though he told his tale as well as a harper in a lord's hall. Later I understood that he must have heard harpers tell this tale many times, though it was new to me. The story was about a boy, an orphaned prince fostered in secret for his own safety. He told how the boy found a sword in a stone that made him High King of Britain and Eire.

This story was like none I had ever heard. We had winter tales, which we told around the fires when snow and dark locked us in and the days shrank down to nothing. Our stories were about local things, or about the Shadow Lands where heroines and heroes lived amid flowers and meadows, knowing neither death nor winter. Thule is mostly cold rock, rent by fires from deep in the earth. Death is no stranger, but it comes through tragic accident or as a fitting end to life. Even during the worst winters, when the living lived off the dead, we ate each other with ritual and all due respect. Christians find this horrible, but all life lives off death. Even those that die in the spring, and are plowed back into the earth, are eaten at harvest time as peas and beans.

Yet in Hands's short story there was more death and destruction than I had heard in fifteen winters. Kings warred with each other, tearing down castles and raising mountains of slain. When they wanted women they forced them, or had their way by magic. It was not the sort of story you dared tell to Mother.

We walked home hand in hand, and the land and sea seemed different to me. If half of what Hands said was true, there were lands very different from ours — lands where men hunted each other like beasts and kept their women confined — and these strange lands of men lay just over the sunrise sea.

THREE HEADS FOR THE HIGH KING

When we returned Maeve and Macha were much put out. Maeve said they had planned to take Hands to some hot springs for a day of warm bathing. She was the twin with the wild ideas. Maeve was even more upset when free time and fair weather rolled around again, because Hands insisted on taking me as well. She said that three was a lucky number for bathing, but four was a bit much. Macha had to make me welcome, since she was the healer who closed wounds opened by her wilder half.

We climbed the cliff behind our home, up to where the hot springs bubbled from a deep cleft. On this holy spot Mother gutted goats at midwinter, mixing their blood with the water and asking for the return of warmth. From the springs we could see the giant stone horse cut into the hills above our house. The spring itself flowed fiery hot, but we had cut channels in the soft stone so the water ran into pools cool enough for bathing. With a good deal of giggling my sisters got us all stripped and into the water.

Before the bath could get too unruly Hands began another story. Out of courtesy Maeve and Macha had to listen, and their hands were occupied in clapping and exclamations. This story was about a royal knight who fell in love with a High Queen, one who was already married to a High King. "A lucky Queen," said Maeve, "to have two lovers." She was hinting that Hands could be as lucky. But the lucky Queen was not happy. Instead of openly enjoying two lovers, or divorcing the old King, she had to meet her knight in secret. The High King behaved horribly, trying to drown the knight and setting headhunters after him; but the lovers were cunning and could not be caught. Even as the Queen and knight outwitted the High King they felt sad because they were sinning.

Sin was also missing from the stories Mother told. Like death, sin added a strange spice to Hands's stories, where knights slunk about with blackened shield doing foul deeds. Maeve and Macha were shocked to find that what they had in mind for the afternoon was sinning. The penalties for sinning frightened and scandalized them. They wanted to know if the sorrowful lovers ever got over their grief, or were they killed by the High King? Death very often terminated Hands's tales. Hands replied that as yet the story had no end, making it all the more real.

Maeve said that fairy tales were fine, but was Hands interested in some sinning right here on Thule, where the Goddess and Sacred Queen did not prescribe such drastic penalties? Again Hands shook his head, asking where she got such ideas.

Maeve said they came naturally, "We are twins, you know."

"Thanks to this bath," said Hands, "I know you are alike head to toe, and at all places inbetween."

"Being born at one birth, we have exactly the same signs and portents. I have the wild side of our soul, so I must be the sinful twin as well. Let us show little Caer how it is done."

Hands still refused to complete my education. "I have sinned a lot of late, and I do not wish to add to the weight I carry on my heart." We all emerged from that bath with nothing more to boast of than clean bodies.

Beltaine brought with it the birds of summer: redwings, wheatears, and meadow pipits. Turnstones had already come and gone, and I showed Hands how to gather the down and eggs from eider duck nests. My sisters gave up on Hands's instruction, because behind the birds came white sails, like banners on the sea. Sailors intent on serious sinning found the bays and fjords of Thule. I alone remained faithful. Hands had a habit of meeting the ships and took me with him. Twice he tried to go alone, but his clumsy furtiveness was no match for a virgin huntress. Both times I spied him speaking Irish or maybe Manx with the two red-haired strangers, the ones who had parted company with him on the beach below our farmstead when he first arrived.

High summer approached, reducing the nights to long twilights. Then Hands found the boat he sought. Some dour fishermen wearing sealskin coats beached their stove boat in our fjord. They were from Lesser Britain, bound for the rich fishing banks off Avallon, beyond the River in the Sea. Hands showed them his sunstones and described the wool Mother had given him as his share of the shearing. They said they would call for him when the boat was whole. I could see my window to the world of men closing. If I had been Brigit I would have demanded that Hands love me once before leaving. Instead I shared his coat on the cold walk home, and bid him goodbye at the leather barn entrance.

The next day three men came walking up from the sea. The strong summer sun was resting on the horizon, and I stood on tiptoe in the twilight, thinking that these were the fishermen coming to collect Hands. Then I saw that they were not fishers of fish, but fishers of men.

The tallest was a knight with a crested helm, kidskin gloves, polished mail, and a silver-handled long sword. He brought an air of jasmine into our barnyard and wore a summer blossom tucked into one steel cuff. His eyes were dark and sad, as though they had seen much he would rather forget. Beside him was a Berber in black mail. The brown face beneath his turbaned helm held no sadness, just cruel humor and crafty eyes. Both men bore blackened shields. Half a step behind them walked a bandylegged headhunter, his blue body naked from the waist up, and his face a tattooed mask. The headhunter

carried a spear and quiver across his back; one blue hand held a heavy bow, the other a leather sack.

Maeve and Macha had run to greet the guests, while Etar and Boann fetched torches to light their steps. Fire flickered over steel as I backed across our threshold, stumbling against Mother. She too had mistaken these men for guests and was coming to greet them in her embroidered dress, the one with horses stamping along the hem. Without a heartbeat of hesitation she stripped off her catskin gloves and handed them to me. "Take the Blackstaff," she said, "and guard the hospitality of our house."

I pulled on the gloves, and took the heavy iron staff from its place of honor by the hearth. Mother pushed me towards the ladder that leaned through the smokehole, then turned to face the mankillers.

I dragged the Blackstaff up the ladder, banging it on the rungs. At the top I turned for a last horrible look through the stinging smoke. The trio had forced their way into our home. The Berber was holding Macha by her hair, pressing a razor-edged scimitar at her throat. Maeve, willful to the death, held on to Macha, refusing to part with half her soul. The headhunter loosed the thong on his sack and two red-bearded heads rolled out. The sightless eyes were open, the lips slightly parted. Last week I had seen these heads alive and speaking on the shoulders of Hands's companions. The fine knight leaned forward on his longsword. His voice was cultured and civil, "Please excuse the intrusion, we have come for the third member of this unholy trinity." I needed to see nor hear no more.

It was night, but not dark. I crawled through the roof grass, slowed by the Blackstaff. The staff was magical but cumbersome; forged from a single lump of iron, starstuff that had fallen from the sky ages ago and far away. I had time, but not much. Mother would stall about, so I could give Hands a warning, but she would not let them kill Macha. Before they did that she would tell them that our guest was sleeping in the barn. The stranger is sacred, but he is still the stranger.

Worming my way uphill, I slid the Blackstaff through the slick grass — shivering whenever it struck a pebble — but reaching the leather entrance without feeling spear in my side or an arrow in my back. I slipped under the leather curtain and through the framework of saplings that supported it. Sheep had not used the barn since winter, but it was still a dark pit smelling of dung and urine. In my haste I forgot that the ground inside had been dug out and leveled. I tumbled down to the earth floor, pulling the Blackstaff behind me. From the back of the barn came the acid odor of birch leaves, and Hands's easy breathing. Hay and straw were too precious for guest bedding, so Hands had laid his sealskin sleeping bag on a bed of birch boughs.

I whispered, "Hands, wake up," as I crawled across the dugout space. Something stirred in the dark V of the natural cave entrance.

"Hands, killers have come for you." I found a bare thigh and shook it.

"Etaine? Is that you? Who has come?"

I was too scared to be disappointed. "No, it is Caer. Killers and headhunters are right behind me."

Hands's nude white body moved like a ghost in the shadows. "What killers?" He lurched towards the leather entrance flap, dragging his tunic and pants.

"Headhunters," I repeated, "a Moor and a man in fine armor."

Hands peered past the leather, pulling on his pants. "Jesus in Heaven, they have come here."

A torchlit procession of friends and enemies was tramping up the hill, with swords and spear points gleaming red in the firelight. For a moment I imagined those honed edges hacking at the beautiful body beside me, because I was too young and foolish to imagine my own murder. Macha was no longer held by the Berber; now it was the knight who had her. His arm was almost protective, circling her shoulder with steel, and his sword was held well away from her body. Maeve still clung to her twin sister, so that alive or dead their soul would stay united.

The rest of my family walked at a wary distance from the mankillers. One of my fathers carried a seal-spear and Etar hefted a cudgel. Boann had her bronze sickle, but Mother held our only real weapon, an ancient double ax.

"Come out, whoreson," called the knight. "A true Christian would not force us to kill innocents."

Hands struggled into his shirt, calling back, "Let the girls go."

"When you have come out, bastard."

Hands turned to me. "You had better go. They mean to kill me and I cannot protect you."

I clutched the Blackstaff through the catskin gloves. "Of course you cannot — Mother sent me to save you."

He laughed, like a man roped for hanging who hears some jest in the wording of the judge. "Caer, you are brave, but bravery counts for nothing against armor and numbers."

Out in the gray twilight the knight signaled to his headhunter. The blue man touched an arrow to a torch and fired. The first flaming shaft clattered against birch shingles. The second thudded into the leather curtain.

I pulled at Hands, trying to get him away from the leather before it began to burn. Arrow after arrow struck. I imagined Mother standing outside with her ax, weighing the lives of Maeve and Macha against my safety. "Mother sent me because I know the cave. It goes deep into the mountain. She is a seeress, and I am sure she saw our escape."

Despite his Christian upbringing

Hands was glad to choose life when it was offered. We collected his cloak and a clay lamp, which there was no trouble lighting. Arrows were flying through the burning leather now, setting the dead birch leaves on fire and filling the barn with acrid smoke. At the dark crevice the Blackstaff banged against the lip of the cave. Hands told me to drop it, but I shook my head. "My Mother saw our escape and told me to take it. She has reasons for everything she says or does."

We edged through the black crack and into The Mother. The crevice narrowed as it angled downward through the rock, and the light from the burning barn vanished after the second turning. Ahead I could feel only the even coolness that fills the earth, day and night, summer and winter. The first turnings were familiar to me, since the cave was a favorite place for winter play. Cold rock pressed in around us, with the gentle weight that turns sand to stone and stone to crystal. Our Mother has all of time to work her wonders, so she never needs to hurry.

Then coolness gave way to warmth and the stink of brimstone. The cavern widened abruptly into a large chamber, a great bubble in the earth, dyed bright yellow with sulfur. Fumes boiled up from a dry sinkhole in one corner. Hands coughed and asked, "Where now?"

Here the familiar turnings ended. "I am not sure, this is as far as we ever dared come."

Hands drew his ivory-handled knife and sat down by the entrance to the chamber. "When they miss my bones in the ashes, they will come here. Cei has come so far for me that it would take more than Hell to stop him."

We sat side by side, watching the lamp burn down, knowing the oil was precious but not daring to blow it out. When the lamp was half gone I decided to make use of the light while we still

had it. I crawled over to the sinkhole, where the sulfur was thicker and I could feel the fires deeper in the earth. Using the Blackstaff I probed into the hot dark hole. Metal rang on a stone slope. "Hands, we can let ourselves down here."

"Down that hole into Hell?" His hanged-man laugh returned. "Caer, I am a Christian, and I would just as soon meet my Maker here."

I waved the lamp at the yellow walls of the chamber. "You know they will not bother to fight you. They will throw fire in and light this sulfur. I know death is always appealing to Christians, but choking on sulfur in a rock tomb is a horrible introduction to hymnsinging at the feet of Jesus."

"Your ignorance of theology is appalling." Hands looked down the hole. Using the Blackstaff to steady me, I went first into the acrid blackness. There was a stinging wall of heat, then the rock opened again into an immense vaulted cavern. The sulfur cave had been only a small antechamber to this great fiery hall within the mountain. Cool and breathable air sank down from the huge dark shaft overhead, mixing with the fumes rising from the middle of the chamber. A hot dark mass heaved and bubbled ahead of me.

"A pool of boiling mud." I had never seen one underground before, but the smells and sounds were unmistakable. I probed with the Blackstaff, but the path we were on led straight to the boiling cauldron. At the edge of the mud was a large stone trough, carved from soft porous rock. "There must be a way through, or Mother never would have sent us down here."

Hands coughed again; the air was so foul it made your throat burn and your head spin. "Maybe your mother never had cause to come here. It took blood-hungry killers to drag us this far."

"No, this is a place of sacrifice," I said, tapping the long boat-shaped altar with the Blackstaff. "Such places are sacred to Brethra the Smith." It was the place where a priestess would come to cast herself into the fires, seeking a quick searing death if age or life became a burden. I did not mention that to Hands, since Mother must have intended more of an escape than that.

"What a place to die," Hands muttered, "beside a pagan altar at the entrance to Hell." He kicked the stone trough and it rocked. I hated to see him do that. When you have seen the ground open up and rock run like water, you have more respect for fire altars.

A stone clattered and torchlight flickered down from the sulfur chamber above. My gloved hands tightened on the Blackstaff. Aside from slapping my sisters I had never fought anyone. Now I was going to get a first lesson in combat from hardened warriors, with my back to a bath of boiling mud.

Hands was on his knees, pushing the stone trough. It grated over the rocks. "Help me push this, it must be light enough to float on the mud."

I thrust the Blackstaff under the altar trough and heaved. My weight was not enough to move the lever. Stripping off the catskin gloves I offered them and the Blackstaff to Hands. At first he refused to take the gloves, but I would not let him touch the Blackstaff barehanded. When he consented, the gloves fit his slender fingers, a good sign.

With Hands working the Blackstaff, the trough slid easily into the boiling ooze. There was no current so it simply lay there, rocking as the bubbles burst beneath it. Hands swung me aboard, and I almost shriveled from the heat. I huddled in the bottom of the stone boat, where the rock hull gave some protection. Hands stepped in behind me and pushed off with the Blackstaff.

The air burned around me and sweat oozed out of my body. Standing above me with his legs spread wide, Hands poled us along the edge of the mud. He kept us against the rock wall where cold air tumbled down into the roaring cauldron. Through a veil of steam we could see torches flickering back on the lakeshore.

"Put out the lamp," Hands choked, "if they see it they will pick us off with arrows."

I smothered the lamp, wondering how we would ever relight it. Heat and blackness swallowed us like a living, breathing animal. We lay together in the boat watching the torches move along the shore. When my eyes grew used to the dark, I saw more light falling from above. Midsummer twilight was fading into day somewhere far above us. If our hunters had doused their torches in the mud they probably could have seen us clearly enough to shoot. Fortunately that is not the thought that occurs to people deep within the earth, where you cling to light like life itself.

I pointed over our heads, "This slope leads to a large vent letting in light and air."

Hands sat up and tested the rock that touched the boat, finding it cool enough to climb. We both scrambled out, happy to be headed up instead of down. The slope was an old lava flow that had cooled and collapsed, forming the vent. Its surface was roped and ridged, easy to climb even in darkness. We each took a glove and used the Blackstaff to pull ourselves along. I lost sight of the torches as the heat of the cauldron faded. A thin sickle moon appeared overhead.

We emerged from the hillside finding the sun already up. I knew where we were at once. Carved into the sod along a western slope was a great stone horse, galloping through the morning light. I pointed southward. "Our farmstead is over that ridge and the hot springs are below us." I looked back down the vent. "I have been to this hole many times, but I smelled the fumes and did not descend. I never knew it connected to our cave." But Mother had known, she was a seeress and must have seen the whole escape even before she handed me the catskin gloves.

Hands had not been listening. He started off down the hill, saying over his shoulder, "I must get away. I should never have stayed. Cei will not harm you if I am gone."

I was up at once, and after him. " Who is Cei and why is he after you?"

"Cei is the dandy with the silver-hilted sword and the kidskin gloves. He is not after me, just my head would make him more than happy. I have broken the High King's law, and Cei wants to deliver my head, before the High King has a fit of forgiveness and pardons me."

"Who are the others?"

"The Berber is named Palomides, and there is a blood feud between his family and mine. He only wants to see me dead, not caring much what happens to my head. I do not know the headhunters, but I suppose they work for wages; even headhunting has lost its honor these days."

"But what law did you break?"

Hands shook off me and my questions. "I have told you too many stories already, and I almost got you killed. Goodbye, as you see I must be going."

"Going where?" I caught up with him again. "I will not let you wander off into the Wilds. We can seek sanctuary from the Sacred Queen. Her Summer Sanctuary is by a northern lake, and the new moon is the moon of Summer Solstice. People are already flocking north for High Summer Festival on Holy Isle. We can cross over to the next fjord and find a ship headed north."

"I can seek sanctuary," said Hands. "You can give me a good start, then go back and tell Cei everything. Hold nothing back for my sake. As I said, Cei is a Christian knight, who will not harm you if there is no advantage in

it."

I sneered at that suggestion. "You do not even know the land well enough to lose me." Hands fought me for a while, wasting time by yelling commands, but finally threw up his hands and fell in behind me.

Fear kept us fresh as we marched through the long summer morning. There was nothing to stop for, because nothing but barrens lay behind our farmstead. These were not the great Inner Wilds of Thule, but they were wild enough if you did not know the way. There was no water for drinking, just hot sulfur springs. Hardy plants clung to rocky soil; eyebright, heath grass, and dwarf willows crowded around the bubbling springs.

Crossing the ridge between fjords, we descended a long green glen and drank from a frigid stream white with glacial milk. At the base of the glen was the neighboring fjord, filled with rags of fog. The farmstead I was seeking sat on a rounded hillock, an island in a hollow foamy sea.

The woman of the house welcomed us at the door. She was a bent and withered crone who spoke of my mother's mother as though she were still with us. Boann had spent a full year studying under her, coming back much the better for it. Before leaving Boann had been like Brigit, sure that she knew what the world had to offer. She returned wiser, and not so sure. The crone was glad to see us, for her farmstead was near deserted. She had no daughters of her own and her sons had married into other households. The old woman laid out a simple meal of honey and oat crackers, which she imagined children would like. The crone counted everyone under half a century as a child, a habit that Boann mut have found irksome.

We ate and slept, then I went down to the fjord to find a boat. Sea fog still filled the fjord; sometimes it hangs about for weeks at a time. Now there was snow swirling through it, wetting my cheek, clinging to my hair and lashes. If you think snow at midsummer is strange, you have not been to Thule.

I asked for a ship headed north, and the fisherfolk pointed out the prow of a longship, a great water insect half-crawled onto the land. As I approached I saw it was slim, single-masted and clinker built, with a shelter for passengers just abaft the mast. Dogs were barking on board.

I went up the gangway and met the Master on the fog-shrouded prow. He was a large gap-toothed man, whose blue nose was part eaten by frost. We struck our deal quickly. He was headed north as soon as his passengers were set ashore. I pledged to get him a passage gift from my family at the High Summer Festival, and he was happy to find any business in this barren place, having brought his ship so far from the sea only because his passengers had business here.

I was thinking that my luck was inexhaustible, when I smelled jasmine on the sea breeze. Two passengers stepped out of the shelter; the first was Cei, and behind him came the Moor. I stood stock still, thanking the Mother that the ship's Master was big enough to hide behind. All I could picture was the blade at Macha's throat, but I suppose Cei had not expected his quarry to come bounding aboard. He did not think to search for me behind the sailing master, but simply said that he would go ashore and that his men would attend to the unloading.

Cei and the Moor descended the gangway and were soon lost in the fog. They were certainly headed for the sod house where Hands was sitting, since the crone's farmstead was the only dwelling this far up the fjord. The armored men were walking with no particular speed, but before I could get over

the side more killers emerged from the deck shelter. Three blue headhunters were followed by a snapping pack of immense Irish hounds. One of the headhunters was letting the Hounds worry a cloak Hands had used, teasing them with it, giving them Hands's scent. My way was blocked by snarling mastiffs and the mankillers trying to keep them under control.

Standing behind the headhunters were Maeve and Macha; roped together at the wrists and wearing the same linen shifts and leather coats they had worn the day before. Their blonde hair was snarled, and Maeve had a bruise over her eye. She had naturally said or done something to annoy them. Macha saw me and her mouth dropped open. She started to speak. Maeve brought her heel down hard on her sister's instep, turning Macha's words into a yelp of pain. The twins had a whole system of silent communication. A headhunter turned and told them to shut up or take another beating.

I took that chance to edge along the rail, kicking at the dogs and keeping my head down. Only one of the headhunters had seen me at the farm, but I was not sure which one that was. Blue skin dye and tattoos made them look much alike to me. I stepped onto the gangway and a hand caught my shoulder. I wanted to shake the hand off and run, but my feet refused to move. Instead I turned and looked straight up the arm.

It was one of the headhunters. His eyes were deep black holes amid a web of tattoos that scared me senseless. The corners of his mouth lifted into a smile, while his free arm displayed an ivory arm ring. "Woman, would you like to warm up the day with me? I will pay."

I dropped my gaze, saying I was not a woman, only a virgin. I added that my mother was surely missing me.

He gave me a squeeze on the breast, then let me go. As I descended the gangway I could hear the others saying that there would be plenty of chances for fornication at the High Summer Festival, but he should mind the hunt ahead — not bad advice, even for the quarry. The disappointed fellow with the arm ring said that if he could only have an hour with the friendly twin he would be happy. They laughed, threatening him with Maeve instead.

I left them arguing and ran like a wraith through the fog, reaching the sod house well ahead of two armored men plodding up a strange path. Seizing Hands, I stammered an explanation, swearing the crone to secrecy in the name of every goddess we knew. She pushed more oat cakes and a couple of cloaks on us, then hustled us out of the house and into the fog.

It was the dogs that I really feared. It would take more than two armored men to get any sense out of a talkative old woman who did not want to be understood. Hounds would be harder to fool. Hands's scent was in the bed and at her table.

Saying nothing, we sloshed back up the white stream that tumbled down the green glen, hoping that the running water would carry away our scent. I suppose that Hands felt guilty for involving me in this disaster. I know I felt frightened. There was only one way out now, to strike straight through the Inner Barrens, across the cold heart of Mother Thule. People had done it before, but we were starting out badly, with wet feet and only a few oat cakes for food.

At the head of the glen Hands asked quiet questions about the route. I pointed out a broad ribbon winding across the flats. "That is the Green Snake. We must follow that river past the Troll's Cap, all the way to its source. When the Green Snake can take us no further, we must turn east into the western lava fields, where the Black River runs down towards the Summer Sanctuary."

"I can follow it," he said.

I shook my head. "You would not make even half the way alone. The Green Snake fractures into a half dozen tributaries. I can spot the main channel; you would get lost in the maze of streams fed by the Troll's Cap. Even if you managed to find the great lava fields, you would never recognize the trails that lead to the Summer Sanctuary."

I did not say this to hurt Hands, but to help convince myself. This was no longer a grand adventure out of Hands's tales. We were not pitting ourselves against men and dogs, but against the most merciless and cruel aspect of Mother Thule. We would have to march quickly, before cold and hunger sapped our strength, but each step had to be taken with care. A wrong turn or a twisted ankle, and Mother Thule would keep me, to add my bones and blood to the land she was still forming. When I grabbed the Blackstaff and went up the smokehole, I had gone without thinking. Now I was picking a path that would very likely kill me. Yet to turn Hands loose would be like kicking him off a cliff. Giving him up to Cei would have been the gentler way.

It took us days just to reach the lip of the barrens, where the Green Snake's flood plain narrowed, shrinking into a steep green notch. We passed tilted fields planted with blue vetch, clover, and half-wild barley; but we saw no one who would feed us. Hands refused to touch the oat cakes, leaving every crumb for me. I argued and pleaded but nothing I could do would make him eat. Hands could be as stubborn as me at times, so I ate the cakes myself, knowing that he would need my strength later. Where the grass ended the Inner Wilds began. We climbed up onto a bouldered plateau. The cracks between the rocks sheltered delicate summer blossoms and tidy piles of mouse turds. Once Hands killed a fox with a well-aimed stone, giving me the meat to eat.

The northern end of this plateau was an upended wasteland of rock, scored and polished by moving mountains of ice. Sea pink and lichens struggled to survive in a landscape stripped bare. Even the leaden sky had all the life pressed out of it, save for a few small birds that flitted by like hard-thrown stones. Long before we reached the white expanse of the Troll's Cap, we met the glacier's children, huge waves of boulders thrown across our path.

This far north there is no night at midsummer, and hardly anything you could call a day. Every so often the sun sank down to a silver thread outlining the southern peaks, then rose again. We walked when we could, and rested when we could not walk. At each rest Hands was weaker. Without food his beautiful body was wasting. When it was time to march he got up more slowly. He started to stumble, and this was no place to stumble. We passed over boulders that trembled under us, turning slips into nasty falls. Hunger sat in our stomachs while cold ate at our strength and morale.

In the end we were moving a pace at a time, with Hands leaning on me and me leaning on the Blackstaff. We were at the northern edge of the Troll's Cap, but I knew that soon I could carry him no longer. I had to hide him somewhere and find food. We waded up a stream that came straight down from the snow-field. The ugly yellow ice water numbed my feet and sliced at my calves, but it hid our scent. I dragged Hands right up to the living edge of the glacier, where the white gleam seen at a distance became a towering wall of dirty ice. Summer melt was full underway, and the moaning wind from under the Troll's Cap carried the sound of rushing rivers and thundering falls. It was a terrifying place, but I had to leave Hands where he could be neither seen, smelled, nor heard.

Wrapping Hands in all our cloaks I helped him into a crystal ice cave, past icicles as long and sharp as dragon's teeth. I told him I had to turn back in our tracks and find our pursuers. They would be bringing food, and somehow I would get it from them. Hands heard this and gave me a wan smile. "Caer, it is best that you do go back. And better still if you would not worry about me. I was born for a bad end and it would be good for the world if I found it here." The foolish man thought this was our last conversation.

Now for food. Using the Blackstaff as a crutch I hobbled back down the dirty stream, hiding my trail. With all the skills of a virgin huntress it did not take me long to find our pursuers. The first sign that I was on their track was a pack of horrible black hounds with mis-shapen heads leaping over the rocks. I screamed and flailed at them with the Blackstaff until the headhunters arrived. As I said, nothing could have been simpler.

They took the Blackstaff away, binding my hands behind me with cruel knots. I told the one with the Blackstaff to set it down because no good would come from holding it barehanded, but he cuffed me across the face for that bit of advice. They dragged me over the stones to their camp. First I smelled woodsmoke and jasmine, then I saw Cei sitting on some baggage and oiling his armor. Keeping metal so shiny must have been a trial in our damp climate. Even his fire was a luxury, since there was no wood to be found in these parts, but I doubted that Cei had been the one who lugged the wood up from the flats. Maeve and Macha were there too, sitting on separate rocks, with their wrists still tied to a rope that stretched between them. They were hobbled at the ankles so they could walk but not run, though in this hungry waste there was hardly anywhere to run to.

Cei bade me sit by the fire. I might

89

have been a lady entering his hall from the quiet way he welcomed me. The headhunters were more professional: one bound my ankles and another laid his knife on some stones so the blade was in the fire.

Cei asked where the bastard was.

I swore by the Goddess that we had been heading up the Green Snake, intending to cross the divide between its headwaters and the Black River that flowed along the lava fields. "When I could go no farther, I turned back to find food." I pointed my chin up the trail, "He is somewhere ahead; I swear I cannot lead you to him." I did not say that it was love, not lack of knowledge, that prevented me.

I do not know whether Cei was fooled, but the headhunters certainly were not. The man who was heating his knife bent down and took it from the fire. By now the blade was blackened, but the tip glowed red. I closed my eyes and prayed to Diana who watches over children and childbirth, saying that the pain could be no worse than what I had seen Mother and my sisters suffer through.

With my eyes closed I heard them arguing. Cei said that torturing defenseless children was not what Jesus preached. I had not personally studied the teachings of Jesus but I hoped there were some parts that supported Cei's opinion.

"She is a pagan," the headhunter protested, *"and those that worship the Beast and bear his mark shall be tormented with fire and brimstone;* Revelations 14:10."

"Who taught you to bandy Scripture with a knight?" There was a weary edge in the gentleman's words.

"My mother wanted me to be a priest," said the headhunter. "It near broke her heart to see me in blue, but the old ways are better." I knew already that he was not a man who listened to his mother.

"Better a good headhunter than a

90

poor priest," said Cei. *"Revelations* refers to the Judgement Day, when God will decide if these girls deserve burning. We will not make hasty judgements for Him. The hounds found her, they will find the bastard."

I opened my eyes. The tattooed torturer was wiping his knife on a scrap of leather. Cei knelt down and gave us a quick lecture on Christian charity. "I am leaving you here. Your virtue is safe, but you will be killed if you try to escape." I was bound hand and foot, the twins were tied together with a length of rope; whatever arrangements he made had to suit us because we were not being offered any better.

Cei told the headhunter holding the Blackstaff to stay behind. "If they attempt to escape, catch them or kill them, but do not let them get away," said Cei. "Palomides should be here in a day or so with the pack ponies. Under no circumstances are you to interfere with them."

"Interfere?" The blue-skinned man with the iron staff lying across his legs looked puzzled.

"He means copulate," said the headhunter who had quoted from Scripture.

"Exactly," said Cei. "Kill them if you must, but preserve their chastity at all costs."

I could see these orders did not set well with the man holding the staff, but he touched his topknot and said he would obey. Headhunters shaved their heads, leaving a long scalp lock tied in a top knot as a sign of consideration for others. They knew that without such handles severed heads were awkward to carry.

Then Cei and the others were off, running behind the baying hounds. The fellow set down the Blackstaff and sat between us and the fire. He started to search through the baggage, saying, "Is it too much to hope that any of you might be virgins?"

Maeve and Macha rolled their eyes

to indicate me.

I said, "You are not supposed to interfere with us."

A grin split his tattooed face. "Yes, and I ask you, where is the sense in that? It would be better for you and for me if his orders were the other way round — copulate with them if you must, but preserve their lives at all costs. Even you will admit that has a better ring to it."

I did not answer, and at last he found what he was searching for, an iron pot helmet and a packet of waxed parchment. Then he got up and sat next to me. I slid away from him.

"Do not worry," he said. "I will not interfere with you, not in that way at least. This Christian pays in silver. Cold silver keeps a man honest, but it makes him do unnatural things."

He opened the packet. "You are a virgin, are you not?"

I admitted that was my condition.

"And you said you were hungry, did you not?"

I admitted that as well.

He opened the packet and I could see it was filled with dried mushrooms, of a type I had never seen. He put them in the helmet, poured water over them, then set the helmet on the fire.

"What is that?" I asked.

"Our dinner," he answered. We sat there without speaking while the mess in the blackened helmet bubbled. When the headhunter judged it done he used his cloak to hold the hot helmet and poured the brew into a wooden bowl. Holding the bowl to my lips he told me to drink.

One whiff took my appetite away. I said the broth was all his.

"Drink," his voice turned hard.

I spit in the bowl, telling him to get it away from my face.

With his free hand he produced a knife. "You heard the Dandy; I have life and death over you. Virgins are preferred for this potion, but not essential.

I can always slit your throat, then see if your sisters are more reasonable." He was smiling in a strange and mad way, as though life and death were equally amusing. I knew he could take my head off, hang it from his belt, then sit down to his mushroom stew without losing a bit of digestion. Hands had said that Headhunting had become a business, but I never knew how routine it was until I felt his knife under my chin.

I told him to move his blade so I could swallow, then I held my breath and drank as much as I could without breathing. The brew lived up to my every expectation, tasting unspeakably vile. My stomach revolted, but my captor clamped a dirty hand over my nose and poured me more.

When I was done with the liquid he offered me the dregs. My stomach was cramping, so I told him that he might as well kill me quickly since I was poisoned already.

The headhunter laughed. Holding my jaws with steel fingers, he speared the cooked mushrooms and fed them to me on the point of his knife. Between bites he gave me friendly warnings not to vomit.

When the meal was over I lay moaning on the rocks, doubled up by the awful pain in my middle. I could see my belly bulging beneath my shift, threatening to burst. Dark colors reeled around me as sunlight dissolved into rainbows. Forgetting his warnings I vomited. From somewhere far away the headhunter was yelling at me, claiming I was wasting his potion. Lying there in my own puke I could hardly care. I was leaving him anyway. Though my hands and feet were still tied hard, I could feel myself moving. I was going to the Shadow Lands, where the world was not only warm, but folk were bound to be civil. The rocky plain around us turned into a rolling, grassy meadow, with sunlight raining down on summer iris and green-gold dandelions. That all this was impossible did not disturb me in the least. I was past caring about what was real or even reasonable.

Two figures rode over the flowered meadow on white horses with red ears, matched mounts foaled from a regal mare. The first rider was a woman wearing a circle of spun gold in her hair. She was a queen with Roman features, her face as fair as a fifteen-day moon. Red-gold hair streamed from under her crown, burnished by the hot sun. Her dress was stiff green silk, pinned by a silver brooch and embroidered with pearls. Though green silk covered her from shoulders to slender ankles, I could see the strong form of her thighs, gripping and urging her mount forward.

Behind rode her king. He was taller and older than Hands, but with the same straight features. There was a circle of gold around his brows and his beard was forked and fair. His tunic took the sunlight and splintered it into a multitude of colors. In his right hand he held a pair of javelins and on his left he wore a dark shield with a red dragon twined around gold bosses. His cloak and mantle were the same deep red as the dragon's skin.

The Queen smiled over her white shoulder, and when her king smiled back he looked even more like Hands. He spurred his horse, but could not hope to catch her. This older Hands kept coming, but she kept laughing and riding ahead. I was both awed and angered by her. Her beauty and richness made me feel small and dirty. It is hard to compete with your imagination, especially when you are lying in soiled leather soggy with vomit.

Then Hands was in my dream too, striding young and strong through the sunlight, long steps carrying him over the meadow. When he passed the King on horseback, his older self grew angry, spurring his steed but falling further behind. The Queen continued to smile.

I suppose she did not care if it was the younger Hands who caught her.

Suddenly they were all brushed away by a great blue ogre with a hideous face. It was the headhunter, destroying my dream and demanding that I drink again. This time the bowl was filled with clear ice water, which woke me and made me want to piss. He placed the empty bowl between my legs and told me to pee into it, saying, "It is about time. I have never seen a virgin with such an enormous bladder."

I was past caring what insults he heaped on me. I just wanted to see him die in some disgusting fashion. Since I could not do that, I peed into the bowl. He cursed at me when the urine ran over the edge, then lifted the full bowl and sniffed it, as though he were judging the aroma.

A smile appeared among the tattoos. "Good girl." he said, and started to drink. When I saw that, I thought I had gone mad, but he drank the whole stinking bowl down, just as clean as if it had been running over with golden nectar. Of course he was a pig, slopping my urine down his front, but still seemed mightily pleased with himself.

He set the bowl back between my legs, saying, "If you feel the urge again, be sure it ends up in the bowl." Then he sat himself down on a rock and smiled. "This is the way to get the dreams without the belly sickness. Passing the potion through a virgin takes the sting out of it."

I fainted again.

When I woke up everything was still, only the summer sun had moved. The blue ogre was sitting on his rock, with a sword across his lap. His eyes were closed and I could tell it was his turn to be visiting in the Shadow Lands.

The twins were watching him too. They were still hobbled, and bound together at the wrists by a length of cord. Maeve looked at Macha, then turned her eyes towards the headhunter. She made a twisting motion with her bound hands, and Macha nodded.

Moving as one they stood up. Keeping the rope between them slack, they stepped lightly over to where the ogre was sitting. Circling in opposite directions they wove a single ring of rope around him. Then they both leaped backwards, pulling up on the rope. As they jumped away Maeve kicked the sword off the headhunter's lap. His eyes flew open. The rope snapped taut under his chin, with the loop around his neck.

The headhunter groped for his sword, then grabbed the rope with both his hands. Each blue arm was fighting the full weight of a strong young body. Maeve and Macha dug their heels into Mother Thule and pulled harder. The headhunter's tattooed face twisted about, his eyes bulging out and his tongue protruding. First one hand, then the other lost its grip on the rope. His knees buckled and he hung forward, supported only by the rope connecting my sisters. Macha looked at Maeve, but the wild one shook her head. They kept pulling until they were sure he was dead.

As soon as they let him drop, Maeve picked up the sword and cut herself and Macha free. Then they were all over me, freeing my limbs, hugging me and kissing me, rubbing life back into my numb hands and feet. I thanked them both, telling them where I had hid Hands, then I fainted again. This time I dreamed I saw Maeve turn the dead headhunter over and start to gut and fillet him with his own sword.

When I awoke the twins were feeding me warm liver, which is both nourishing and tasty if taken in small servings. We found Hands in his ice cave, and fed him too. He insisted on having his headhunter cooked, though he was too famished to ask what meat it was. Which was just as well, considering his Christian stomach.

The magic in the mushrooms wore off slowly, and the days that followed were long, even for midsummer. We turned our backs on the Troll's Cap, heading due east towards the great lava fields. This was the harder route, through the worst of the barrens, but not the way Cei had headed. We crossed the headwaters of the Black River where serpents of snow wriggled down the passes amid a whitecapped sea of peaks. We kept to the east bank of the Black, turning further eastward when we saw a cairn that marked the trail to the Summer Sanctuary.

In a huge depression between the lava streams we found the Sacred Queen's summer home, where she dwelt during the endless days beside a lake of surpassing beauty. Rushes and waterfowl dotted the entire surface of the lake, for even in the center the waters were hardly over a tall woman's head. Above the lake towered a ring of volcanoes and smoking craters, their images thrown back by the great watery mirror.

Cei and his morose men had arrived ahead of us, not one whit happier for being a headhunter short. They had seen the remains of their companion and knew what had happened to him. It was no use pretending that his body had been nibbled up by foxes, because Maeve had broken open the long bones to suck out the marrow. That was not strictly necessary to support life, but it was tasty eating none the less. She was the wild and sinful twin, and could hardly control her nature.

The Sanctuary stood well above the lake, in a grove of mountain ash carpeted with alpine flowers. The Sacred Queen was seated on her ash chariot, wearing a cloak made from the skin of a great white bear and a dress of plated silver that ended just beneath her breasts. Her nipples, hair, and lashes were dusted with powdered silver, giving her a cold, distant splendor. Cei and

93

Palomides were washed and scrubbed, wearing clean clothes and polished armor. The headhunters had on fresh skin dye. With our torn clothes and slime-spattered bodies, we looked as guilty as Cei claimed we were. He accused us of a long list of heinous crimes: treason, murder, cannibalism, outlawry, mayhem, and wife stealing are the ones I remember. My family was there, and Mother spoke for us; but Cei brushed aside her counterclaims, pointing out that no member of our family had been badly harmed, much less eaten.

The Sacred Queen listened, then made her judgement. "I must dismiss outlawry because their crimes are not yet proven, likewise treason, which can only be committed against me."

Cei protested, "I meant treason against the High King."

"When next you are on British or Irish soil, you may make your complaint to him," said the Sacred Queen.

The Queen then turned to us. "Eating strangers out of season, and without permission, is indeed a serious offense against our customs. It will be up to me to review the circumstances and decide if the Goddess was offended, but that is a private matter for me as High Priestess. The only criminal complaints are murder and mayhem. The deceased was a stranger, does he have relations present?"

The two remaining headhunters stepped forward. Despite their fresh skin dye, they seemed uneasy at the center of attention.

The Queen continued. "If you lived among us, the blood-debt might be worked off through labor and services; since you are strangers you must accept silver." She reached down and tore a handful of silver from the hem of her dress, tossing it at their feet. The metal sparkled among the wildflowers. "You may either accept this bloodmoney, or seek physical satisfaction by fighting the male members of these girls' family."

94

ily."

Etar and my current fathers stepped forward. They were now more properly armed with slings, seal spears, stone headed clubs and stiff leather jackets. The headhunters bowed before the Sacred Queen and said they were more than pleased to take the silver. They assured her that their cousin himself was a great respecter of silver who would want his family to find some profit in his loss, and indeed would have done the same had he been the survivor.

The Sacred Queen turned to Cei. "This leaves only the crime of wife stealing. Whose wife did these girls steal?"

"The charge is not against them, but him," Cei pointed at Hands.

"This is a crime that is not known on our island," said the Queen. "Here women are not owned and cannot be stolen. We have a crime called rape, but only if the woman was unwilling."

"Why then, rape it was," said Palomides, stepping forward. The Moor seemed anxious to bring the proceedings to a speedy conclusion.

Cei cut his companion short. "No, the woman was willing, though it hurts me to say it. As a Christian knight I will not lie even to a pagan court."

The Queen glared at Palomides, "Aside from possible perjury, there are no crimes remaining."

Cei ground his kidskin gloves together. "The woman's husband was High King of Britain and Eire."

"King or commoner," said the Queen, "what cannot be owned cannot be stolen."

"Suppose I told you he was the King's bastard," said Cei, "which makes fornication with his step-mother incest as well?"

For the first time the Sacred Queen addressed Hands. "Is the High King your father?"

Hands hung his head. "My mother

refuses to be bound by any marriage oath. Any man could be my father; I was not there to see."

The Queen turned back to Cei. "Was he an acknowledged bastard, raised in the High King's Court?"

"No, thank God," said Cei.

"Then there is no legal tie between him and this woman on which to base a charge of incest, and no proof of rape. Unless he convicts himself from his own mouth he is free to go." She turned back to Hands. "Did this woman offer herself, and did you treat her with respect?"

"Yes, she did and I did," said Hands.

Those words set Hands free, but brought tears to my eyes. He was the knight in his stories, in love with some strange Queen across the sea.

Cei gripped his sword. "You may set him free," he said to the Queen, "but as soon as he steps outside this precinct he is mine."

Hands looked up. "Do you really want my head?"

Cei spat at his feet.

"Then fight me for it," said Hands. "If you win my head, it is yours. If I win, you and your dogs must go home to Britain."

"No," said the Moor, "there is my quarrel too. His brother killed my closest kinsman."

Cei held a gloved hand before the Moor. "Affairs of state take precedence over personal revenge. When I kill him for treason, your blood-debt will be paid as well."

"So you mean to settle the case by combat," said the Queen. Both men nodded. "I expected as much from the beginning," she said. "This is now a thing between men, and there can be no combat in the Sacred Precinct. One last word for the survivor. I often have serious cases to judge. If you have future need for law in Thule, do not bring complaints to me unless you plan to heed my judgements."

Her male attendants entered, their bodies painted and naked, carrying axes and wearing antler horns. They led us away from the grove, followed by female members of the court drawn to the excitement of a male rite. Free now, I walked beside Hands, carrying the Blackstaff.

The antlered attendants stopped just beyond the sacred grove and chanted in low voices as they trod out a level ring at the base of a cinder cone:

Man must die to feed the corn,
All that falls shall be reborn.
Seeds planted by winter moon,
Bow heads to the blade so soon.

Rain clouds darkened the sky, so the men lit torches. Cei had his sword, armor, and blackened shield. Hands stripped off his sodden shirt and I gave him the catskin gloves, then the Blackstaff. He kissed me for the first time and stepped into the ring.

With eyes locked the two men circled each other. The hands on the Blackstaff flexed and my love smiled. "Cei, here they call me Fair Hands. That is not a lucky name for you."

"Bastard," Cei spit again, "your brothers are not here to help you now."

What followed was a beating, for fight there was none. The Blackstaff feinted high and Cei's shield went up. Hands reversed the staff and hit Cei's leg between boot and armor. The heavy iron snapped his leg bone and Cei went down. Reversing again, Hands swatted the wrist that held the sword, sending Cei's blade spinning into the crowd. Batting the black shield aside, Hands pressed the Blackstaff against Cei's throat. "I could kill you now," said Hands, "but she would be sorry. When you return to Court, thank the Queen for your life."

Palomides looked almost pleased to see Cei beaten. He stepped into the ring behind his own blackened shield, cutting little patterns in the air with a scimitar as curved and wicked as his smile. Hands sprang back, then crouched down. Grasping the Blackstaff at one end, he swung it in a vicious arc at ankle level. The Berber was faster than Cei. He pulled both his feet into the air, letting the staff pass under him. Landing lightly, he closed with Hands.

Cei was up on one elbow yelling for Palomides to stop.

"No," said the Moor, "I will have my man."

"You are the High King's man," said Cei, "and I am his Seneschal. Take another step and you can count yourself an outlaw." Palomides hesitated, caught between Hands's Blackstaff and Cei's threats.

"I promised we would leave if I lost," said Cei. "It is not your duty to make a liar of me." This was noble of Cei, but he would have lost either way. Hands would have killed his Moor, or Palomides would have succeeded where Cei had been beaten.

"What of my family's honor?" Palomides protested.

"How much will you have with your lands and titles forfeit? The bastard has half-brothers at Court who will gleefully enforce any order given against you, with scant regard for your family and honor."

Wealth, I suppose, may be a burden. A poorer man might have found death or satisfaction, but the Berber backed out of the ring, never letting his guard down, never admitting defeat.

Hands straightened up and handed back the Blackstaff with pain in his eyes. My bare hand touched the cold iron and for an instant I could see clear to his soul. Hands was the sort of Christian who wanted what his religion would not give. He wanted another man's wife and hated himself for wanting her.

When his boat sailed for Avallon I stood on the sand, seeing him off. Screwing up my courage I said, "You must not love his High Queen much if you are sailing off to Avallon."

"I love her too much," Hands replied. "Perhaps my mother can give me peace." He stepped aboard the small, single-masted boat.

"Will you come back?" I called from the wet sand.

He shook his head. "Not if you are lucky."

"At least give me a real name to remember you by."

He stood in the stern of the boat, a black-cloaked figure against the metal sky. "You would do better to remember me just as Hands, but I will tell you — not because it is wise but because I owe you much. My name is Modred and the mother I seek is Morganna. The woman I love is Gwynyfar, wife to High King Arthur."

Waves curled over my feet, while gulls screamed and wheeled overhead. I watched my window into the world of men sail away to the west. ▲

MISTER BLACKWIDOW . . .

Mister Blackwidow spoke with remorse.
"I have reason to fear intercourse."
    Then he wistfully said,
    As she bit off his head,
"I believe I would like a div——"

— Ray Nelson

PORTFOLIO: J.K. POTTER

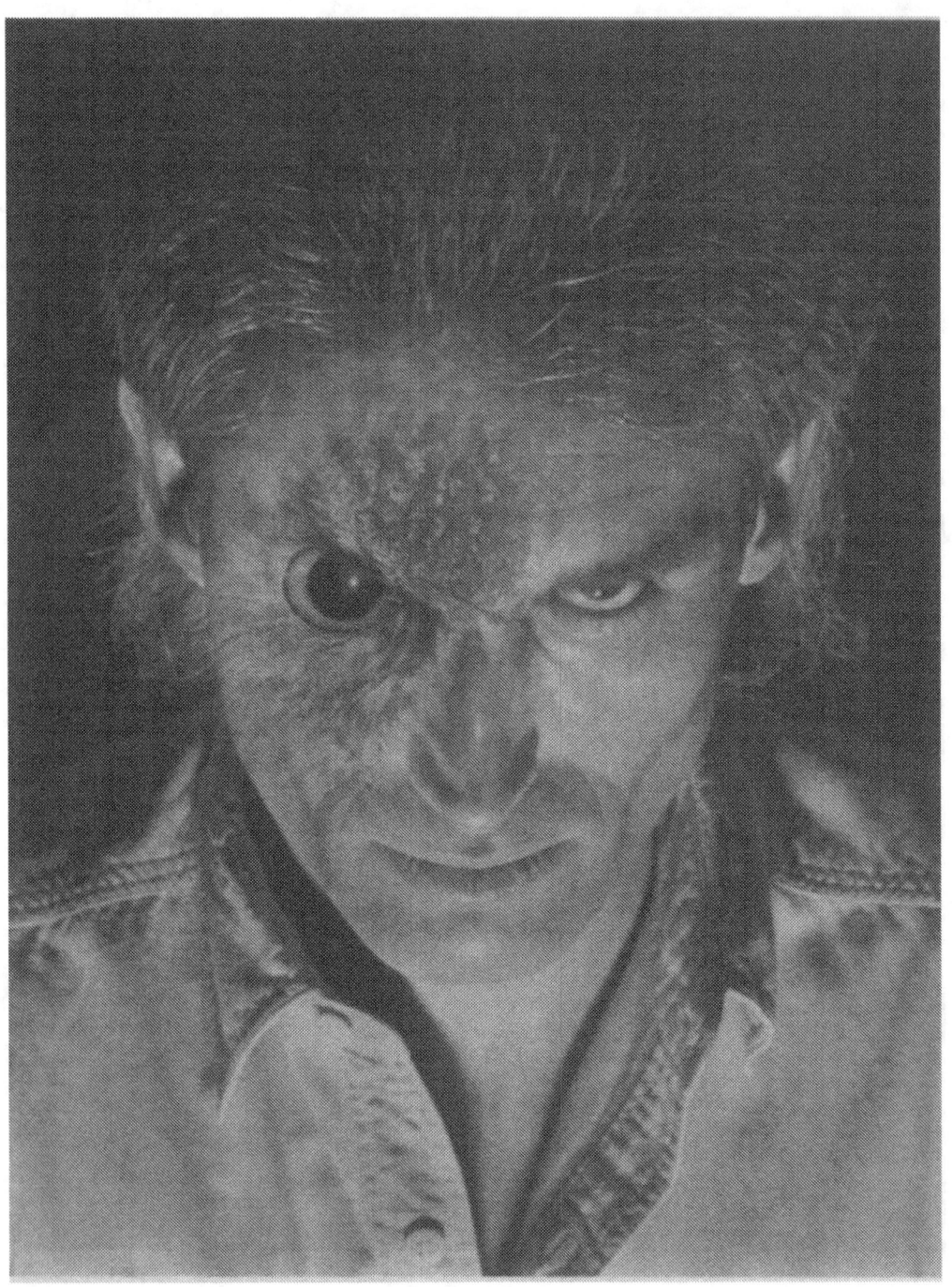

THE HIGHWAYMAN

by Lois Tilton

It was the day he would be hanged.

As the muffled bells of St. Sepulchre's began to toll, the din of Newgate Prison hushed. Prisoners crowded forward for a glimpse of the men to be led out of the condemned cell.

Walter Rowland nervously smoothed his claret-colored coat and adjusted the lace at the front of his shirt. It had cost him dear in garnish to the gaolers, but he was determined to put on a brave show this day. The doeskin breeches fit his legs well, and his high boots were polished to a gloss. Manacles clanked as he bent down to give the leather a final rub.

Young Wat Rowland, the highwayman bold — that was what the broadsheet ballads were calling him. There would be thousands in London today, come to see him die game on Tyburn Tree. Walter smoothed back his dark hair, tied into a black ribbon. Despite the prison pallor, he was the very image of a gentleman highwayman, young and handsome enough to make the maidens cry out for shame that he had to hang.

He was prepared for that, as much as a man could be, though he had always planned that they would never take him alive. And afterward, to be hung on the gibbet in chains — well, that would cause him no pain. Only . . . *Oh, Bess!*

Walter's hand went to the half-healed scar under his shirt. They had planned to meet the very night the soldiers intercepted him on the road. Someone had betrayed him. Not Bess — he would

wager his soul on that. Nor his partner Jemmy. But who else had known the hour he would be on the road? And why hadn't he heard from her since that night?

Walter paced the cell, agitated, chains clashing.

"Here," called a fellow-sufferer, holding out a bottle, "steady yourself, lad."

Walter gulped raw gin, gasped thanks. Just then the turnkey came to take the condemned out into the press-yard. As they stood in line to have their fetters struck off, the ordinary stood by with his prayer-book. *"I am the resurrection and the life,"* he intoned.

Resurrection. Walter suddenly put a hand into his pocket and pulled out a thin strand of filaments fine as hair. It was colorless and braided — no, twisted like a rope.

The woman had come to the press-yard two days ago, handing a coin to the gaoler. Walter had sensed that here was no common, morbid curiosity-seeker, come to gawp at the condemned. Under a black, hooded cloak was a thin, hooked nose like a knife-blade and small black eyes pinched together above. She lacked only the wart to be the very image of a witch. The tiny eyes had strayed over the inmates of the prison yard, then fixed directly on Walter. She beckoned with one bony hand for him to come to the gate.

"So you are Young Wat Rowland, then?" Her tone was mocking. It grated on the ears.

Walter flushed in anger and turned away. He had no intention of putting himself on exhibition for the likes of her.

"Nay, wait. Nan Jenkins has something for you, lad."

He paused, because even the barest comforts of Newgate were ruinously expensive. Supercilious lordlings would often amuse themselves by tossing a coin into the press-yard. But what she held out was not coin. It was the twisted strand. And she whispered to him, "What would you give for resurrection, lad — to come down alive off Tyburn Tree?"

He caught his breath, for what felon did not know the tales of men revived after they were cut down from the gallows? Resurrection was the secret hope of all who went up to Tyburn. But witchcraft? Peasant superstition.

"Aye, you know what I mean," she went on despite his obvious doubts. "But no need to talk of payment now. Wear this round your neck when they take you up Tyburn Hill. *After,* well, then we can talk about what you could do for old Nan Jenkins, eh?"

And then she had laughed, a screech so shrill, so piercing, even for Newgate, that heads turned in their direction. Walter shuddered to remember it. But he had taken the strand. And now . . . what harm, after all, could there be in wearing it? What could happen to him worse than hanging? And if, by some chance, it did work . . .

He reached up with his newly unfettered hands and placed the strand around his neck.

He had no more leisure to consider what he had just done. A roar from outside the gates announced that the Sheriff's men had come with the carts to convey them to Tyburn for the hanging-match.

Walter straightened his back, adjusted his coat, the lace at his throat. He strode to the front of the press-yard as the warder called out his name. Chained hands reached out to him,

102

voices called: "Fare ye well, lads!"

"Buy the Devil a pint for me!"

"Die game, now!"

Die game, Walter whispered to himself.

As the gates opened, the spectators surged forward to view Young Wat Rowland on his ride to the gallows. He forced a gay grin and waved, gave them a mocking bow, altogether the gentleman highwayman in his claret-colored coat.

A hanging-match was always a holiday. Crowds lined the London streets as the carts proceeded down Snow Hill, up High Holborn. Ballad-hawkers sang out, men cheered, girls cried. Walter waved a flower that someone had thrown into the cart. The procession halted at taverns along the way so ale and wine could be handed up to the condemned.

The drink and the excitement of the throngs made Walter dizzy. His stomach churned with mixed anticipation and fear. He felt like a hero in triumph, or a bridegroom on the way to his wedding. And his eyes went to every slender, black-haired young lass on the streets with a desperate hope that it might at last be his Bess.

As they came up Tyburn Road, the crowd swelled into a mob roaring at the approach of the carts. 'Prentices and fishwives, orange vendors, pickpockets and whores — all London was eager for their sport.

Then Walter caught sight of the gallows rising above their heads. His waving arm dropped, his heart lurched with dread. Suddenly, he was cold with sweat.

He was to be the first. The hangmen knew better than to thwart the demands of the mob.

The cart drew up beneath the gallows. The rope hung ready only inches from his face. Walter stared upward at the beams of the scaffold, at the triangle of sky they framed.

Two hangmen jumped up into the cart and pulled back Walter's hands

THE HIGHWAYMAN

behind him. He tried to draw them away, but they pinioned his arms before he could resist. *Die game,* he reminded himself, lifting his head, straightening.

Now a hush was spreading through the mob in anticipation of hearing his final speech. Walter tried to swallow. He had a speech prepared for this moment, but it stuck in his throat. Better to say nothing.

He shook his head.

"Brave words," the hangman sneered, giving a final tug to the bonds on his arms. "Now let's see how you dance."

No! Not yet! Walter was face to face with the man, his florid, unshaven cheeks, the dribble of tobacco down his chin, the leer as he dragged the rope down over Walter's head, snugged the knot around his neck. The hemp rasped his skin. He knew he was afraid to die.

The clamor of the mob was secondary now to the sound of his own breathing, the pounding of his heartbeat. He wavered and had to lock his knees to stay upright in the cart.

Heavily, the hangman jumped down, and Walter felt the cart lurch. He desperately caught his balance. But then it was moving. Panicking, he felt the rope pull him back, he braced himself against it until it grew taut, choking. Then his footing was gone and he fell . . . into the grasp of strong arms.

They held him around the thighs and knees, and he heard a rough voice laugh, "We'll just let you down nice and slow, eh, lad?"

Oh, God, no! Walter twisted and tried to kick out against their hold, but the hangman grated, "Oh, no! Not so fast, I said."

And slowly, with tender care, they lowered his body, letting the rope take his weight gradually. The noose tightened around his throat as the slow strangulation began.

It hurt! The weight of his body made the hemp cut into his skin, bruised his windpipe. He couldn't breathe! His diaphragm heaved, struggling to draw air into his lungs past the constricting rope. His whole body writhed with the effort, his legs kicked for purchase on the air. He twisted, his bound arms strained to reach the noose.

Somewhere in Walter's mind was the knowledge that his struggle could end only in death, but the instincts of survival were overriding. If there had been anyone in the mob who might have run forward to add their weight to his for a quicker end, he would have tried to kick them away.

But he had no friends among them, and his torment was prolonged. His lungs were aflame, and his head felt as if it would explode, his eyes about to burst from their sockets. His vision crimsoned. The roaring in his ears drowned out the crowd's cheers as he danced the Paddington Frisk.

Walter's thrashing kept constricting the noose until it was embedded into his flesh. Harder and harder he strained to draw breath as his bruised larynx swelled to block his windpipe from within. Congested circulation turned his face purple. Blood ran from his ears. His tongue protruded obscenely.

Of these things he was unaware, of the jeering spectators, of the piss that flooded his breeches. It was all one profound anguish. But eventually his vision darkened, hearing faded. Finally, even the pain began to recede, along with his life.

His unconscious body jerked at the end of the rope for minutes longer before it finally stilled. Then the throng surged forward to touch the corpse as the hangman began to cut the rope.

His throat hurt. He tried to swallow, and the pain flared into voiceless agony. Every breath he took was torture.

He had been hanged. Walter's whole body convulsed. His hands flew to his throat, tore at the rope. It was seconds before the awareness penetrated that there was no rope, that he no longer hung suspended from Tyburn Tree. Only gradually did it occur to him that he ought to be dead.

It was dark, as if in a grave. He touched the raw flesh once more, with fearful care. It had happened, then, it had been real. He sobbed, weakly, painfully. No tears came.

There was the sound of footsteps, a light approaching. Then, with a fetid odor, a face bent over him. A hand felt his pulse, turned his head to one side and back.

"Back with us, are ye? Here, take this." A spoon was held to his lips. He took it, swallowed — Oh, God, it hurt! But the sweet syrup soothed the rawness. He was beginning to remember. That hideous face, that voice . . . the press-yard . . . the thin twisted strand around his neck. . . . He lifted his hand to his neck again, but found nothing.

A shrill burst of laughter answered his unasked question. "Looking for something, lad? This?" He had a glimpse of twisted filament held briefly before his eyes. "But you won't be needing it any more, now, will ye?"

The laugh came again, and Walter shivered with unease. Was this hag really the witch that she looked? There was no denying he was alive. He felt there was something else he ought to remember, but it slipped from his mind as the drug took hold and he could no longer keep his eyes open. He had a moment of panic, then, that this was all a dream and he would wake again in the condemned cell on the morning he was to hang. But sleep claimed him.

The next time he woke it was light enough that he could see his surroundings. He stirred, and a figure rose from a chair, approached him with heavy footsteps. Walter blinked. The man was broadly muscled like a dray horse, with a dark, heavy-jawed face, dark gray in color. Circling the thickly massive neck, almost hidden by the neckcloth of his shirt, was a broad, livid scar.

Walter levered himself up to a half-seated position. He shared something with this man, then. They had both worn the hempen collar.

Broad hands pulled Walter to his feet, held him there until he was steady, then proffered a folded bundle of clothing. Walter glanced at the black garments, frowned. But, of course, the hangman would have had his own things. He recalled now the care he had taken with the claret-colored coat, its shining buttons, all for a brave display on the gallows. Bile rose into his throat. He reached for the black clothes and dressed without the need for assistance.

There was a small mirror on a chest. When he was clothed, Walter sought his reflection. He caught his breath. It was his own face looking back at him, with haunted shadows around the eyes. His own face, but — He had seen the grotesque, blacked features of other men cut down from the gallows. Now, for a moment, such an image had stared back at him from the mirror.

He shuddered and rubbed his face. An angry red collar circled his throat, and he wrapped the neckcloth higher to hide it.

He rubbed his face once again.

Then a hand fell on his shoulder. The silent man gestured him to follow. The noose had doubtless crushed the fellow's voicebox, Walter thought. He was led up a flight of creaking stairs, and his guide rapped on the door at the top, then pushed it open, gesturing for Walter to go through.

The room was hazy with a foul, oily smoke. Crocks and bottles and wrapped bundles covered several tables and much of the floor. And in the middle of this scene of disorder the beldame named Nan Jenkins sat at a desk. She looked up at Walter and laughed. The sound scraped against his ears.

"Well, Young Wat Rowland, time for the reckoning now, eh?"

Walter grimaced in distaste, but he did suppose he was in her debt. Whether or not her amulet had kept him alive on the gallows, she must have snatched him away, after. Else he would be presently adorning some gibbet, wrapped in chains and soaked in tar for the better preservation of his remains.

"Mistress Jenkins," he whispered hoarsely, "I would gladly pay any amount you might name. But at the moment I am altogether without funds."

"Nay, lad." Her tiny eyes seemed to glitter. "It wasn't for gold I saved you. Look!" She dragged out a chest from within her desk and flung the lid up. It was heaped with coins.

"It's your service I want, Wat Rowland. I have need of a strong lad with your qualities."

Walter was ready to turn away with a curse when he felt a large hand come down on his shoulder from behind. The mute. "What about him?" he asked instead.

"Cully is very useful, true. Ha! It was Cully who got you away from Tyburn, and quite a struggle he had of it, too. I can rely on his loyalty," she added pointedly.

"But you are a gentleman. And you have other talents I can use, Young Wat Rowland."

At her beckoning, the mute Cully came forward, carrying a swordbelt and a brace of pistols. Walter could easily read the warning in the big man's eyes. He was loyal, she had said. He would likely cut his throat at a word from her. Walter reached out to take the weapons, keeping all traces of a smile from his face. Well, then, let the witch see how long she and her lout could hold him here!

Walter soon learned he was lodged in the Clerkenwell neighborhood, near Hanging-Sword Alley. No one there cast too close a look at another's affairs — a good place for a man with no wish to arouse the attentions of the authorities. Walter had come to realize he would need such a refuge for a time. The publicity of his trial and hanging had made his face too well known.

So he would stay, he decided reluctantly, for a time in Nan Jenkins's service. Only, though, until it was safe to go his own way. And until he could get word to Bess.

A frown darkened his face. It would be risky, not knowing who had informed. It might have been her father, or the ostler, anyone who had overheard their plans. But he would find a way. They could go away together, to the colonies perhaps, once he found coin for the passage. And Nan Jenkins's guineas could very well be the solution to that problem.

It made him grin, that she had picked a thief to guard her chest. The witch had a good custom, he did admit, though most of it came from the neighborhood's whores, buying charms to prevent pregnancy or the pox. All quackery, of course.

Yet there were other, more sinister aspects to her trade. One night a cloaked figure brushed past Walter at the head of the stairs and hurried out into the street. As soon as the man had gone, his mistress summoned him.

Her eyes pierced him. "Did you mark the man who just left here?"

Walter nodded.

"He thinks to get Nan Jenkins hanged on a charge of poisoning. Too clever, that one. I want him stopped before he can call a constable. Go, hurry!"

Cully was waiting as he came down, with a grimy boy at his side. "This way!" the urchin called, leading them swiftly through dark alleys and byways where Walter would have been lost without a guide. He wondered as he ran — did the old hag really trade in poisons? And how had she known to have Cully waiting? Who was betraying whom?

Then the child stopped and pointed to a figure ahead. "There 'e goes!"

Walter scowled. Though it was past midnight, they were on a lamplit street with groups of roisterers still idling on the pavement. Their quarry wore the blue coat of a naval officer and he gripped the hilt of a sword, looking from side to side for trouble. He appeared to be lost.

Walter thought an instant. Then he grasped the lad's arm and whispered urgently into his ear. The boy nodded once and ran off after their man as Walter waved Cully back into a darkened corner.

The boy ran up behind the sailor and tugged on his coat pocket. Then he turned and fled. The man wheeled, felt his pocket, then, bellowing, ran after him. A few bystanders jeered but no one else took up the chase. They were all thieves themselves in this place.

In a moment the lad had pelted around the corner where Walter was waiting. Breathing heavily, the naval officer followed, straight into Walter's ready sword.

From his side, Cully gave a grunt of satisfaction. Walter glanced over, saw the bludgeon ready in his hand. He suspected the big mute would have been as willing to use it on his skull as on their victim's, if Walter had failed this test.

They stripped the body and dragged it between them to the Fleet Ditch.

Walter knew he would have to be cautious. Nan Jenkins indeed dealt in poisons, and other wares, more sinister still. She would arrange an assassination as readily as a resurrection, and her victims, too often for Walter's peace of mind, seemed to die without a hand laid on them.

Then afterward, as she added the guineas to the gold in her chest, she would laugh, the strident screech that always set Walter to shivering. "Look at it,

106

Young Wat Rowland," she taunted him. "Gold enough for ye?"

Cully, she mocked as well. "Aye, we wouldn't want them to know about *this* at the Old Bailey, would we?" she would say. "But, then, who's to tell them? Not my Cully, eh? Can't talk nor write, can he? Not my Cully."

Walter could see Cully's face grow even darker, his fists clench when she called him that. The big mute was no idiot. He must know that without the two of them to protect her she was only a helpless old woman. With a tempting chest of gold.

He began to consider Cully a possible ally instead of his gaoler. Once, after she had mocked the man, Walter tried to make his proposal, but Cully only looked nervously back over his shoulder at the stairs. His hand went up to touch the dark-purple scar tissue around his neck. Walter felt a tremor of unease and turned his eyes away from Cully's lead-gray face.

He would do the job on his own, then. By this time, he had had enough of the hag's service, her constant mocking laughter. Let Cully endure her taunts if he must, if his superstitions kept him prisoner. Walter longed for a horse and the open road. And for Bess. When he came to the alley's whores, they would turn away from the sight of his dark, bloodless face.

But once he had Nan Jenkins's gold he would buy a horse and ride to Bess's father's inn at Tunbridge. She would be there waiting for him, a ribbon in her black hair. He would swing her up to his saddle, and they would ride away together, her long black hair flowing in the moonlight.

It was just before dawn when Walter crept up the staircase. He was sweating. Somehow, in the darkness, the treads seemed to creak more loudly than he remembered. He wished this business was over — he was a highwayman, not a house-breaker.

THE HIGHWAYMAN

The door at the top groaned as he eased it open. The familiar acrid odor of smoke intensified. He could just make out the furniture of the room by the gray light that came through the window. He dared not carry a candle.

He went on soft feet to the desk, exhaled with relief as he tried the lock. It was open. He recalled now that he had never seen her lock it. He pulled out the chest, lifted the lid. His hand closed around the coins.

Then light flooded the room. He wheeled around, guineas spilling from his hand, as her laugh pierced the silence. In one hand was a candle, in the other . . .

She was twisting something between her thumb and forefinger. Walter felt a constriction in his throat. It had been a trap! She had taunted him with the gold, knowing he would not be able to resist. Now she laughed with malicious triumph.

"Were you thinking of leaving me now, Young Wat Rowland? And taking my gold, too? Nay, that won't do at all! Not after all the trouble I took to bring you back from Tyburn Tree!"

Walter choked. An invisible rope was tightening around his neck. Guineas fell to the floor as his hands grew numb. He dropped to his knees, strangling, fighting for breath.

"Did you never stop to think, Young Wat Rowland, how you come to be alive once you were hanged? Look here, my lad. Remember?"

Through a haze of red, Walter saw a thin filament held before his eyes, knotted into the shape of a noose. Her words pierced through the pounding in his ears. "Aye, *here* is your life, Wat Rowland. You died slow, did you not? A guinea to the hangman for that. So slow your life left you — into this! Oh, aye, you danced bravely, my fine young highwayman!"

Walter had already fallen to his face, writhing as he had at the end of the rope. But still he could hear her laugh as she pulled the knot closed and the constriction around his throat grew tighter.

"But you have to learn not to try to rob old Nan Jenkins, don't you? My lad Cully, now, he's learned his lesson well. You will, too, in time."

Slowly, Walter died once again, while she watched, shrieking gleefully as his face blackened, as his body convulsed in the struggle for breath. Only when it had stilled at last did she carefully straighten out the thin bloodstained strand.

Walter gasped for air and sat bolt upright in the bed, screaming. His hands tore at his throat. Gradually he registered his surroundings, fell back with a cry. He had dreamed . . .

But then he became aware of the damp stench of his clothing. Had he fouled himself in his sleep? Or . . .

The pain in his throat! Fearfully, he swallowed. The flesh felt raw.

There was something clutched in his fist. Slowly he opened his hand, revealing the guinea. *Oh, God!* Walter wanted to weep, but no tears would come to his eyes. The dead have no tears, and he was twice dead now.

He stumbled from the bed. The reflection from the mirror caught his eye. He snatched it up, stared. The band of scar circling his throat was still half-healed, but his face . . . He pressed his hands against his eyes. The skin had darkened to a leaden gray.

Behind him, hinges creaked. Walter looked up to see Cully filling the open doorway. *I tried to warn you,* said his eyes.

Now that her trap was exposed, Nan Jenkins took malicious delight in flaunting her power over Walter. The sound of her voice made his throat constrict, and it would hurt even to whisper.

107

There was only one way to escape her grasp on him. But it would have to be done with care. He would lie awake in his bed at nights, staring at his loaded pistol, hearing her footsteps overhead. She had known he was coming. She had been waiting for him. No longer could he doubt she had ways of dealing with those who tried to cross her.

But he never doubted he would have his chance. Until then, he waited. And he dreamed, still, of Bess, her black hairflowing, her white breasts beneath her bodice, her red lips on his. Her memory was becoming an eidolon for him, waiting loyally and timelessly in the moonlight.

But Walter's mistress had other tasks to occupy his nights. Hanging-days were of particular interest to her. After one splendid match at Tyburn when a good fifteen were turned off, Walter and Cully were dispatched on another of her grisly errands. At the crossroads, the moonlight illuminated the gibbet where the corpses of three felons hung in chains. Walter knew that there were thieves who would pay in gold for the hand of a hanged man holding a candle made of human fat. The Devil's candle — in its light a thief could go unseen. Walter wondered — with such, could he approach the witch herself?

They came to the gibbet cautiously, for fear of witnesses, but the crossroads was quiet this far out of London. There was only the sound of chains chinking as the wind made the bodies turn. Cully reached up and began to use his knife on the dead flesh.

Walter swallowed uneasily. He glanced up to the distorted face above him, compelled by the knowledge that, but for Nan Jenkins, this could have been himself.

A sob of horror rose to his throat. The swollen, blackened features were familiar. This was his partner Jemmy! Gay young Jemmy, whom he had left at the Bull's Head inn the fatal night

he had ridden off to meet Bess. They had ridden the roads together, as close as brothers.

The knife dropped from Walter's hand. It was more than he could endure. Frantically, he backed away from the gibbet, stumbling. Cully looked over from his task. His eyes widened; he shook his head, *no!*

But Walter had scented escape. They were already outside the city, on the road to Tunbridge, where Bess's father kept his inn.

"Stay back," he whispered to Cully, pulling free his sword. The big mute halted, his expression twisted as he strained for the power to cry aloud.

Walter spun around and ran. He had forgotten the gold, his plans to do away with Nan Jenkins. Now he cared only to get as far away as possible from the witch's influence, never again to hear that grating laugh. Surely her powers could not reach this far!

Too soon, he was panting with exhaustion, limping. A horse, he had to find a horse. Free on horseback on the open road — then nothing could touch him. Bess would be waiting. At last he found a stable where the dogs did not run baying at his approach. He quickly saddled the best animal, swung onto its back.

He kicked the horse into a run. The wind hit his face. Then he could not restrain an exultant cry as he took the beast over a fence, onto the highway and freedom.

Two miles further down the road, he coughed. There was something wrong, his throat . . .

Oh, God, please, no! Walter desperately whipped his stolen horse to the limits of its speed. If he could only get far enough away from her . . .

But within seconds he could feel his arms starting to go numb, his legs to twitch helplessly in the stirrups. The animal started to slow as the reins fell from his hands. He fell heavily onto the roadway, where he lay choking. By the time dawn finally came, and the cart from London, he was still.

Hot tallow dripped onto his face. Walter started, gasping for breath. His eyes focused on the hideous candlelit face of Nan Jenkins. Tearlessly, he turned his face away, but there was no escaping her voice.

"So, Wat Rowland, gone travelling, were you? Thought you'd go visit your dear Bess, eh?"

Walter's eyes flew open again, he croaked with the effort of his question.

"Oh, yes, my lad, I know all about your Bess. You were riding to meet her the night the soldiers shot you down and brought you back to hang. Someone peached, didn't they? Someone gave away your meeting-place.

"Oh, not your Bess, no. I hear it was some lad in her father's stable, fancied the lass for himself if it weren't for her handsome highwayman. It was too bad, wasn't it, that she rode herself to warn you of the trap. Poor lass, shot down on the road like a bitch-dog, she was."

Walter's hands went to his ears in a vain attempt to shut out the sound of her laughter. Now, if ever, he would have shed tears, but their source had long since dried up. They were as dead as the focus of all his hopes. Yet he had known she would never betray him. He would have wagered his soul, if a soul he still had.

Then the witch's tone changed. "Get on up out of bed, now," she ordered.

"There's much to do this night. I've already lost the whole day, bringing you back. No thanks to that fool Cully, letting you go. *He* at least, I thought, had learned his lesson."

Her face took on a horrible, gleeful grin, showing long yellow teeth. "This time, mayhap, he will."

In the candlelight, Walter could see a thin filament dangling from her fingers. "No!" he croaked, springing clumsily from the bed.

She backed up, tiny eyes showing alarm. Like a magician's, her hand was now holding a second strand. "Stay back," she warned, "unless you would feel the rope again this night!"

Walter hesitated, then he lunged for her. She shrieked, dropping the candle to the floor, tallow splattering. The knotted strand drew tight, and Walter's throat constricted. He felt his death begin once again and knew how much time he would have.

One hand grasped her bony wrists. The other jerked the strand free. For a moment, while he began to choke, he watched her struggle, knowing soon she would break free of his weakening grip. Then he dropped the strand to the floor, into the pool of flaming tallow.

With a hiss, it burst into ash, just as the candleflame went out.

"You fool!" she screeched, as Walter fell to the floor, strangling.

But this would be the last time. He had finally escaped her power.

Or so he prayed, through every endless moment of his dying. ▲

A BRIEF INTRODUCTION TO KARL EDWARD WAGNER

by David Drake

In early 1970, Manly Wade Wellman told me that a young friend of his in medical school wanted to write like Robert E. Howard — and had even sold a book. I was amazed that someone with enough brains to get into med school nowadays would also have the very different talent needed to write a publishable novel.

Karl Edward Wagner — Manly's 'young friend,' and as close a friend as Manly had until Manly's death in 1986 — is an amazing man, and an amazingly fine writer.

Karl was born in 1945 and raised in Knoxville; his father, a long-time TVA employee, retired a few years ago as Chairman of the Board of that organization. A city kid in the 1950s could find not only EC Comics on the stands but — if he had a mind to — *Weird Tales*® and other pulps in the used-book stores. Karl absorbed both (and by 1982 had *completed* his set of *WT*: the second issue was the tough one).

By the time Karl entered high school and began to write with an eye to publication, he'd added a third element to that literary amalgam: the Gothic novels of the 18th and 19th centuries.

The heroic fantasy stories Karl wrote in high school didn't sell. Sometimes they didn't even come back. He enrolled at Kenyon and continued trying. These later stories didn't sell either — at the time.

There were a number of reasons for Karl's lack of success. Markets for short

heroic fantasy were as circumscribed then as they are now; and besides, Karl's stories were *different*.

The characters in them talked like normal human beings instead of mouthing a mixture of Elizabethan and bull-puckey, forsooth. Kane, their hero, was . . . well, he was a Byronic hero-villain with intellect, power, and the ruthless amorality he brought from an age when men were very thin on the ground. Present-day readers have to remember that one authority of the '60s (yes, it was a period which accepted Lin Carter as an authority) seriously suggested that a proper 'swords and sorcery' novel was one in which the hero fought a river dragon in Chapter One; fought a ghoul in Chapter Two; fought a sea serpent in Chapter Three; fought a . . .

But you get the idea. Then add the fact that in Karl's fiction, the monsters were as apt to be fighting for the hero (a term of convenience) as against him.

Kenyon wasn't a complete waste of time. Karl graduated *cum laude* with an AB in History (with Honors), a Phi Beta Kappa key, and acceptance at UNC Medical School in Chapel Hill, NC.

In Chapel Hill, Karl met Manly Wade Wellman, a freelance writer since 1926 who was still going strong. (Manly continued to sell stories until his fatal illness.) And, in an off-campus soda shop, nestled among the westerns and the porn, Karl found a new line of heroic

110

fantasy put out by a California firm called Powell Publications. Powell looked open to innovation —

And they did indeed accept *Darkness Weaves* in 1969, when Karl expanded it from novella length into his first true novel.

The money wasn't great; but a sale is a sale, and maybe that's what broke Karl out of the slush pile with Paperback Library (now Warner Books). Paperback Library took a Kane collection, *Death Angel's Shadow*, in 1970 and optioned the novel that would become the blockbuster *Bloodstone*. Karl dropped out of med school to write the book.

And the bottom dropped out of the heroic fantasy market. *Bloodstone* came back by return mail, and *Death Angel's Shadow* was pulled from the schedule indefinitely.

The next few years were rough, but there were compensations. *Darkness Weaves* attracted the first Wagner fans. F&SF bought a horror story with a modern setting, though the magazine returned a Kane novelet which they'd already copy-edited.

Karl started his own publishing house, Carcosa, to retrieve stories which would otherwise moulder in pulp collections. Through Carcosa, he met Lee Brown Coye and heard the story which Karl himself transformed into 'Sticks,' widely acknowledged as a modern classic.

And finally, Karl finished medical school and became a staff psychiatrist at a state mental hospital. Besides the pay, the experience became grist for his World Fantasy Award nominee 'Into Whose Hands.'

But after a year of drunks and psychotics, the reawakening fantasy market brought Karl back to full-time writing. *Death Angel's Shadow* appeared. It was followed by *Bloodstone* — the contract negotiated by a new agent, Kirby McCauley, and the cover painting the first of the stunning Frazettas that have graced the Kane series.

Writing full time sometimes means writing the book somebody else wants written. Karl did a Bran Mak Morn novel, *Legion from the Shadows*. It was created with a care for Roman history, Pictish prehistory, Howardian non-history, and general quality as fiction — which made it greatly more difficult to write than a straight fantasy novel of Karl's own. It is also nearly the only Howard pastiche which is, in my opinion, an excellent, self-standing novel. (More about the 'nearly' in a moment.)

The next Kane novel, *Dark Crusade*, bothered some people because of its realism. The villain is punished exactly as Richard Nixon was . . . which is to say, not at all. Warner signed Karl to a three-book contract, leading off with an uncut *Darkness Weaves* (you have to read the Powell edition to see how much it had been cut) and followed that with the Kane collection *Night Winds*.

Karl accepted the editorship of *The Year's Best Horror* series from DAW. For Bantam, he did a Conan pastiche, *The Road of Kings* — and was again faced with the problem of trying to write two novels, one of them another man's work, in the same volume. *The Road of Kings* is an excellent book; it was an honor of sorts; and it paid the bills for a goodly while.

But the book which made explicit the new direction of Karl's writing was *In a Lonely Place* from Warner in 1983, collecting a decade of Karl's modern-setting horror stories. The stories were all well-crafted; they were all unrelievedly horrifying; and they — with different choices for different tastes — contain at least part of *any* reader's list of the three best horror stories ever encountered.

Heroic fantasy had been Karl's first love, but he'd come to realize that no matter how good he was, he wouldn't be able to reshape the field singlehandedly into the form he wanted it to take. Reviewers were going to treat heroic fantasy as a lowest-common-denominator dreck without bothering to read it; and for most of each year's new crop of thirteen-year olds, the lowest common denominator was plenty good enough. Modern horror, on the other hand, had a chance of being taken seriously as literature.

The other factor influencing — and limiting — Karl's fiction output was his growing involvement with film and television. In recent years he's done (on commission) teleplays from his own works and those of Robert E. Howard, among others; and has done film scripts (again on commission) for projects as widely different as Conan and adaptations of Japanese folk-tales.

Karl's work with visual media has paid the bills and will — one of these days — introduce an even larger audience to his artistic vision; but it's necessarily cut into the time he has available for prose. Nonetheless, 1987 saw the publication (by Tor) of another modern horror collection: *Why Not You and I?* Like the first volume, this one contains a number of award-winning stories — and some of the most vivid nightmares you're going to see in print any time soon.

What can we expect from Karl in the future? Excellence, because his work has always been excellent. And a variety of forms, because that too has been a facet of Karl's work from the beginning.

We can, in other words, expect more stories like this one, written for the magazine you hold. . . .   ▲

THE REVENANT

(From the French of Charles Baudelaire)

Like a dark angel, feral-eyed,
I will return and softly glide
Into the silence of your room,
Wrapped in the shadows of night's gloom.

And you I'll give, my sweet delight,
Kisses cold as the moon's cold light
And chill caresses like the crawl
Of snakes around a pit's dank wall.

You'll find, when comes the livid dawn,
The vacant place I've lain upon
Where a strange cold shall bide till night.

Though some by love and tenderness
Would rule your youth and zestfulness,
Me, I would seize your soul by fright.

— **Richard L. Tierney**

AT FIRST JUST GHOSTLY

by Karl Edward Wagner

I. Beginning Our Descent

His name was Cody Lennox, and he was coming back to England to die, or maybe just to forget, and after all it's about the same in the long run.

He had been dozing for the last hour or so, when the British Airways stewardess politely offered him an immigration card to be filled in. He placed it upon the tray table beside the unfinished game of solitaire and the finished glass of Scotch, which he must now remember to call whisky when asking at the bar, and this was one of the few things he was unlikely to forget.

Lennox tapped his glass. "Time for another?"

"Certainly, sir." The stewardess was blonde and compactly pretty and carefully spoke BBC English with only a trace of a Lancashire accent. Her training had also taught her not to look askance at first class passengers who declined breakfast in favor of another large whisky.

Lennox's fellow passenger in the aisle seat favored him with a bifocaled frown and returned to his book of crossword puzzles. Lennox had fantasied him to be an accountant for some particularly corrupt television evangelist, doubtlessly on an urgent mission to Switzerland. They had not spoken since the first hour of the flight, when after pre-flight champagne and three subsequent large whiskies Lennox had admitted to being a writer.

Fellow passenger (scathingly): "Oh, well then — name something you've written."

Lennox (in apparent good humor): "You go first. Name something you've read."

In the ensuing frostiness Lennox played countless hands of solitaire with the deck the stewardess had provided and downed almost as many large whiskies, which she also dutifully provided. He considered a visit to the overhead lounge, but a trip to the lavatory convinced him that his legs weren't to be trusted on the stairs. So he played solitaire, patiently, undeterred by total lack of success, losing despite the nagging temptation to cheat. Lennox had once been told by a friend in a moment of drunken insight that a Total Loser was someone who cheated at solitaire and still lost, and Lennox didn't care to take that chance.

Eventually he fell asleep.

Cody Lennox liked to fly first class. He stood a rangy six-foot-four, and while he still combed his hair to look like James Dean, his joints were the other side of forty and rebelled at being folded into a 747's tourist-class orange crates. He was wont to say that the edible food and free booze were more than worth the additional expense on a seven-hour flight, and his preventive remedy for tedium and for jet-lag was to drink himself into a blissful stupor and sleep throughout the flight. Once he and Cathy had flown over on the Concorde, and for that cherished memory he would never do so again.

He still hadn't got used to traveling alone, and he supposed he never would.

He looked through the window and into darkness fading to grey. As they chased the dawn, clouds began to appear and break apart; below them monotonous expanses of grey sea gave way to glimpses of distant green land. Coming in over Ireland, he supposed, and finished his drink.

He felt steadier now, and he filled out the immigration card, wincing, as he knew he would, over the inquiry as to marital status, etc. He placed the card inside his passport, avoiding looking at his photograph there. There was time for another hand, so he collected and reshuffled his cards.

"We are beginning our descent into London Heathrow," someone was announcing. Lennox had nodded off. "Please make certain your seatbelts are fastened, your seat backs are in the upright position, your tray tables are . . ."

"The passengers will please refrain," prompted Lennox, scooping up the cards and locking back his tray. "Batten the hatches, you swabs. Prepare to abandon ship."

"Do you want to know why you never won?"

"Eh?" said Lennox, startled by his seatmate's first attempt at conversation since the Jersey shore.

The mysterious accountant pointed an incisive finger toward the cabin floor. "You haven't been playing with a full deck."

The Queen of Spades peeked out from beneath the accountant's tight black shoes.

"The opportunity to deliver a line such as that comes only once in a lifetime," Lennox said with admiration. He reached down to recover the truant card, but the impact of landing skidded it away.

Probably the really and truly best thing about flying first class across the Atlantic was that you were first off the

114

plane and first to get through immigration and customs. Lennox had a morbid dread of being engulfed by gabbling hordes of blue-haired widows from New Jersey or milling throngs of students hunchbacked by garish knapsacks and sleeping bags. "Americans never queue up," he once observed to an icily patient gentleman, similarly overrun while waiting for a teller at a London bank. "They just mill about and make confused sounds."

"The purpose of your stay here, sir?" asked the immigrations officer, flipping through Lennox's passport.

"Primarily I'm on holiday," said Lennox. "Although for tax purposes I'll be mixing in a little business, as I'm also here to attend the World Science Fiction Convention in Brighton some days from now."

The officer was automatically stamping his passport. "So then, you're a writer, are you, sir?" His eyes abruptly focused through the boredom of routine, and he flipped back to the passport photo.

"Cody Lennox!" He compared photo and face in disbelief. "Lord, and I've just finished reading *They Do Not Die!* "

"Small world," said Cody imaginatively. "Will you still let me in?"

"First celebrity I've had here." The immigrations officer returned his passport. "Your books have given me and the wife some fair shivers. Working on a new one, are you?"

"Might write one while I'm here."

"I'll want to read it, then."

Lennox passed through to baggage claim and found his two scruffy suitcases. They were half-empty, as he preferred to buy whatever he needed when he needed it, and he hated to pack. He also hated carry-on luggage, people who carried on carry-on luggage, and cameras of all sorts. Such eccentricities frequently excited some speculation as to his nationality.

Cody Lennox was, however, Ameri-

can: born in Los Angeles of a Scandinavian bit-player and a father who worked in pictures before skipping to Mexico; educated across the States with two never-to-be-completed doctorates scattered along the way, and now living in New York City. He had had eight best-selling horror novels over the last five years, in addition to some other books that had paid the bills early on. His novels weren't all that long on the best-seller lists, but they were there, nonetheless, and film rights and script work all added up to an enviable bundle. He had been on *Johnny Carson* twice, but he had never hosted *Saturday Night Live*. His books could be found at supermarket check-out counters between the tabloids and the *TV Guide*s, but only for a month or so. It was a living. Once he had been happy with his life.

Cody Lennox hauled his pair of cases through the green lane at Heathrow customs. He had made this trip a dozen times or more, and he had never been stopped. Sometimes he considered becoming a smuggler. Probably he looked too non-innocent for the customs officers to bother examining his luggage.

He looked a little like an on-the-skids rock star with his designer jeans and t-shirt and wrinkled linen jacket. He still had the face of a young James Dean, but his ash-blond hair was so pale as to seem dead-white. His left ear was pierced, but he seldom bothered to wear anything there, and his week-old smear of a beard was fashionable but too light to be noticed. He wore blue-lensed glasses over his pale blue eyes, but this was more of necessity than style: Lennox was virtually blinded by bright sunlight.

Lennox adjusted his scarred watch to London time while he waited to cash a traveler's check at the bank outside the customs exit. He saw no sign of his seatmate, and for this he was grateful. Bastard might have told him about the

missing card.

The Piccadilly Line ran from Heathrow to where Lennox meant to go, but he was in no mood for the early morning crush on the tube. Still feeling the buzz of a long flight and too many drinks, he joined the queue for a taxi — nudging his cases along with his foot, as he endured confused American tourists and aggressive Germans who simply shoved to the front of it all.

Lennox was very tired and somewhere on the verge of a hangover, when the next black Austin stopped for him. He tossed his cases into the missing left-side front seat and pulled himself into the back. After the 747 the back seat was spacious, and he stretched out his long legs.

He said: " The Bloomsbury Park Hotel. Small place on Southampton Row. Just off Russell Square."

"I know it, gov," said the driver. "Changed the name again, have they?"

"Right. Used to be the Grand. God only knows what it was before that."

II. Lost Without a Crowd

It was not much after nine when the cab made a neat U-turn across Southampton Row and landed Lennox and his cases at the door of his hotel. In addition to changing its name, the Bloomsbury Park Hotel had changed management half a dozen times in the dozen or so years that Lennox had been stopping there, but the head porter had been there probably since before the Blitz, and he greeted Lennox with a warm smile.

"Good to see you again, sir."

"Good to be back, Mr. Edwards."

It had been about a year since his last stay here, and Edwards remembered not to inquire about his wife.

The newest management had redone the foyer again; this time in trendy Art Deco, which fitted as well with the original Art Nouveau décor as did the kilt on the golden-ager tourist who was complaining his way across the lobby in tow of his wife.

Jack Martin was at the reception desk, scribbling away at a piece of hotel stationery.

"Hello, Jack."

"Cody! I don't believe it! I was just writing you a note telling you where I was staying."

"Synchronicity, good buddy. When'd you get here?"

"Flew in Sunday from L.A. Still coping with jet-lag, but I walked over here to see whether you'd checked in yet. Had breakfast? Guess they fed you on the flight. How was it?"

"OK. Anything you can walk away from is OK. Here, better let me register."

Lennox filled in forms while Martin worked on a cigarette. No, his room wasn't ready yet, but Lennox had expected that, and the porters would see to his cases in the meantime.

The girl at the desk was auburn-haired, Irish, and half Lennox's age, and he wondered if she'd been here last time. Probably so, or else she was instinctively cheeky.

"You're very popular, sir. Two calls for you already."

"More likely ten, judging by my usual luck with hotel switchboards." Lennox studied the messages. "Mike Carson says to give him a ring and I owe him a pint. And the other one — from a Mr. Kane?"

"He said he'd be getting in touch."

"Never heard of him. Social secretary from Buckingham Palace, isn't he? Come on, Jack. Let's go get something to drink."

"Pubs won't open until eleven," Martin pointed out.

"Let me show you my private club."

There was a minimart just down Southampton Row from the hotel, and Lennox bought Martin a carton of orange juice and two cans of lager for himself. Cosmo Place was the alleyway that connected onto Queen Square, where there were vacant benches beneath the trees. Lennox was just able to keep his hands from shaking as he popped his first lager.

Martin was trying to solve the juice carton. "So, Cody. How are things going?"

It was more than a casual question and Lennox hated the glance of watchful concern that accompanied it, but he had grown accustomed to it all and it no longer hurt so bitterly.

"Can't complain, Jack. *They Do Not Die!* is still hanging high on the lists, and Mack says the sharks are in a feeding frenzy to bid on my next one."

"How's that been coming along?"

Lennox killed his lager, stretched out with a sigh, and thoughtfully opened the second can. He said: "Cathy and I used to come here and sit. Place close by on Theobald's Road sells some of the best fish and chips I've ever had. Used to carry them back, sit and eat here, and then we'd walk back to The Sun and wash it all down with pints of gut-wrenching ales."

He closed his eyes and took a long pull of lager, remembering. When he opened his eyes he saw the worn benches stained with pigeon droppings, the dustbins overstuffed with cider bottles, the litter of empty beercans and crisps packets. The square smelled of urine and unwashed bodies; the derelicts slept all about here at night.

"Let it go, Cody."

"Can't. Nothing left to hang onto but memories."

"But you're just killing yourself."

"I'm already dead."

The church steeple tolled ten. Lennox had always suspected that its bells were an array of old iron pots. A deaf gnome banged on them with a soup ladle. The steeple was a ponderous embarrass-

117

ment that clashed with what remained of the simple Queen Anne architecture.

"The Church of St. George the Martyr," Lennox said. "Loads of history here. See that steeple? Hawksmoor had a hand in it."

"Who's Hawksmoor?"

"The hero of a famous fairyland fantasy trilogy. Did you know, for example, that the church crypts here are connected by a tunnel beneath Cosmo Place to the cellars of that pub on the corner — The Queen's Larder?"

"Didn't know you read guidebooks."

"Don't. Old pensioner Cathy and I used to drink with there told us. Name was Dennis, and he always drank purple velvets — that's stout mixed with port. Haven't seen him since then."

"With that to drink, I'm not surprised." Martin tossed his juice carton into a bin. "So why St. George the Martyr? I always thought old George slew that dragon. Must have been another George somewhere."

"Or another dragon," said Lennox. "Let's just see if my room is ready by now."

His room was ready. Lennox poured himself a glass of Scotch from the coals-to-Newcastle bottle in his suitcase, then phoned Mike Carson. Carson said he'd meet them at The Swan soon after eleven, and he did.

Lennox was at the bar buying the first round. The day was turning warm and bright after last night's rain, and they had seats at an outside table on Cosmo Place.

"You ever notice," observed Carson, "how Cody always seems to bring good weather when he's over?"

"No, I hadn't," said Martin. "Just must be luck."

Carson offered a cigarette, and they both lit up. "Cody once said to me," he said, inhaling, "that the English carry umbrellas because they expect it to rain. Cody says he never does, because

he expects the day to be clear."

"First optimistic thing I've ever heard about that Cody said."

"It's not optimism," Carson explained. "It's bloody arrogance."

Martin turned to peer into the pub. Lennox was still waiting to be served. Martin said: "God knows it can't be good luck. Not with Cody."

"So, then. How is he?"

"God knows. Not taking it well. I'm worried."

Jack Martin was short for his generation, neatly groomed with a frost of grey starting in his carefully trimmed beard, and there was a hint of middle-age spread beneath his raw silk sport jacket. He had known Lennox from when they were both determined young writers in Los Angeles, before Lennox had connected and split for New York; and while his own several books in no way competed with Lennox's sales figures, he had scripted at least three successful horror films (one from an early Lennox novel), and he had a devoted following among discriminating readers of the genre. Martin's ambition was to become an emerging mainstream writer. He had known Lennox as a friend since high school days.

Mike Carson was taller than Martin, shorter than Lennox, and spare of frame, with short black hair and a brooding face. He wore a long overcoat, loose shirt and baggy trousers, and stopped just short of punk. He looked like an unbalanced and consumptive artist who was slowly starving in a garret; in fact he was Irish and scraping out a fair living between moderately frequent assignments and his wife's steady job. Carson had done the British paperback covers for the last five of Lennox's novels, and, although Lennox had never said so, Carson knew that Lennox had insisted that his choice of artist be included in his contracts. Carson had known Lennox since the first time Cody and Cathy had visited London — when

West End pints cost 30p, and Carson had made the mistake of trying to drink him under the table.

"Two bitters, and here's your lager, Jack," said Lennox, sloshing their pints on the pebble-grained aluminum table. "Christ, I hate these straight-sided glasses. They look like oversized Coca-Cola glasses."

"Cheers."

"Oh, thanks, Cody."

They drank.

"Well," said Lennox, halfway through his bitter at a gulp. "So who else is over here?"

"Haven't seen very many stray American writers," Martin told him. "Still a bit early, I guess. Geoffrey Marsh is here — staying over at the Wansbeck. Saw Sanford Vade coming out of an off-license with two jail-baits and a bottle of Beam's Choice. Oh, and I did run into Kent Allard in the lobby this morning. He asked if you were coming over."

"He would." Lennox finished his pint. "You said you were staying at the Russell?"

"That's right."

"I'll get these." Carson downed his pint.

"I'm still OK." Martin sipped at his lager.

Lennox belched. "Crazy town where you have to do your drinking between eleven and three — and then try to find a loo. At least this time next year they'll have twelve-hour opening."

"Why don't you come down to Mexico with me sometime?" Martin suggested. "We could stay a week for what a day here costs. I know some great places."

"My destiny lies here."

"Bullshit. You can get just as drunk in Mexico for a lot less money."

"Money means nothing to me."

"Bullshit."

"Besides, in Mexico I might run into my father."

Carson crashed down three pints.

Martin had started to raise a hand in protest. The aluminum table tipped. Martin's fresh pint of lager rocked and tilted. Lennox reached across his own pint glass to catch Martin's. His heavy wristwatch band shattered the top off of the straight-sided glass. Lennox caught Martin's pint and set it safely upright.

"Reflexes," said Lennox proudly.

"You're bleeding," said Martin.

"No, I'm not."

Carson pointed. "Then where's all this blood coming from?"

Lennox examined his wrist, then pulled out the splinter of glass. "Shit. I've ruined my pint."

It was a minor cut, but it bled stubbornly. Martin gave him a crumpled tissue to use until Carson returned with several paper serviettes and another pint of bitter.

"Don't drink the other," Carson advised. "It's all full of glass and blood."

"I'll hide the evidence," said Lennox, dabbing at his cut wrist. He carried his broken glass to the sewer grating between The Swan and The Queen's Larder. As he bent to pour out the blood-tinged mess, he noticed a playing card balanced against the grating. It was the Queen of Spades.

Lennox reached down for it clumsily, but a splash of his blood was faster and struck the edge of the card, flipping it into the darkness below.

III. Wicked Malt

"I understand you just slashed your wrist."

"Hello, Kent," said Lennox without enthusiasm. "Nice to see you again. Been over here long?"

Kent Allard had joined their table while Lennox was disposing of his shattered glass. Kent looked like any well-to-do Hollywood hustler — permanently tanned and forever 35. He wrote

119

about writers, made books about books, and had ghosted half the celebrity kiss-and-tell autobiographies of the past decade. Lennox had heard that Allard was somehow related to one of the Great Departed. Martin liked Allard and called him a demonic genius in wolf's clothing; Lennox saw in Allard most of the reasons why he had fled from Los Angeles.

"What a coincidence," said Lennox, reaching for his fresh pint.

"Slashing your wrist?"

"No. Running into you here."

"It's all because of the Harmonic Convergence," said Allard. "Synchronicity is in the air. Besides, I'm staying down the block at the Russell, and Jack said you might be meeting here for lunch. So, how are things going for you, Cody?"

"Keeping busy. What's the Harmonic Convergence?"

"You mean you missed it? August 16–17? Scant hours ago."

"I was in transit. Just got in scant hours ago."

"Didn't really miss anything. Now, what about lunch?"

"I'm on jet-lag," Lennox begged off. "Think I'll just mellow out with a few more of these and hit the sack."

"I ate just before coming over," Carson lied.

"You and me then, Jack," said Allard. "I'm in a mood for Italian. Anyone know a good place?"

Martin pointed. "One right here's a good one."

They left, and Lennox said to Carson: "Let's get out of here."

Lennox kept dabbing at his wrist, but it had long since quit bleeding. He and Carson ended up at the Nellie Dean in Soho, for no particular reason. Inside it was crowded, loud, smoky and hot, so they leaned against the wall outside and drained many pints. Lennox had twice already bashed his head on the rafters going downstairs to the gents'.

120

"English pubs have a distinct aura," said Lennox.

"What's that?"

"A smell of strong tobacco, spilled bitter, stale clothing, sweat and breath."

"That's aroma you meant."

"Very possibly." Lennox glanced at his watch, saw no blood, decided they had less than half an hour to drink. "Have you noticed that all the women are dressed in black?"

"It's the fashion," Carson explained.

"Black everything. Neck to their shoes. Everything very tight. And those wide belts to cinch their waistline. Do you know what it all signifies?"

"My round," said Carson.

"It's the return of *fin de siècle* decadence. This is 1987, the dawn of a new *fin de siècle*. A new age of decadence. All of it kicked off by the Harmonic Emergence."

Carson remembered that Martin had asked him to look after Lennox. He bought another round.

"Some wicked malt," Carson nodded.

She was dressed in a black leather mini and might have been 17. They solemnly watched her parade by on her stiletto heels.

"Christ, I'm horny." Lennox downed his pint. "And I need to piss. And I need some sleep."

"It's your round," prompted Carson.

And soon it was three o'clock closing time.

The walk back to the hotel was a staggering muddle of crowded sidewalks and near-misses when crossing streets. Carson served as a guide of sorts.

"Here, have you seen these?"

They were leaning against a telephone kiosk, catching their breath and getting their bearings.

"Seen what?"

"These here."

The inside of the booth was papered with a dozen handprinted stickers, all offering sexual services and a phone number to call:

. . . PUNISHMENT FOR WENDY — NAUGHTY SCHOOLGIRL & UNIFORMS . . . LET'S GET ON YOUR KNEES, BOY . . . TIE & TEASE TV RUBBER . . . WANT SAFE SEX? GET BREAST RELIEF . . . PUNK BOYS AGAINST THE WALL . . . NAUGHTY BOYS GET BOTTOM MARKS . . .

"Here." Carson abruptly began peeling off stickers, handing them to Lennox. "In case you get lonely."

Lennox dutifully stuck the torn patches into his notebook. "I don't think I'm really into caning punk boys until they cry and all that. I'm just horny. Do any of them say anything about just that? I mean, just screwing?"

"You said you were decadent."

"Well, not that way. What happens when you call one of these numbers? Do the cops come around?"

"Don't know. Never tried. But I know this geezer who did. Woman comes up to his hotel room, and there's a big bloke lurking back down the corridor to make sure there's no trouble for her."

"What happened?"

"She let the ponce in, he bashed the geezer, and they took his wallet and watch."

"Did he have to pay extra for all that?"

It was about four by the time they managed to get back to his hotel. Lennox was feeling the double effects of jetlag and too much booze on an empty stomach. Carson dutifully saw him to his room, had a glass of whisky with him, then left Lennox with the advice that he have a lie-down. Lennox did.

He slept soundly, which was rare for him these days, and it was past ten when he awoke. Lennox sensed the familiar throb of an incipient hangover, so he washed his face, changed shirt and jacket, and headed for the residents' bar.

He was briefly confused, as the new management had moved the residents' bar into the former restaurant on the ground floor. In the course of remodeling the foyer, they had evidently inserted some striking stained-glass panels beside the steps leading to the downstairs bar. Some sort of heraldic designs, Lennox noted in passing, one of them a little garish.

Lennox decided on a large whisky, then chased it with three aspirin and a pint of lager. The lager settled in nicely, and he had another — drinking it slowly as his hangover receded. He began to feel almost alive once again, and with his third pint he was chatting up the willowy blonde barmaid. She was patient, if not receptive. The bar was nearly empty, and Lennox might have pressed onward, were it not for the table of blue-haired widows who were discussing the quaintness of the British in voices that probably carried all the way back to New Jersey.

Lennox finished his fourth pint and gave up. He stopped by the front desk on the way to his room. There were two messages: one from his British agent and one from a Mr. Kane. Both said they would ring back.

Lennox was just able to manage the plastic card that unlocked his door. Supposedly this improvement over the old metal keys made his room secure from hotel thieves. Lennox wished said thieves the possession of his dirty socks.

He poured himself a generous shot of Scotch and slumped into a chair. The nightcap had no apparent effect, so he tried another. The long nap had left him restless, and it was still early bedtime in New York. Digging out his pocket notebook, Lennox decided to tally the day's expenses. Must keep the IRS happy.

And there he found the peeled-off stickers from the phone booths. Lennox had almost forgotten the incident, and he chuckled as he re-read them:

"MISS NIPPLES"

"SLAP HAPPY BITCH"

"FUN AND GAMES"

It might be fun to phone one of them, just to hear what they'd say.

Lennox studied his collection. Most of the stickers had torn when Carson pulled them off, and Lennox had stuck them all in a jumble onto the pages. No, he didn't want to talk to the enema specialist. Lennox closed his eyes, stabbed a finger onto the notebook. There was a phone number under his finger, but nothing more; the sticker had torn in half in coming away, and all Lennox had left was a badly smudged phone number.

Better that way. Strictly random. Besides, he had no intention of telling Ms. Switch or whoever where he was staying. Was that a 2 or a 7?

Lennox had a third drink and just was able to sort out the buttons on the phone. He was still chuckling while it rang.

Three rings, and someone picked up the receiver.

"Howdy there!" Lennox answered the silence. "My name's Bubba Joe McBob, and I'm here from Texas, and I sure could use a little action. What you all got for me, honey?"

"Do you wish me to come to you?" The voice was coldly formal, but at least it was a woman's voice.

"You bet I do, sugar britches."

"As you wish, Cody Lennox."

Lennox stared stupidly at the phone. There was only an empty buzzing from the receiver. He started to dial again, then began to laugh.

"That barmaid," he chuckled, hanging up. "She's watching switchboard, now that the bar's closed down. Cut into my call."

He struggled out of his shoes and considered trying another call. Was that barmaid going to come up to his room after work? She just might. She'd taken

122

the trouble to remember his name. Why miss a chance to sleep with a famous author?

That last drink had made him sleepy. Lennox turned off most of the lights and stretched out on his bed to await the hot-to-trot blonde barmaid. Almost immediately he began to snore.

Lennox was certain he was awake when his door opened and the woman entered his room.

Passkey, he thought, raising himself on his elbows.

It wasn't the barmaid.

"Well, hello now," he said, thinking, *so much for plastic keys and burglar-proof locks.*

She stared at him as if he were part of the furnishings — her eyes slowly taking stock of the room. She was dressed entirely in black, and he could barely see her pale face beneath her low cap. If her eyes hadn't so dominated, he might have seen her face.

Lennox cleared his throat, wondering how to handle the situation. Was she just a hotel thief, or did these call services have some sort of high-tech tracing device? The hotel management wouldn't be amused if he phoned down for them to evict the call girl he'd summoned. Besides . . .

"Cody Lennox?" she asked, and it was the voice on the phone.

"At your service," said Lennox. "Or vice versa, I suppose."

She pulled off her cap, and her hair was straight and short and black. Its blackness accentuated the paleness of her face — devoid of any color other than the black-red bruise of her lips. Lennox thought her eyes must be black as well.

She had many rings on her fingers and her nails were varnished black. She unclasped the wide cinch at her waist, and when she tugged off the black turtle-neck, her breasts were small and her erect nipples were as pale as the rest of her body. She kicked off her black stiletto pumps, then wriggled free of black tube-skirt and tights with a sinuous motion that reminded Lennox of how a snake would shed its skin. Her hips were small and well-rounded, and her pubic hair was a narrow black vee against her white skin.

Lennox remembered to close his jaw.

She sprang onto the bed — cat-like, thought Lennox — and all of this was moving much too fast. Her black-nailed fingers clawed at his belt and zipper, and his jeans were jerked down and away from his growing erection.

"Whoa!" Lennox protested, trying to unbutton his shirt. "Hey, let me just . . ."

And the door must have opened, because there was another man suddenly in the room.

The woman froze.

"Hey," said Lennox. "You're shit out of luck. I put everything in the hotel's safe deposit."

His voice trailed off. He sensed tension, far too much tension, and he knew this was not just a hotel burglary, and he desperately hoped it was only a dream.

The man was not as tall as Lennox, but he was built like an all-pro NFL lineman. He was wearing kicker boots, punker black leathers, and a lot of chains and badges and things. His combed-back red hair and short beard were like rust surrounding a brutal face, and his eyes were cold blue and malevolent. Lennox quickly looked away. It was time to try pinching himself. He tried. It hurt.

"Stay out of this, Kane!" said the woman, backing away like a cat before a pit bull.

"It's you who should go," said Kane, "while you still can."

"We grow stronger."

"But not strong enough. I was in time."

"Hey," said Lennox. "Are you two

sure you're in the right room? Or, just tell me if I've made a . . ."

She made a gesture. A globe of blue fire darted from her fingers toward Kane. It faded before it reached him.

"Pathetic," said Kane. "Now, get out."

She made a virginal dash for her clothes, clasping their bundle before her, and Lennox almost failed to notice that her feet were changing into cloven hooves. Then she was gone. Like that.

"I'll let myself out," said Kane.

"This is the weirdest dream yet," Lennox congratulated him. "If I can remember this when I wake up, you guys are going into my next book. You got an agent?"

"Remember this, Cody," said Kane. "Just because you're paranoid, it doesn't mean someone isn't really shooting at you."

And Lennox must then have drifted back into dreamless sleep, because he didn't remember when Kane left, and he didn't remember how the pair of black stiletto pumps came to be at the foot of his bed.

IV. Blue Pumps

Lennox awoke at around noon with the grandfather of all hangovers and the maid clattering at his door. He managed to get into his clothes, looked at his face in the mirror and swore never to drink again. As he headed for the bar, he told the maid: "Previous guest left her shoes under the bed. You take them. Not my size."

Two pints of lager put him right, and Lennox remembered that he was supposed to meet Jack Martin for lunch. A third pint, and he was able to paw through his notebook for the time and place. He gazed curiously at the clusters of stickers from the telephone kiosks in Soho. No sign of the number he had dreamt that he called last night.

"We thought you was dead," said

Mike Carson, sitting down beside him. "Sorry I'm late, but the bus was held up in traffic. How's the wrist?"

"What?" Lennox was surprised to note a small scab and swelling next to his watchband.

"Don't you remember? You karate-chopped your pint yesterday. Is it lager you're drinking?"

Carson carried over a round just as Jack Martin hustled down the steps into the downstairs bar. "I'm sorry I'm late," he said, "but it's not my fault."

"Is it lager you're having?" asked Carson.

Lennox finally found an indecipherable scrawl that seemed to indicate he was to meet Martin and Carson here at Peter's Bar at noon. He felt a little smug as he closed his notebook.

"So," said Martin, cautiously. "Are you rested up?"

"Slept like the dead," said Lennox. "A lustful lady in black visited my dreams."

"Whoa!"

"She was chased away by Hulk Hogan before I starched the sheets." Lennox was feeling much better. "What do you say we drink up and wander over to The Friend at Hand? They do a super pub lunch there."

Lennox was able to cope with a ploughman's lunch with Stilton, and he only hit his head once on the eccentric copper lanterns that hung from the fake wooden beams. The food steadied him, and after three pints of bitter he felt up to laying waste to London.

Martin dropped all of his change into a fruit machine, despite his avowed prowess with the Vegas slots, and when he asked for just one more 10p, instead Lennox stuffed the coin into the machine himself and collected five pounds. "Synchronicity," explained Lennox, who had pushed buttons purely at random. Beginner's luck, he decided privately, and converted his winnings into pints.

124

It was close and crowded inside, so they found a table outside next to the door. They watched the crowds hurry by along Herbrand Street behind the Hotel Russell; it was a shortcut from the Russell Square tube station to Southampton Row and on toward the British Museum. Tourists wandered in confusion, consulting guidebooks. Office workers strode purposefully by.

"Blue pumps," said Lennox.

"Eh?" Carson was headed inside for his round.

"My next book," Lennox confided. "You got your camera, Jack?"

"Sure. Why?" Martin was carefully picking out the bits of kidney from his steak-and-kidney pie.

"In this Our Harmonic August of Our Lord, 1987," said Lennox, "London women are all wearing pumps."

"Training shoes?" Carson glanced at Martin's Reeboks. "I think you mean stilettos." He continued inside.

"Sorry, I do not speaka your language so good. No, look. The tourists are all wearing tennis shoes or something ugly and comfortable. London women all wear stiletto pumps. And they have that quick, purposeful stride, and they never look about; they know where they're going even if they don't want to go there."

"Didn't know you had a foot fetish," Martin said.

"A lovely turn of the ankle," Lennox went on. "Pure *fin de siècle*."

"Skirts are a bit shorter though."

"We'll get a cab," said Lennox. "Drive all around London. You take pictures of their pumps. I'll write the commentary. *Blue Pumps*. Retitle it *Blue Stilettos* for the UK edition. Coffee table book. Pop art. Sell millions of copies. You got enough film?"

"I've got to piss," decided Martin. "You going to be all right here?"

"Steam into this," invited Carson, bringing fresh pints. "You feeling any better?"

"Never better." Lennox was staring back into the pub. "See her?"

"Where?"

"Girl in black."

"Which one?"

"Back by the corner — next to the cigarette machine. Near the Gents'. Jack just walked past her."

"I can't see who you're talking about."

"She's the Lady in Black from my dream."

"Here, sink your pint, Cody. It'll steady you a bit."

"No, wait." Lennox made it to his feet. "I'm going to check this out. Ready for a slash anyway."

Lennox passed Martin as he entered the pub, and Martin gave his back a worried look.

She was standing alone by the bar, her back was to him, and she was dressed all in black. Beside her, talking to one another, stood a group of workmen wearing white boiler suits, somewhat smudged with soot and grime. The side door, which opened onto a sort of tiny alleyway named Colonnade, let circulate a welcome breeze to part the dense tobacco smoke.

She was pretty from the back, and her tight black skirt set off her figure. Lennox figured to walk past her, buy a pack of cigarettes from the machine, then turn to glance at her face. Next he'd casually move beside her at the bar, order a large Glenfiddich (very impressive), open his cigarettes, politely offer her one, and conversation would follow. He was aware that Carson and Martin were observing his progress from beyond the other doorway.

Lennox had almost reached her, but one of the workmen — a rather large bloke — turned away from the chattering group and leaned a thick arm across the bar to block his way. Lennox started to say something.

"Don't," said Kane, turning to face him. "It's another bad move."

Lennox had only a vague memory of his face, but his eyes were not to be forgotten, and the man in the white boiler suit was the man from his dream.

Lennox found drunken *sang-froid*. "Have we met?"

Kane ignored him, not removing his arm from the bar. He said to the Lady in Black: "Turn around, Bright Eyes."

She slowly turned her head toward Lennox. Beneath the black cap, her face was a leathery mask of tattered flesh clinging to a blackened skull.

Lennox felt his beer coming back up.

"Leave us," Kane told her. "Lunchbreak is over."

Lennox closed his eyes tightly, battling to hold his stomach under control. She — whatever he had seen — wasn't there when he opened his eyes again.

Kane was. "That's twice now," he said. "You and I need to talk, Cody. How about over dinner? I'll have my girl get in touch."

Lennox pressed his hand to his mouth and surged toward the Gents'. Kane let him pass.

"Catch you later," Kane called after him.

Kane was gone when Lennox stumbled out of the Gents'. When he had toweled himself clean, his face in the mirror was ghostly pale. He stopped at the bar and quickly downed a large whisky. He was shaking badly, but the second whisky settled him down.

Carson and Martin were studiously trying not to watch him too closely as he stumbled onto his seat.

"You OK, Cody?" asked Martin.

Lennox wanted to say: "I'm all right, Jack." Instead he said: "I'm not sure."

"Ought to go easy," Carson suggested. "Jet-lag."

Lennox swallowed his pint. "Look, did you see her?"

"See who?" Martin exchanged glances with Carson.

"Look. What did I just do?"

"What? Just now?"

"When I got up from this table a minute ago."

Martin put down his cigarette. "Well, Cody, I wasn't really paying much attention. You told Mike you thought you'd recognized some girl at the bar and that you needed to take a leak. Then you groped your way past one of those workmen and vanished into the loo. Mike was about to look in on you when you staggered out, tossed back two shots, and found your way back here. I really think you ought to get a nap."

"The girl! The girl in black at the bar. Where did she go?"

"There was never a girl at the bar," said Carson. "Not that we could see."

"My round, I think." Lennox gathered up their glasses and lurched for the bar.

"Don't let him drink too much," Martin cautioned Carson.

"He's really not taking it well," said Carson, "about Cathy."

Martin shook out another cigarette. "What could you expect? I just hope one good drunken binge of a vacation over here will be the catharsis he needs. Otherwise . . ."

Lennox slammed down the pints, spilling relatively little. He was really feeling lots better. Hair of the dog was a sure cure for DT's. "So, Jack. You got your camera?"

"For *Blue Pumps*?"

"That, too. But mainly so that next time you can take a picture of me with my girl friend."

"Are you Cody Lennox?"

Cody saw her dark blue pumps and followed the nicely filled dark blue hose up to the short denim skirt and jacket. Her breasts were small and firm, and he supposed he could see the rest of them if he unbuttoned her badge-covered jacket. She had that peculiarly perfect British complexion, with a fashion model's features and short red hair in a sort of spiked crewcut. Behind her mirror shades her eyes would have to

be blue, and she was almost as tall as Lennox. She was holding out a copy of *They Do Not Die!*

"I apologize for being so forward," she said. "But I'm a fan of yours, and I'd heard you were coming over for the big convention in Brighton. Well, I'd just purchased your latest book at Dillon's, and then I saw you seated here and looked closely at the photograph on the dust jacket. It's a match. Please, do you mind?"

Lennox did not mind. He dug out his pen. "Would you like this inscribed to . . . ?"

"Klesst. K–l–e–double–s– and one t."

He was trying to place her accent. Not quite BBC English. Hint of Irish? "Last name and phone number?"

"Just 'Klesst,' please."

Lennox wrote:

All My Best to Klesst.
Signed at Her Request.
Love from London —
Cody Lennox
8/19/87   1:18 PM

He closed the book and set it down on the table. "Here you go. Care to join me and these other debauched celebrities for a drink?"

"Thanks ever so much, but I've got to run." Klesst scooped up her book. "But I'm sure I'll be seeing you again soon." And she hurried away toward the Russell Square tube station.

"Blue pumps, but too long a stride," observed Lennox. "Can't be a native Londoner."

"Christ, but is she 21?" Martin craned his neck to watch her vanish around the corner.

Carson pointed. "She left you a note, Cody. See if it's her address."

There was an envelope lying where the book had been. Lennox turned it over and read *Cody Lennox,* penned in a large masculine hand across the front. He opened the envelope. There was a short note in the same hand and written upon his hotel's stationery:

> 8/19/87   1:20 PM
> Cody —
> Let's do dinner.
> Meet you in the lobby of the Bloomsbury Park Hotel at 6:30 this evening.
> My treat.
>   — Kane

"Shit," said Lennox.

Martin reached out. "Let me read it."

Martin read it. He handed the note to Carson. "You know what I think?"

"What do you think?"

"Kent Allard. It's just exactly his sort of twisted humor. Got some pretty fan to pass this to you instead of just phoning you at your hotel. Bet he's watching us from his hotel across the street there, laughing his head off."

"Seems more like M. R. James's 'Passing the Runes'," said Carson, returning the note to Lennox.

Lennox wadded note and envelope and stuffed them into the ash tray. "Anyway, I know where I *won't* be at 6:30 this evening. Jack, it's your round.

V. As I Wander Through My Playing Cards

Lennox made it back to his hotel, had creatively opened his door, and found his bed. There he remained until 5:30, at which point his headache awakened him. He washed down six aspirin with swigs of Scotch, then decided to kill the rest of the bottle. He sat on the edge of his bed, looking at his hands, thinking about Cathy.

At 6:00 he washed his face, combed his hair, brushed his teeth, and went out in search of adventure. After having parked his lunch in the Gents' at The Friend at Hand, his stomach was raw and uncertain about the whisky. He supposed he really should eat some-

thing, so he steamed into a pub by the British Museum and had three pints of lager.

Much improved, Lennox strolled through Soho and into the theatre district. *Follies* was playing at the Shaftesbury Theatre, but he'd already been told that tickets were impossible. He stood outside, wishing he might press his nose against the glass, and a scalper exchanged a Stalls ticket for only thirty quid. Lennox was delighted, and he managed to stay awake throughout the performance, despite an overpowering headache and sense of lethargy. He enjoyed himself, and it was quite a disappointment when he had to go back alone to his hotel instead of having a late dinner with Diana Rigg.

Instead, Lennox stopped in at the first pub he passed. By closing time he had drunk six large whiskies and had won twenty quid from the fruit machines on an investment of 50p. He was getting looks from the barmen as he left. Lennox had played the machines out of boredom, never really understanding what the buttons were supposed to do. Jack Martin, eat your heart out. Lennox decided he'd present Jack with a handful of tokens when they meet for lunch tomorrow.

Lennox was in good voice by now. He considered that a walk back through Soho to his hotel would count as an evening constitutional, all the better because the narrow side streets provided superb echo for his medley of Bon Jovi hits. Lennox had screamed out all that he could remember of "You Give Love a Bad Name," when he found the Queen of Diamonds.

She was lying in the gutter, somewhat soiled: a lost playing card with a buxom and nude lady, very much early 1960s *Playboy* centerfold, and quite demure by Times Square standards. He pocketed this.

Another chorus, a sudden turning, and he found the Queen of Clubs. She

127

had been trod upon, but was in fair repair: a lovely black girl with dusky skin and a fetching smile. Lennox added her to his jacket pocket and proceeded along the turning.

He was quite lost by now, but completely confident, when he found the Queen of Hearts. She was propped against a lamp post, and she was a tall redhead who reminded him of Klesst, whose name had stayed in his memory. Lennox carefully included her with the others and stumbled into another darkened side street, certain he would find the Queen of Spades.

His voice was growing hoarse, and he reckoned he could use another drink, and he realized that he was seriously lost, and then he noticed that five people were closing around him from out of the darkness.

One was the Queen of Spades, dressed all in black, her face a pale shape in the darkness. The others were four ragged, shuffling winos — blowlamps, was that the expression in cockney rhyming slang for tramps? Whatever. More to the point, they had very long knives.

Of additional interest, as they closed in, Lennox saw that their clothes weren't actually ragged, but rather they were rotted, as were their faces.

"Take him now," said the Lady in Black.

Lennox started to run.

Kane stepped out of a black passageway as Lennox flung past. He was wearing a three-piece pin-striped business suit that was obviously the best of Bond Street, and he had a distinctly professional appearance with his neat beard, bowler, and umbrella.

Kane petulantly threw the closest attacker against the wall. As the wall was on the opposite side of the street, the man hung there for a moment, before sliding down like a filthy and shattered doll. By then Kane had pulled the head off the next assailant and tossed that bit somewhere in the direction of

the Lady in Black. The third dead thing lunged for Kane with his knife, but Kane disarmed him, throwing arm and knife into the darkness, and then deftly ripped out his heart.

Hanging back, the last assailant threw his knife at Kane, and, while Kane was catching the blade, rolled behind a large dust bin and pulled an Uzi from beneath his rain coat.

Kane shoved Lennox onto the pavement, as a burst of 9 mm slugs ripped over them. Twisting away, Kane tugged some sort of pistol from his shoulder holster and pointed it at the dust bin. Dust bin, gunman, a parked car, and most of the wall opposite blew apart into glowing cinders.

The Queen of Spades had disappeared.

Tires howled, and a black Jaguar convertible took the turning on two wheels.

"Pitch him in!" Klesst shouted. She was wearing a black leather jumpsuit, and she was already reversing as Kane tossed in his bowler, umbrella, and Lennox, then tumbled in after — all but crushing the lot.

Perhaps thirty seconds had elapsed from Kane's first appearance. Lennox was in a state of shell shock.

Kane propped up Lennox against the back seat, as Klesst turned Soho streets into Le Mans.

"Well then, Cody," Kane shouted. "I really don't think you should have broken our dinner engagement."

VI. This Ain't the Summer of Love

"You've got dead bits all over your suit," Klesst scolded.

Kane muttered and dropped Lennox onto a leather sofa; he had been carrying him pendulant from his jacket collar, and Lennox collapsed like a stringless puppet.

Lennox said: "I need a drink."

"Single-malted. No ice." Kane nodded to Klesst. "Rather a large one, I think. Same for me."

"You just blew up half of Soho," Lennox remembered.

Kane was shrugging out of his suit jacket, eyeing his carrion-smeared hands in distaste. "Threw in a mundane this time. Wonder whether for you or for me? Play hostess, Klesst. I need a quick wash-up."

Lennox noticed the weapon in Kane's left-hand draw shoulder holster. It seemed to be made of almost translucent black plastic, and it reminded Lennox of the Whitney Lightning .22 automatic he had lusted over in the outdoors magazine ads of his youth.

"He just blew up half of London," said Lennox, accepting the glass from Klesst. "Is that really a raygun?"

"Cosmic ray laser, as close as you'd understand."

Lennox watched Klesst over his glass as he drank. "Oh, sure. I've read too much science fiction for that. Which hand holds the fusion reactor or something?"

"That's just a selective transmitter. Broadcast power on tight-contain. Trans time-time. Two black holes locked in an anti-matter matrix. Dad worked on it for a long real-time."

"Am I supposed to believe any of that?"

"No, Cody. It's really just magic."

"Carried off by Emperor Ming and his charming daughter. This is where writers get their ideas, you know." And for a while he sipped his drink and waited to wake up.

"May I have another?" Lennox handed her his empty glass. She was very long-legged and very lovely in tight black leather. He decided that DT's were nothing to be afraid of, after all.

"You know, my friends did warn me it would come down to this in the end," he told Klesst.

"Still think you're hallucinating,

Cody?" Kane had scrubbed his large hands and switched into formal evening attire. They seemed to be in a spacious sort of oak-paneled study. Lennox looked about for the butler and a stuffed moose's head.

"I'm not prepared to argue with a hallucination."

"You might, if I began to pull off your fingers, one at a time," suggested Kane.

Lennox turned to Klesst. "You're not really related to this ogre? You don't look a bit like Myrna Loy."

Kane nodded to Klesst, and she left the room.

"Have we been properly introduced?" Lennox gulped his imaginary drink. Excellent dream whisky.

"Only if you bother to count the three times I've recently pulled your ass out of the fire. I'm Kane."

"Charles Foster Kane?"

"Just Kane."

"So, Kane," said Lennox, sitting up. "How you been? I heard your old folks got evicted. You and your brother still not getting along?"

"Chance?" wondered Klesst, returning with an agate box.

"Not likely. He has the power, but not the control. That's why they want him. And why they can still get to him."

Kane opened the box. It was filled with a white powder. "Care to partake of a few numbers, Cody? Time you were getting back to some semblance of lucidity."

"You Brits manage some awesome coke," Lennox approved. "Let's toot up and party till dawn. You're a great host, Kane, you know, and I'm sorry I called you an ogre. I'm really going to miss you when I wake up. By the way, how old's your daughter?"

"Old enough to break your back," Klesst assured him.

"Kinky." Lennox dipped a golden coke spoon into the white powder, snorted, and refilled for his other nostril. "Smooth." He quickly repeated the

129

process and handed box and spoon to Kane.

"My special blend," said Kane. "Took some work to get right. First one's free."

"Shit," said Lennox. He was experiencing a rush like nothing he'd ever felt before. A moment ago he had been close to dropping off into an alcoholic stupor — assuming he hadn't already passed out somewhere. The drug — clearly not cocaine — cut through the alcohol-soaked blur of his consciousness as shockingly as splinters of ice thrust into his brain. Lennox felt suddenly sober, suddenly aware that he was seated in an opulent study with a leather-clad young lady and a very large and very intimidating man in black tie, and suddenly he began to suspect that this might not be a dream.

"So glad that you could finally join us, Cody," said Kane. "If you care to stay alive very much longer, there are a few things you really need to know about yourself and about those others who already know all about you."

Lennox looked at his hands. They should have been trembling, but they weren't. So, this still had to be a dream.

"Do you understand the popular expression 'synchronicity' as used in the sense of 'coincidence'?"

"Easy one, mine host. Random events or experiences that appear to align in non-random patterns. You start to call your great-aunt Biddie to whom you haven't spoken in years, and as you reach for the phone, it rings, and it's your great-aunt Biddie. Some call it ESP. Paranoids see patterns in it all."

"And you know about the Harmonic Convergence?"

"Some sort of alignment of the planets. Supposed to unleash all sorts of astrological forces, mumbo-jumbo, etc., etc., etc., and change the world forever. What's your sign, by the way?"

"Not on your zodiac. Give him another hit, Klesst."

Lennox helped himself to a couple

more generous snorts. "It's some kind of speed, right? Maybe crystal meth mixed with coke?"

"Old world secret," said Kane. "I'll send some home with you, perhaps."

He settled into a leather chair and sipped his drink, watching Lennox. "Suppose a person had the power to control random events?"

"He'd be a very wealthy gambler."

"Won much on the fruit machines, Cody?"

"Now, whoa!"

"Suppose the conscious wish to talk to great-aunt Biddie were powerful enough to cause her to phone up in response to the wish?"

"Suppose great-aunt Biddie's wish to talk to me was the cause of my suddenly thinking of her? *Touché,* I think."

"Rather, that's the whole point, Cody. Cause or effect? Because if synchronicity is not a random phenomenon, then who controls it? Who is the master?"

"Klesst, sweetheart — go fetch your father his nightly Thorazine, while we discuss the one about the chicken and the egg. By the way, where did you buy that outfit?"

"Kensington Market. I have a stall there. Come visit. We also do tattoos and piercing."

Lennox was starting to fade, despite the drug. "Already had my ear pierced."

"That's just a start."

"What a coincidence," said Kane. "Klesst, why not give Cody a sample of your jewelry stock — something to remember us by?"

Lennox was helping himself to the whisky. "I really should be waking up — I mean, getting back. This really has been real, gang. I just hope I can remember it all tomorrow long enough to write it down."

"You will," Kane told him. "I've seen to that."

Lennox tossed back straight whisky, then poured another. It was his dream, so he could do as he pleased. "So what about the Moronic Confluence?"

"The Harmonic Convergence was a cosmic expression of synchronicity. It unleashed certain forces, certain latent powers. Your powers, for instance."

"So now the world will become a better place for all?"

"Afraid not, Cody. It only unleashed forces which you would consider forces of evil."

"Bummer!"

"Try this." Klesst handed Lennox a silver pendant affixed to a French hook. It was a sunburst, about the size of a one-pound coin. A circle of somewhat serpentine sunrays framed a sun whose face was that of a snarling demon.

Lennox gazed at the amulet uncertainly.

"Allow me," said Kane. Very quickly he inserted the silver hook through Lennox's left earlobe. Lennox winced, touched his hand to his ear, saw blood on his finger. It had been some time since he had had his ear pierced, and the opening must have begun to close.

"Looks good," approved Klesst.

Lennox remembered that you weren't supposed to feel pain in a dream, but then he also felt like he was about to pass out, and that wasn't right for a dream either.

"Where's that coke?"

"Don't want to overdo it first time, do we, Cody?" said Kane. "I think you've had enough to handle tonight. But not to worry: I'll be in touch tomorrow. Too late for a taxi, I'm afraid, but we'll see you safely to your hotel."

"Keys," said Klesst, and caught them as Kane tossed.

"I was really very sober there for a minute or two," Lennox explained, bouncing against Kane's huge shoulder.

"Short-term effect," said Kane. "Just be glad of that."

"How come only evil forces were released?"

"Because there are no good forces."

"So, then. You don't believe that there is a God."

"There was a god."

"Well, then. Where is he now?"

"I killed him," said Kane.

VII. Strange Days Have Found Us

Lennox awoke when his bedside phone began ringing at noon. He was in his hotel room, but he hadn't the slightest as to how he had arrived there. He had some confused memories of the night before . . . But first, the phone.

It was Carson. "Wake up, you lazy sod. We're all waiting on you."

"Where?"

"In the downstairs bar. Me and Jack, Geoffrey Marsh and Kent Allard. Come on, you're missing your breakfast."

"Be right down."

Lennox automatically went through the motions of dressing. The morning after a blackout was nothing new for him. He wished he had time to shower, but settled for splashing cold water over his face and shoulders, toweling vigorously. The towel caught on something on his left ear, tugged painfully. Lennox wiped cold water from his eyes and saw the sunburst amulet dangling from his left ear.

"Get serious," he told his reflection. Must have bought it off a stall during one of his blackouts. But it was all coming back. Vivid memories of Kane and zombie assassins. No way. Another all-too-real nightmare. Maybe he really should cut down on the booze.

Lennox fingered the silver amulet, but the French hook seemed to be fixed within his earlobe, and it hurt to try to draw it free. No time to fool with it now. Lennox splashed a little whisky onto his ear to guard against infection, finished dressing, and took the stairway to the downstairs bar. Art Nouveau stained-glass windows, brightened by the midday sun, made each landing a sort of kaleidoscope, and Lennox was winded and dizzy by the time he reached Peter's Bar.

"Steam into this," Carson said. "Reckoned you'd fancy a lager."

Lennox wedged into the table and drained half the pint in a long swallow. "God, that feels good!" He was surprised to notice that his hands were steady. Must have made it an earlier evening than he'd thought. Good job, that. He was aware that they were all trying not to watch him.

"So, where do you guys want to go for lunch?" Jack Martin asked. "Is there someplace near here where we could, like, get a real pizza?"

"Pizza Express in Soho has American-style pizza," offered Geoffrey Marsh. "How've you been, Cody? Enjoying your trip?"

"So far, so good." Cody shook hands across the table. "Good to see you, Geoffrey. Jack said you were over."

Marsh was an athletically fit man whose hair was starting to thin and whose brown beard was showing grey. As he was the same age as Lennox and Martin, the two consoled one another that workouts and tennis evidently could not slow the aging process, and that therefore there was no point in their mending their ways. Marsh wrote what he liked to call "quiet horror" under various pseudonyms, several of which sold very well indeed. He, Martin, and Lennox had been friends and colleagues long enough to become regarded as "the Old Guard" of the horror genre.

"Nice earring, Cody," said Kent Allard. "Are you turning cyberpunk on us?"

"More likely cyberdrunk," Lennox said, finishing his pint. "I caught *Follies* last night, then crawled back here somehow. Look at all the loot I won on the way."

As he poured forth a handful of fruit machine tokens, Lennox asked casually: "Hear about anything going down in Soho last night? Could have sworn I heard some sort of gunfire or something."

"Probably just yobboes," suggested Carson.

"Check the papers, maybe," said Marsh.

"I never read beyond page three," Allard said.

Martin was looking hungrily at the fistful of tokens. "Let's try the machine here. Will it take these same tokens?"

"Just watch me," Lennox said. "I'm on a streak. Has to do with the Harmonic Convergence."

As he and Martin made for a fruit machine, Marsh watched them with concern. He asked Carson: "How's Cody doing? Really."

Carson was acutely aware of Allard's attention, and Allard was a notorious gossip. "He's doing OK," he lied. "Good as any man might after his wife and her lover are found dead in bed in some posh hotel room. He'll get through it."

"I wonder," said Allard.

"Just watch him, Mike," worried Marsh. "I don't think he's in control just now."

"Was he ever?" Carson wondered.

It took Martin most of ten minutes to lose all of Lennox's tokens in the fruit machine, plus the five quid Lennox won for him by suggesting when to hold. Martin then said: "I'm ready to . . ."

Lennox was already starting for the door, but he stopped short. Martin's voice had halted, as had the plume of his cigarette smoke. Lennox turned about. No one was moving in the pub. Nothing was moving in the pub. Totally freeze-frame. Awesome.

"Same again, mate?" asked Kane, filling a pint mug from behind the bar. "Lager, isn't it?" He was dressed as a hotel barman.

"What have you done?" Lennox took the pint.

"Time-time," said Kane, helping himself to a pint of Royal Oak. There were bits floating in it. Kane waited for them to settle.

"It isn't three yet," Lennox protested. The pub and all within were entirely motionless.

"I really like your sense of humor. Actually, I meant I'm holding time-time at stop just a bit. Did you know, Cody, that the energy currently being expended could create two moderately large star systems?"

"All right, I'm impressed," admitted Lennox. "Are you real, or am I really over the edge?"

"Right on both counts, Cody." Kane lifted his mug. "Cheers."

Lennox knocked back his pint, set it down on the bar. Nothing moved, save he and Kane.

"Same again?" Kane asked.

"Might as well. Can anyone else see you?"

"Confusing me with Harvey?" Kane refilled their pints. "And after I've just saved your ass yet again."

"How's that?" Lennox drank, because there was little else he could do about matters.

"A horrid and malevolent tentacled thing was lurking about. Here. Just now. Looking for you, I think."

"Didn't notice one. Where? In the Gents'?"

"No. Behind the fireplace over there. Take a closer look at its tiles, by the way."

"I've seen them. It's St. George slaying the dragon."

"I said, a closer look. Take it from an experienced dragon fighter: George isn't doing all that well. Could have been you just now."

"I need to sit down."

"I'll join you later."

"I'm going back to my room."

"In that case, that's four pounds eighty, please."

Lennox passed Kane a five pound note, and suddenly everything was moving again.

". . . go get something to eat," said Martin, banging on the fruit machine.

"I need out of here!" Lennox was headed for the stair.

But Kane was already seated at their table. He was wearing stone-washed jeans, a Grateful Dead t-shirt, and mirror shades. Lennox was grateful for that last.

"Hello, Cody," said Kane. "Been so looking forward to meeting you at last."

"This is Mr. Kane, said Allard, breaking off their earnest conversation. "He's brought us all invitations . . ."

"I'm out of here."

". . . to the publishers' party tonight . . ."

"Please do sit down, Cody," Kane invited.

The tugging pain from his ear pendant abruptly dragged Lennox back onto his vacated seat.

"That's better," said Kane. "I've always wanted the two of us to have a chat."

". . . for all of his authors," Allard concluded.

"And you must be Jack Martin." Kane stood up to shake hands. "I've read all your books. I like the one about Damon."

"Are you a writer?" asked Martin, wincing. "Or what?"

"He's a what," said Lennox, gulping Marsh's lager.

"Mr. Kane here — or is that your first name?"

"It's just Kane. Like Sting or Cher or Donovan."

"Kane here," Allard continued smoothly, "recently acquired Midland Books. He's now our major British publisher. I guess you guys hadn't heard the news."

"Just cut the deal. I know it will prove to be a good investment. But, hey, we're all of us in this outlaw profession together." Kane raised his mug. "Death

133

to publishers."

"And Midland Books is having a party for its authors tonight," Allard informed them, thinking good job he'd phoned his agent this morning for the insider information.

"So, do you write yourself?" Martin persisted.

"Barbarian fantasy," said Kane. "Under a pseudonym. Some time back. I'm sure you've never read any of it."

"Can the rest of you guys see him, too?" wondered Lennox.

"Invitations, Kent, as promised," said Kane, distributing engraved cards. "Relatively small gathering of some of my authors and staff. Please do feel free to bring along friends. It's just over at the Hotel Russell, so I know you can find your way."

"You're not British, are you," said Lennox.

"A citizen of the world," Kane explained helpfully. "And by the way, I believe I owe you 20p change." He handed Lennox a coin.

"A pre-convention bash, is it?" asked Marsh.

"Naturally we'll discuss business matters amidst the champagne. Must do it up proper for taxes, after all. And I'm particularly interested in talking over your current projects, Cody."

"I'm writing a novel about demonic trilobites who gobble people's brains. It's called *The Biting.*"

"Much to be explored there. Is the small community in New England or California?"

"How'd you know to find us here?"

"Synchronicity."

"Mike, let's go get something to eat." Lennox stood up.

"Actually, Kent phoned the office to say you were meeting here for lunch."

"Kane is taking us all to lunch," Allard said smugly. "I love this man."

"I got a previous engagement. No time. Come on, Mike."

"Tell Klesst I'll be counting on her as

hostess again tonight," Kane called after them.

"You've got to sort of make allowances for Cody," Marsh told Kane. "Sure, he's drinking too much. But he's really been through Hell lately."

"And he's likely to remain there," said Kane, "without a little help from his friends. And I already count him as my friend. My round, I think."

VIII. A Big Chrome Baby and a Black Leather Doll

Carson was examining the engraved invitation. "Do you think I might bring along some prints to show tonight?"

Lennox was searching for a cab. "Kane's no publisher."

"We can take the tube. It's just over there."

"Horrid and malevolent tentacled things lurk beneath underground platforms."

"So, where are we really going?"

"Kensington Market. I need an obscene tattoo and some gross t-shirts."

Lennox secured a cab, and they piled in. "Ken High Street. Anywhere near Holland Road."

"You're missing lunch, and your publisher's paying. What do you think about the prints?"

"Do you know anything about Kane? Anything at all?"

"Never heard of him before today. Kent said Kane's bought Midland, and Kent would know. You know how it is with publishers today — new owners taking over one after another and then selling to the next one. Doesn't do you good to walk out on your publisher. He was going to buy us lunch. Maybe just a few prints, what do you think? He'll have seen some of the covers I've done for Midland."

"The pubs are still open, and it's my round. What was your impression of Kane?"

"Intense. Mega. Crucial. Must work out twice a day." Carson then turned serious. "Buys our lunch, but I wouldn't want to have him come round to the flat after closing. He looks as though he might break you in half if he wanted."

"I never saw Kane before just now. At least, I don't think I *really* did." Lennox found some cigarettes, poked one toward Carson. He'd almost quit. "But I've dreamed about Kane. I've seen Kane before, and I've talked with Kane before, and it all seemed totally real. In my dreams. In my nightmares."

Carson lit their cigarettes. He said, cautiously: "Sometimes, when you've been drinking bad . . ."

"I only hope that it is just the booze. I can sober up tomorrow or next week. Then, what if Kane's still here?"

"What's your worry? It's just that he's your new publisher. You must have read about him in the papers, seen pictures of him somewhere. Let's just go have a pint, Cody. It'll steady you some."

"We're here," announced Lennox, rapping on the Austin's glass partition. "Just let us out anywhere."

"What's here?" asked Carson.

"Kensington Market. Klesst said she has a stall here."

"The wicked malt whose book you signed yesterday? The original lady in blue pumps?"

"She says she's Kane's daughter."

"And when did she tell you all this?"

"She said she has a stall here. She said that in one of my dreams. What if my dreams are true?"

"Then we'll find her, and then we'll all steam into the closest pub."

"That would mean that it wasn't a dream. That it was all true."

"What's true, then?"

"Kane. And all the madness he's told me."

"You've just met him. All of us just did. He's only your publisher."

"I used to do a whole lot of acid back

in my Haight-Ashbury days," Lennox confided.

Carson was getting major worried. "Let's just have a look through, and then we'll find a pub. Maybe an off-license, and we can sit on the benches out behind the church across the way."

Kensington Market enclosed three or so floors crammed with many tiny shops, catering primarily to the latest punk styles. Latex and leather fashions, all glistening black and tailored like a second skin, crowded the aisles — reminding Lennox of the fetish boutiques in L.A. and New York. He guessed that PVC probably meant vinyl or something, and while it was all very shiny and kinky, it looked very hot to wear, and it was sweltering in here. The place smelled like a tire graveyard on a hot day, and was about as organized. It was all a bit too trendy, more sideshow than sordid. Punkers were everywhere, and Lennox suddenly became aware that, for once, his was maybe the straightest appearance on the scene. He felt more secure when he noticed that some eyes were glancing toward the omnipresent photographs of James Dean, then turning back to study his face.

Carson was thoughtfully looking at Dead Kennedys records.

The sunburst pendant in his ear seemed to turn Lennox's head and his attention away from the record stall. It was very, very hot. And claustrophobic. Images came to mind of Doré illustrations for Dante's *Inferno*. He moved aimlessly along the crowded aisles. He wished he had a drink.

"Hello, Cody. So good of you to drop by."

Klesst had a stall just down from Xotique. She was wearing a black leather bra, a very brief black leather miniskirt, an exposed suspender belt holding up black stockings, and black stiletto boots. This much Lennox took in at first glance. At second glance he

135

saw that she wore an ear pendant similar to his own, but it was her face on the sunburst.

"Klesst?" Lennox's voice was uncertain. This was probably just another hallucination. Got to keep thinking of them as dreams. Nothing more.

"So, Cody. You recovered from last night. Dad was off looking for you earlier. You see him?"

Lennox faltered, then gave it up. "He caught up with me at the hotel bar. Gave me an invitation. To a party. Tonight. Said to remind you that you're to be hostess."

"Boring."

"What are you?" Lennox's voice held panic.

"Good question. What are we all? Why are we here? Do you know Jean-Paul Sartre?"

"Not socially. He doesn't hang out much these days."

"Next question."

"What's happening to me?"

"I thought Kane started to explain that to you last night."

"Sometimes I can't tell my dreams from reality."

"Sometimes there is no distinction."

"I think I'm starting to lose it."

"Are you going to stand here paralyzed in some existential dilemma, or are you going to buy something?"

Lennox stared without focus at her clutter of punk jewelry and studded leather accessories. Extreme. From the corner of his eye, he could see Carson still flipping through the record display. He supposed he ought to re-enter the real world if he could find it, or at least go through the motions. Did he really need a spiked collar?

"Perhaps an earring."

"Then I'll just pierce your other ear. No charge."

"No problem. I'll just take this one out."

"Can't be done."

"Say, what?"

"Do you remember last night?"

"I got very drunk as is my custom. I had some crazy dreams. You were in them. And Kane. That's all. What would you know about my dreams?"

"That was near-time, but real enough. Kane put his mark upon you. Now you bear the mark of Kane. There's no removing it. Ever."

"Tell that to Vincent van Gogh."

"Never fancied pictures of flowers. You're signed and sealed."

"Come again?"

"And be glad for it. They'll try to kill you, now that they can't possess you. What actually do you think happened to you last night?"

"I got very drunk and walked back to my hotel."

"Kane thinks they were trying for him as much as for you. They never else would have called in a mundane. The Harmonic Convergence has increased their powers, but they still have no control of time-time."

"Look. I read *The Sun* today, page three and all of it. Nothing about Soho being devastated or stray bits of zombies found strewn all about."

"I told you: that took place in near-time. Very dangerous. Kane has much less power there, and that's why they lured you there. But now that you're aligned with Kane, they'll come looking for you in real-time as well."

"Are you from around here?"

"Not hardly."

"And is Kane really your father?"

"Obviously."

"He doesn't look old enough."

"You'd be surprised."

"And your mother?"

"Kane killed her."

"And how did you feel about that?"

"She meant to sacrifice me to a well-known demon. She'd made a pact at my birth."

Lennox wondered if he were the only sane person here. And how sane was that?

"Klesst, you're a really beautiful person. May I even say, you're devilishly intriguing. And if I were twenty years younger I'd deck myself out in some of these outrageous costumes they sell here, and I'd carry you off to some dingy basement club where people dance till dawn by bashing their heads together, and afterward I'd tell Kane we were running off to live together in my gentrified loft in New York's SoHo, and if he objected I'd just have to punch him out. However, I'm not twenty years younger, and Kane is bigger than me, so instead I'd like to fix you up with a really good psychiatrist."

"I'm lots older than you think."

"Delighted to hear you say that. I wasn't sure about British laws on the matter."

"So, are you going to buy anything?"

"I haven't really looked about. Maybe a nice leather bra for my closet."

"Have you had your nipples pierced? I can do it here, and I have some lovely golden rings."

"Not today."

"But I'd like that." Klesst moved toward him suddenly, and Lennox as suddenly was afraid.

"Christ, you really did find your lady here." Carson wandered into the stall, holding a Nico album in a plastic bag. He was looking at his watch, calculating how many pints might be sunk before closing.

"She wants to pierce my nipples," complained Lennox.

"Why not just get a tattoo?" Carson compromised. He rolled up his left sleeve. Lennox saw a devil's head above the numbers **666**. "Can't remember where I had it done. I'd been pissed for weeks before I noticed it."

"I did it," said Klesst. "Looks great."

"This is Kane's daughter," said Lennox. "I've mostly seen her in my dreams, but I think she's real enough."

"You might find out how real tonight."

"See there, Carson. They throw themselves at me. Klesst, why did you say that I was aligned with Kane?"

"Ought to be more careful about what you sign your name to, Cody. Yesterday. The book."

"I like the British," said Lennox. "You just have to get used to their odd sense of humor."

"I'm not British," said Klesst. "And you still haven't bought anything. Let you have that spiked collar for a fiver."

"Are the pubs still open?" Lennox asked Carson.

"Try it on."

"We'd best be going," said Carson.

Klesst moved very quickly, and it was over before Lennox could think to struggle.

"Radical," she said. "That's a fiver."

"Klesst, you're beautiful, but you're a true space cadet. Close up, and I'll buy you lunch. You're really from California, aren't you? That can be cured."

"So can reality, Cody. See you tonight."

Lennox fingered his studded leather collar. It chafed his neck, but he paid her anyway. He was aware that he was in serious danger of becoming sober, and he intended to remedy that without further delay.

"I think I'm on to something here," he told Carson. "She was coming on strong to me. Real strong."

Carson looked back. "She's not there now."

Lennox turned around. The labyrinthine aisles of stalls seemed to be shimmering in the stagnant air. He couldn't pick out Klesst's stall. He couldn't see Klesst.

"Whoa! Wait a minute here." He started to go back.

Carson took his arm. "Let's just go have a pint."

Lennox fumbled with his collar. "I think this is locked."

"Get the key after the pubs close."

IX. Say a Prayer in the Darkness for the Magic to Come

Lennox nearly slept past the party, but his hangover and the pain from his earlobe woke him up around seven. He found a half-bottle of Scotch and medicated himself. In the mirror his earlobe did not appear to be inflamed, and it no longer hurt. He tugged at the ear pendant, but it didn't want to come loose. Probably encrusted. Lennox dabbed more whisky onto his earlobe as a safeguard.

He wondered what he was doing wearing a spiked collar, then remembered that Klesst had locked it there and kept the key. He fumbled with its lock, wishing it would open, and the catch snapped. Must be a trick to it, he thought, dropping the collar onto his table.

Just time for a quick shower. The cold water helped to wake him up. He had some vague memories of sitting on a bench behind some church in Kensington and drinking several cans of strong lager, while he explained to Carson all about synchronicity. Carson had managed to get him into a cab and back to his hotel.

Lennox felt much better after he finished with the shower, and he took time to trim his near-beard. He put on a baggy cotton designer shirt and matching trousers, a narrow necktie loosely knotted, and his favorite linen jacket. Got to look the part for your publisher, and besides there was Klesst.

Kane had reserved a large suite of rooms at the Hotel Russell, so it was just a short walk along Southampton Row. Lennox found his somewhat crumpled invitation, rechecked his image in the mirror, and sailed off in high spirits.

The party had already started, and a hulking biker in a dinner jacket met him at the door and wanted to see his

invitation.

"Let him in, Blacklight," Klesst called out. "He's one of us."

Klesst gave him her hand. "Champagne?"

"For sure."

She was wearing some sort of gleaming black sheath dress that laced openly across her breasts and back. The latex dress and stockings clung tightly to her very lovely body, and Lennox decided that these kinky London fashions weren't all that bad, and that having an affair with his publisher's spaced-out daughter was worth checking out.

"Here we are." Klesst lifted two glasses from a passing tray and handed one to Lennox.

"Cheers," he said, touching their glasses.

"Ah! There you are, Cody. So glad you could make it. I see Klesst is taking care of you."

Kane shook his hand. He was casually dressed, as were most of those in the room, and he was playing the perfect host.

"Lots to munch on over there. I imagine you already know most of the people here. Mingle and enjoy. We'll talk later on."

Lennox downed his champagne and reached for another glass. He did know most of the thirty or so people here. It really was just another publisher's party. Jack Martin had seen Lennox and was working his way over to him.

"Well, Klesst," Lennox said. "That's a very lovely dress you almost have on. Are you the Queen of Spades?"

"Wrong card. Have another drink, Cody."

"You're right. She's not a redhead. But you're both in my dreams." Cody grabbed another glass. "And you're much cuter."

"How's it going, Cody?" Martin had just been talking with Mike Carson about the afternoon's adventures. He was close to panic and wondering about commitment laws in England.

"Ms. Klesst Kane, meet famous writer, Jack Martin."

"I already know her," said Martin. "Blue pumps. We all met yesterday at The Friend At Hand. Nobody told us you were the publisher's daughter."

"My secret identity," said Klesst, and then she smiled and left them to greet the always fashionably late Kent Allard.

"Everything OK?" asked Martin.

"No. I don't think so." Lennox emptied his glass.

"You missed a really great lunch. You really ought to eat something. Just look at all this food here!"

"Had a late lunch with Carson. Wonder if Klesst might like a late dinner?"

"Cody!" Kane's massive arm gripped his shoulders. "Grab a glass of champagne, and let's sit down for a minute in the other room. I want to talk about your next book. Jack, please excuse us for a minute. Business."

"Business," echoed Lennox, reaching for another glass as he followed Kane.

Kane closed the door behind them. "So, how's your day been?"

Lennox sipped his champagne. Kane was pulling a fresh bottle from the ice. "Very pleasant. I dropped by Klesst's shop. Nice place for your daughter to work."

"Kids these days." Kane popped the cork. "Heard you bought some neckwear from her. Not wearing it tonight."

"Took it off. Didn't go with my tie. Had trouble with the catch, though."

"Good job, Cody. There was no key to that lock." Kane refilled their glasses. "I'm impressed."

Cody stood up and bunched his fists. "No way do I believe any of this. I'm blitzed out of my skull just now, and I know I need to cut down on my drinking. Let's do lunch tomorrow, if you really exist, and then we can talk about the next novel. I'm sorry if I'm perhaps not making a lot of sense just now, but

life's been a bitch."

"Do a couple hits of this, and then you'll be sober enough." Kane tossed him a phial of white powder. "I need you tonight."

Lennox delved into the phial with the attached spoon. "Kane, you are very weird."

"Take a couple hits. Nice big ones."

Lennox blinked and looked about him. He was sitting in a hotel room across from a huge individual who at best just might be mad. And Lennox suddenly felt sober for the first time in months. Then last night . . .

"Much better," said Kane, retrieving the phial. "Just take a moment to get used to it all."

"You're not a publisher."

"For the moment I am. Needed a real-time framework. Bought Midland Books and kept the staff. Nice cover, and I may even turn a profit. Want to talk about the advance for your next book?"

"Those other times when I saw you. All of that really did happen?"

"Trust me, Cody. It really happened."

"So, I'm not losing my mind."

"Afraid not, Cody."

"So, then." Lennox rubbed his forehead and wondered whether he was over the edge beyond return. "If I'm not crazy, and you're for real, then who are you?"

"A friend, Cody. Haven't I saved your life?"

"That was real?"

"All of it. And anyway, you already knew that beneath the alcoholic fog you've been hiding in. Head in the sand, Cody. Doesn't work. *They* can still see you."

"No, *this* is reality: I'm sitting in a hotel room in London talking with my publisher and there's a party going on. One or both of us is quite mad. I think I'll mingle."

"It takes a bit of getting used to," said Kane, escorting him back to the others. "That's why I'm trying to bring you

139

along slowly." He squeezed Lennox's shoulder in a comradely way, and Lennox sensed that beneath the friendly grip there was latent strength that might crush him in an instant. "Now go enjoy yourself. Busy night ahead."

Carson greeted him with a glass of champagne. "So then, did you make a deal?"

"I'm afraid I may have." Lennox tossed back the champagne. "Mike, I'm beginning to think that all of this is really happening to me."

"Best get some food inside you," Carson said, looking about for Martin for help. Martin was chatting up Klesst.

"What I need is some air. I'll just have a stroll around Russell Square. Back in a flash."

"I'll come with you."

"No. I just want to be alone for a minute. Stay here and talk to Kane. See what you make of him."

Allard had cornered Kane, and Lennox waved as he made for the door. "Just getting some air."

"Catch you later, Cody," Kane shouted back, and Blacklight let Lennox out the door.

Feeling somewhat conspiratorial, Lennox did not cross into Russell Square, but instead walked along Southampton Row and turned down Cosmo Place into Queen Square. With a shudder he made to ignore the human wreckage hunched over their bottles and their benches about the cobbled pavement, and he passed through an iron gate onto the green. It smelled less of urine and unwashed bodies here, if he kept away from the shrubbery which sheltered the enclosing iron fence. The trees deadened the noise of London at night, and the grass felt cool beneath feet bruised by endless pavement.

Lennox walked slowly toward the end of Queen Square, toward the woman's statue there, formerly thought to be a statue of Queen Anne but now believed to be that of Queen Charlotte,

Consort of King George III. He paused there, his thoughts aimless — vaguely wondering, as he had so often done before, as to what Queen Charlotte's downward stretched right hand might be pointing.

It was there and then that Lennox found the Queen of Spades.

She was dressed all in black, and at first he just saw her face, ghostly in the darkness. Lennox stared, and the rest of her emerged from the night.

He said: "Hello, Cathy."

"Hello, Cody."

"You're dead, Cathy."

"You should know, Cody."

"So this is it, then. It's not just the booze and all that. I really am completely mad."

"You must have been to cast your lot with Kane."

She moved toward him, swaying bewitchingly as she balanced forward to keep her stiletto heels from digging into the sod. She had on glossy black stockings and a black ciré sheath minidress that would have clung to her waist even without the wide leather cinch. Her dress was strapless and exposed a swath of pale skin from above her breasts to her bare shoulders, where the tops of her long black evening gloves reached the neckline.

Her black hair was gathered in a high chignon, so that her pale face and shoulders seemed to be an alabaster bust floating out of the darkness. Perhaps a plaster deathmask. Lennox recognized the familiar sensuous mouth and finely boned features, and he knew the shade of green of her eyes even before she gazed into his own.

Lennox grasped her bare shoulders. Her flesh was cool but certainly solid beneath his touch.

"Are you really Cathy?"

"If that's what you want."

"Cathy is dead. There was a funeral, and I stood there. It's been more than a year."

"There's nothing permanent about death, Cody. Not when you have power."

"This is another of Kane's tricks."

"I'm not one of Kane's minions. You are. I'm trying to help you break away from Kane."

"All right, that does it. I've been called a lot of things, but never a minion. No more of Kane's white powder, because God knows what's in it, and it's too much for my mirror. I'm going back to my hotel room, where I will curl up with a bottle of Scotch and find oblivion. If I'm still like this tomorrow, I'm really and truly this time for sure going to seek professional help."

Cathy seized his arm and firmly halted his departure. "I can take you to someone who can help you."

As Lennox spun about, the sunburst pendant on his left ear faced her. She instantly released him and stepped back.

"Please," she said. "Please come with me, Cody. Anyway, what have you got to lose?"

"Plainly, not my wits. My sanity is history. I'm standing in a London park talking with my dead wife. You can not be Cathy."

"I can be anyone you want me to be."

"Really? Did you leave your shoes in my room the other night? And did you develop severe acne in the pub the next day? And do you loiter about non-existent streets in Soho in the company of rotting zombies? Because if you answer yes to any or all of the above, then you are not Cathy. Cathy had her secret life, but nothing this extreme."

"I think you need a drink, Cody. Let's go to my place. There we can talk." Cathy took his right arm.

"You know," Lennox told her. "I think I'm handling all of this very well. It's that mega coke that Kane gave me, isn't it? I learned back when I used to do lots of acid that if the trip starts to get too weird, it's best not to fight it and just go with the flow. So, take me to

your leader."

Cathy held fast to his right arm and steered Lennox in the direction of the Russell Square tube station. "You really haven't a clue, do you?"

"I am totally clueless."

There were still meth-men and blow-lamps sprawled in the bushes and folded onto benches.

"Promise no more zombies."

"You're marked by Kane."

There were tired tourists and late revelers hurrying along the streets toward the underground for the last trains. Cabs busily scooted past, braking as they dared a zebra crossing, and all of this was very reassuring to a man out on a stroll with his deceased wife.

"Can you see her, too?" Lennox asked a cluster of blue-haired ladies who were puzzling over their maps outside the tube station. He received bifocaled glares and a muttered "Disgusting!" as Cathy dragged him through.

"Let's get a cab," he protested.

"I'm just down the way."

"We'll need tickets."

Lennox stumbled and touched one of the automatic ticket machines. The machine spat out two tickets, and Cathy captured them before he could react.

"I hate these lifts," she said. "Let's take the stairs."

The Russell Square station had a pair of wooden-slat lifts that probably dated back to its Victorian construction. Their open cages crawled down a sooty shaft of geological strata to the depths of London, and often they stuck there when overloaded with too much compressed humanity. Present construction to replace the aged lifts with new shiny steel boxes only added to the congestion.

"These steps go down a hundred miles," Lennox argued, pointing to a sign which advised caution to all those rash enough to attempt the descent. "It's like climbing to the top of the Empire State Building."

"But this is all downhill, Cody. Stop

whining and come along."

The stairway bored into the depths in a tight spiral. Cathy's heels made a rhythmic echo, and Lennox began to feel dizzy. Not many people took these stairs, and just now they met no one at all.

"Cathy," said Lennox, pausing for breath. "If it's really you, I just want to say how glad I am to see you again."

The stairwell was hot and claustrophobic, and Lennox felt certain they should have reached the platform by now.

"Cathy, do you remember when we saw that film, *Deathline*? Parts of it were shot down here."

"Come on, Cody."

"I think the print we saw was retitled *Raw Meat*."

"Right. That was some birthday treat, Cody."

"We had fun afterward."

"Right. You pulled one of my stockings over your head and chased me around the apartment, waving a rubber chicken and yelling: 'Mind the doors!' "

"Was that before you began seeing Aaron?"

"Just keep walking, Cody. We're nearly there."

"I can't hear the trains."

"So, what made you throw in with Kane?"

Lennox grasped at the railing. The brass was warm and seemed to be filmed over with slime. He stumbled and leaned hard against Cathy.

"He bought out my British publisher, acquired all my contracts. Hey, I jut met the guy. He has some awesome coke and a lovely daughter. Inasmuch as you're dead, you'll forgive my lust, won't you?"

There seemed to be steam filling the spiral stairway. Droplets of something fell onto his face, and Lennox wiped them away curiously. The brass railing began to look more like an uncoiled intestine. He hoped he wouldn't throw up

on the steps.

"I think we've been walking too far." The steps were so slimy as to feel gelatinous beneath his feet. Lennox clung to Cathy.

"You're more likely to recognize his name when it's spelled *C a i n*," she said.

"As in the fratricidal horticulturist? Surely, he's dead by now."

"Immortal," said Cathy. "Unless you can help us stop him. That's why he's bonded you."

The stairway ended, and they walked onto an underground platform of sorts. The overhead tunnel was oozing tendrils of gluey foulness through misshapen tiles, the rails seemed to be writhing like salted worms, the platform and all were clogged by enveloping steamy mist.

For as far as Lennox could see into the mist, hundreds of would-be passengers aimlessly shuffled against one another, rotting in their tatters of medieval clothing.

"Sorry about the mess," said a figure standing on the platform. "Been holding this lot here for quite some years. Really in remarkably good state of preservation though, all things considered — don't you think?

"Cody Lennox?" The man stepped closer. "Please allow me to introduce myself. My name is Satan."

"I think this has gone far enough," Lennox decided. "And anyway, I'm an atheist."

"No problem," said Satan, but he did not offer his hand. He was a tall, dark man with a widow's peak and neatly trimmed black beard, dressed rather theatrically in cape and medieval costume.

"There are no horns and tail," said Satan. "Or would you feel better if there were?"

"You're a theatrical overstatement."

"First impressions," said Satan. His image blurred, and he was much the same but attired in formal dinner dress, fashionable about 1900. Cathy was suddenly wearing a black evening gown from the same period.

"Go away!" begged Lennox, anxiously hoping to awaken.

"Doesn't really matter, does it?" said Satan. "Appearances are deceiving. Like yours. We need to talk."

"That's what Kane told me."

"Cody, I can see that you're confused. Who wouldn't be? So you cut your first deal with Kane. We can renegotiate. What do you want? I've already brought Cathy back. No obligation."

"That's not Cathy," Lennox insisted.

"She could be Cathy. Or whoever you want. Look about you, Cody. Anything you want. Name it. It's yours."

"This is not a mountain top. This is a very horrible subway tunnel, and I don't see anything here that I like. Get thee behind me."

"Good job, Cody," said Kane. He was carrying two glasses of champagne, and he handed one to Lennox. "We missed you at the party, so I came to look."

"Clever move, Kane," Satan said. "So, he led you here."

"Sorry. I should have brought another glass. Satan, is it? Is that what you're going by now? Don't mind if I slip and call you Sathonys out of old acquaintance?"

"Kane, you shouldn't have meddled into this."

"Nice place," approved Kane. "I like the décor. Giger out of Bosch. It's the catacombs beneath Coram's Fields Playground, isn't it? Connects through beneath Queen Square. Very convenient. And I see you've been recruiting from the plague pits."

Lennox made his voice calm. "Kane, are we in Hell or something?"

"What we're in is deep shit," Klesst answered him. "Dad, we're going to run out of champagne."

"The delectable Klesst!" said Satan. "My, how you've grown up!"

"Blacklight can ring room service," Kane told her.

"Klesst," Lennox asked, "is this the well-known . . ."

"We've all been around for a long, long time, Cody."

"Best be getting back to the party," Kane decided. "Can't trust Blacklight to cope on his own."

"A truce," Satan offered. "We've fought on the same side often enough before."

"But this is my turf now," Kane warned him. "And I don't like your plans for renovation."

"You can't stop this."

"Lighten up, Sathonys. You're like a brother to me."

"Oh, shit!" said Klesst.

Kane's left hand moved, and there was a gun in it, and Kane fired the gun.

Satan had instantly vanished, but the point where he had stood coalesced into a seething mass of flaming destruction.

"Cody, get your ass behind me!"

Dead creatures began tumbling from the walls, crawling over the slime-covered paving. Kane fired another annihilating burst. Part of one wall melted into glowing rubble.

Klesst tugged what might have been a derringer from beneath her skirt. She aimed it at the line of rails just as their tentacled lengths were reaching outward. Most of the platform and rails vanished in a consuming flash that hurtled the three of them backward over the slime and toward where the staircase no longer was.

The ceiling began to crumble. Kane fired pointblank into a collapsing tier of ravenous dead creatures. Stones were falling heavily from above. In seconds nauseous smoke clogged the warren of tunnels. Continuous bursts from Kane's and Klesst's weapons provided a strobe-light vision of disintegrating masonry and mindlessly advancing dead. Beyond that spasmodic glow of destruction, ill-defined shapes hunched toward

143

them.

"What do you say, Cody?" Kane shouted. "Want to go back to the party?"

Something long dead reached out of the buckling catacomb walls and clawed at Lennox's throat. The sunburst pendant at Lennox's ear blazed with instant power, and the desiccated arm vanished into ash.

"I want out of here!" Lennox screamed.

It was instantly quiet. It was very dark. Dank walls still compressed them.

"Just up these stairs, I think," said Kane, holding his gun at alert. Cover our back, Klesst. Move along, Cody."

"Where are we?" Lennox cursed as he stumbled and bashed his knee against the unseen steps. Klesst powerfully grasped his arm and kept him from falling into uncertain darkness.

"Not on the Russell Square station staircase, as I'd hoped," Kane answered. "That's where we began to follow you. At a guess, we're coming up from beneath Queen Square."

Lennox stumbled again, but Klesst held him upright.

"Can you both see in the dark?" Lennox asked her.

"Yes." Klesst squeezed his arm comfortingly.

"I want out of here."

"Good one, Cody!" Kane congratulated him. "Here's a door that should open onto the cellars beneath the Queen's Larder. We're going to make an awesome team."

Kane snapped the bolt and pushed open the trap door.

"Or, maybe not," said Kane.

Kane shoved away the debris, and they emerged.

The Queen's Larder was a blackened ruin, as were all of the buildings in sight, save for the Church of St. George the Martyr across the way. The sky was a sodium-flame yellow and outlined an endless horizon of blackened heaps of fused stone and glass. There was no

144

clear evidence of sun or moon through the glowing haze. Occasional and distant shapes seemed to sail on black wings across the dead skies; otherwise there was no sign of life. No sign of any sort of life whatsoever.

"Shit," said Kane.

"You sure threw one hell of a party," Lennox managed. He sat down on a seared heap of wall. "Look, my sanity reserve has been running on empty for too long. Where does one get a drink here?"

"You bastard!" Klesst yelled at him. "You brought us through the wrong way!"

"Whoa! I was only following your dad. You're the ones who can see in the dark — remember?"

"This is worse than it looks," Kane told them.

"Well, it looks really bad, Kane," Lennox agreed. "Whatever happened to time-time, and where's the party?"

Kane suddenly turned the full power of his eyes upon Lennox, and for the first time Lennox was irrevocably convinced that all of this was really happening to him. And then Cody Lennox knew real fear.

"I've tried to bring you along by stages," Kane said. "The problem is that I need you, and I need you now. What you're looking at right now is a near-time reality — for your entire world."

"Global nuclear holocaust?"

"Worse than that, Cody. It's more like Armageddon or the Day of Judgement. The Harmonic Convergence gave them the power. They'll open the Gates of Hell and raise the dead. Only no one's flying up to Heaven. It won't be a pretty sight. Look about you."

"Straight answers this time, Kane. Was that really Satan?"

"To the best that your theology can comprehend: yes. Disregarding Judeo-Christian myth, that was the Demonlord. What you saw was a physical embodiment of a hostile and predatory force alien to this world."

"And are you also a Judeo-Christian myth?"

"Very possibly. But don't believe everything you read. There are at least two sides to every story."

"And are you human?"

"Yes, and no."

"I was just wondering," said Lennox. "Except for all the muscles, I'm having a very difficult time telling you and Satan apart."

"I am a physical entity," Kane promised him. "Just as is Klesst. Just as are you. Satan, as you saw him, is a physical embodiment of a trans-dimensional force."

"And Cathy?"

"What you saw was a succubus. Another demon, as your theology interprets such matters. Don't blame yourself for summoning her. You've been set up all along."

"Why?"

"Because you can control synchronicity, Cody. It was a latent power, unconsciously used. The Harmonic Convergence has intensified your powers. You haven't attained real control yet, but I can teach you."

"Why should I trust you?"

Kane waved his arms. "Just look at what will happen. At what *has* happened. This is reality, Cody."

"I thought you could control time, Kane."

"Time-time, Cody. And real-time within limits. We followed you into near-time to find their center of power. They shunted us future-forward on the way back to real-time. I have only physical power here. I need you, Cody, to get back, to keep all this from happening."

"Do it, Cody," Klesst encouraged him. "This place is really boring."

"So. What do I do? I forgot my ruby slippers."

"If you break open the way," Kane said, "I can draw through the power.

Think of it this way: you unlock the door, and I come through with the shotgun."

"Kane, I think we'd best just call a tow-truck."

"I really do admire a sense of humor in a man who's facing an unpleasant end." Kane stepped closer, and Lennox was suddenly uncertain as to where the immediate danger might lie.

"It's all random patterns, Cody. It's like a gigantic interlocking puzzle with infinite and equal solutions. When the pieces come together and form a final pattern, it's real-time. Near-time is still in flux. Synchronicity can determine the way the patterns come together. You can control synchronicity. Do it, and get it right this time."

"Do what? Is this where I make an expressionless face and unfocus my eyes?"

"The monster's from the id, Cody. All you have to do is to want something to happen. I'll see that it does."

"I don't begin to understand any of this."

"You don't have to." Klesst put her arm around him. "Hey, don't you wish we were all back at the party and having a good time? Like, here's the three of us together in the bedroom, talking away. Then Dad leaves you and me alone, while he goes to check on the champagne. Our eyes meet, and then our lips crush together."

"Let's party!" Cody shouted.

This time there were no blasts of weaponsfire to mask the shock of ripping apart the space-time pattern . . .

"Sorry, but there's always business," Kane apologized to his guests. "Blacklight, how are we doing on the champagne?"

"Cool," said Blacklight. "Ordered up two more cases. Had some gate-crashers. Bad-looking dude in a tux and a comely Gibson girl in a black formal. Said they were old friends of yours, so

145

I let them in. Don't see them now. Anyway, they said they'd be back."

"I'm sure they will. Carry on."

"Hey, Kane!" Kent Allard lurched toward him. "Did you find Cody?"

"We did."

"We were worried about him. You know . . ."

"Cody is fine."

Lennox and Klesst chose this moment to emerge from the bedroom. They were arm in arm and talking together furiously.

"Well, well," observed Allard. "Fast mover, our Cody."

"Champagne, Cody?" Kane invited.

"Maybe just one," Lennox said. "Please excuse us for a moment, Kent."

"Of course. Go for it, guy."

Lennox snagged a tray of champagne as he guided Klesst into a corner beside Kane. Each took a glass.

He said: "Kane, I'm not sure I really believe any of this, but I'm throwing in on your side."

"Good decision, Cody."

"Only one thing still bothers me, Kane. Granted, I've met the forces of Evil . . ."

"Only *inimical* forces, Cody. It's all so relative."

"We'll argue this later. So, when do I meet the forces of Good?"

"Already told you, Cody. There are none. I'm the only hope this world has."

Kane and Klesst touched glasses with Lennox.

"To us," said Kane. ▲

COMING IN OUR WINTER, 1989 ISSUE!

Our Special *Brian Lumley* issue

— *featuring* —

3 stunning new stories by Brian Lumley

— *plus* —

Uncanny new tales by

ROBERT SHECKLEY : KEITH TAYLOR : PHYLLIS ANN KARR

Artwork by Vincent Di Fate!

Don't miss a single issue — turn to page 38 and subscribe today!

www.ingramcontent.com/pod-product-compliance
Lightning Source LLC
Chambersburg PA
CBHW070556180626
46817CB00005B/1870